DRIVEN

A RITA MARS THRILLER

BY
VALERIE WEBSTER

DRIVEN

A Rita Mars Thriller

Valerie Webster

Driven: A Rita Mars Thriller

Valerie Webster

Published 2021 by Valerie Webster
with Ignited Ink Writing, LLC
2076 Skylark Court
Longmont, CO 80503
www.valeriewebster.com

Cover design by Larry Ingram and Bill Holtsnider

Library of Congress Number: 2021900405

ISBN: 978-1-952347-03-0

First print edition published in 2021
Printed in the United States of America

Chapter 1

"Rita Mars, this is a voice from your past."

"Who the hell is this?" Rita demanded.

It was eleven o'clock, and the dreary end of a long day. A miserable October rain tapped on the office windows. Through the water washed glass, Baltimore's Mitchell Court House next door was a smear of grey and black.

"I first met you devouring Hershey bars in the newsroom at midnight." The man was gleeful.

"That narrows it down."

Great clue. Hell, she'd been a reporter for seventeen years before she started the agency. Rita cradled her chin. The police department snitch who gave up the narcs ripping off drug dealers? The accountant with the guilty conscience who squealed on the HUD housing contracts?

"We were a pair and then again we were not."

"Look, pal, I don't know—"

"I was the snow king and you were the fire breather."

Rita started to hang up, but there was something eerily familiar about that line.

"You never know when you've had your last chance," the man said.

"Bobby Ellis." Instinctively, Rita touched the worn chrome Zippo in her pocket that bore those very words. Chills ran along her arms and the hair bristled at her neck.

"Bingo," Ellis said.

"God, I'm so glad to hear from you. Where are you? When can I see you?"

"Sunday."

"Halloween?"

"The Overlook Inn in Harper's Ferry. Breakfast at ten. I'll have a lot to tell you. A story for above the fold. "

Rita scribbled his instructions on a blank notepad. "Tell me now." Above the fold on a newspaper's front page was reserved for big time news.

"Just be here."

Rita thought he was hanging up.

"By the way—ever think you'd see me alive again?" Ellis asked softly.

"No," Rita said. "I never thought I would."

Chapter 2

Rita Mars sang along with the Shirelles. She glanced at the Jeep's speedometer and then at the rearview mirror to check for approaching troopers.

The West Virginia countryside blazed with yellow and scarlet. Sunlight sprinkled the rock-strewn pastures with brilliance and made the car's white hood shimmer like a snowfield. Even the black and white Holsteins seemed brighter than usual as they ripped up the last shreds of yellowed pasture grass.

Though it was late October, Rita had the top down on the Jeep. It was good to ride on this open road alone with the sun and wind. She couldn't really be forty-five this year. She ran thirty miles a week and could still get into jeans the size she'd worn in college. Rita peered over the top of her Raybans and took another look in the mirror. Ok, so her dark hair was shot through with silver.

She smiled. It made her look more interesting. After all, how many older women had she fallen madly in love with in her younger years?

Rita flipped the radio off and concentrated on her meeting with Bobby Ellis. She hadn't seen him in forever. Yes, she had thought he might be dead. A superior journalist, he'd thrown it all away with a coke habit that he paid for with a career and a marriage. No one had seen or heard of him now for more than two years.

After he disappeared, a malaise had set. Rita abandoned investigative reporting and spent her time working on a detective's license. She was going to right wrongs instead of writing about wrongs as she described her abrupt life change.

She sighed. She wanted to return to the happier thoughts that had so recently danced in her head.

A red truck with a rainbow sticker on the front bumper appeared in the oncoming lane. Rita's smile came back and she waved as they raced past each other.

"We're everywhere. We're everywhere," she hummed to herself.

She returned to her former mood of excited anticipation. She was seeing Bobby again.

They had been reporters together on the *Washington Star*. More like brother and sister than co-workers, they had fought over editorial recognition, wept on each other's shoulders, and held each other's hand during their respective long, dark nights of the soul.

Rita tried sweet talk at first when his habit began to devour him. Then she got tough. They fought bitterly. In the end, he surrendered everything to the white powder.

She'd been as angry with herself as with him. She couldn't make him stop. Like a flashback, the feelings were the same when she thought about her childhood. She hadn't been able to stop the runaway train her father rode either. Alcohol carried him far and fast. In the end, he stuck his police revolver into his mouth and killed his pain.

Bad memories again. Rita shook her head and switched the radio back on.

"There she was, just a walkin' down the street . . ." Rita sang along at the top of her lungs and pushed the accelerator just a little farther with her docksider.

Five miles and three oldies but goodies later, she slowed as the road narrowed to the twisting mountainside lanes that led to Harper's Ferry. Down the sheer embankment on the passenger side, she could see canoes below on this rocky segment of the Potomac. She took a deep breath. The cobwebs of leftover memory cleared. It was a gorgeous day. At the top of a steep winding hill, Rita spied the flag pole that stood in the center of the Overlook Inn's circular drive. Old Glory ruffled its red stripes in a soft October breeze that seemed more spring than autumn.

The parking areas along the drive were jammed with American made pickups and SUVs. Lots of military bumper stickers and window decals. Families just out of church hopped out of cars and headed for the Inn's dining room and Sunday brunch buffet.

As she reached the crest, she had to slam on the brakes. The drive was blocked by two Harper's Ferry sheriff's cars, a

West Virginia trooper vehicle—blue gumball lights twirling—an ambulance from nearby Ransom, a fire truck, and a dented beige Crown Vic with county plates.

Guests and townies milled around the west annex. A tall, grim-faced sheriff's deputy held them at bay.

"What the heck is this?" Rita jumped out of the Jeep.

Inside the interior of the Overlook lobby was cool and dark. The desk clerk was a woman with long red nails and a plunging neckline to her sundress. Her blue eye shadow made her look like an alien. Oblivious to Rita, she leaned across the far end of the registration counter to stare out the front door toward the commotion outside. Rita pulled off her Raybans.

"What happened?" Rita asked.

"Man killed hisself." The woman continued to lean and stare over the counter.

The taste of metal rose in Rita's throat. "Killed himself?"

"Room 107. Maid found him." The clerk's sense of duty returned and she walked toward the center of the counter where Rita stood. "Can I help you with something?"

Rita felt icy from the inside out. She dug her hand into her pocket to touch that Zippo talisman she always carried.

"I came here to meet someone." The words jumbled in her mouth.

"Name?" The clerk absently flipped the registration book behind the counter.

Rita said nothing.

The clerk looked up then and said once more. "Name?"

4

"Bobby Ellis," Rita whispered.

The two women stared at one another.

Ignoring the angry comments as she elbowed her way, Rita plunged through the people gawking around the Overlook's west annex.

"Lady, you can't go back there." The tall sheriff's deputy in charge of crowd control barred her way with his nightstick.

"I came here to meet him." Rita pushed at the deputy's stick. He towered over her slim, five-foot frame and easily brushed her back.

"Meet who?" He kept the nightstick between them.

"Bobby Ellis. The man in room 107." Rita pushed harder this time.

"I said you can't go back there. Police business." The deputy almost knocked her off her feet.

"I have a right. He's my friend." Rita grabbed the stick this time.

The deputy yanked the stick, pulling her toward him and he leaned his face inches from hers. She could smell the nasty scent of Skoal on his breath.

"You are not goin' anywhere if I say so." He twisted the stick, Rita still hanging on. She let go when her hands ached from the tension.

Tears and rage streamed across her face. Her hands clenched into fists as she raised them once more to do whatever damage she could. Motion behind the deputy on the path to the rooms at the back of the annex stopped her.

"Coming through." A med tech in navy pants and a starched uniform shirt guided the front end of a stainless gurney behind the deputy. On the gurney was a black vinyl body bag.

"Bobby." Rita lunged forward as the deputy stepped aside to make way.

But the deputy was quick. He snatched at the back of her denim shirt, catching her so that the banded collar cut into her throat. Rita gasped.

"Lamar!" A booming command came from behind.

The deputy let go and Rita tumbled against the tech.

"I'm sorry," the tech said. "Nothing we could do when we found him."

Another big paw touched her arm. It was gentler this time. This was the giant who pulled Lamar's chain, a giant with a sheriff's badge and sweet, sad eyes.

"I know this is hard, miss. But I'd like you to come down to the hospital with us and help with a positive ID. Then I'll help you any way I can."

The sheriff put an arm around her shoulder. "I'll walk with you and we'll get him into the ambulance. Is that all right with you?"

Rita nodded.

Her knees were like water, but she walked. Crying, stumbling, held now and then by the giant. She kept one hand on the gurney, the other frantically worked the worn engraving on the lighter in her pocket.

Chapter 3

On this Halloween eve, a gold crescent moon suspended above the valley at Harper's Ferry. On the dark mountainsides, flickers of light signified the little cottages that clung to the steep rocky slopes. It was a clear and perfect night.

Rita saw this through the smudged glass doors of the Harper's Ferry Hospital emergency room. Out there the world was in order. In here, on the other side of a few inches of glass, was chaos and the dread of loss.

As she watched she saw a man standing in the dim edge of the light pool cast by the parking lot lighting. He was dressed in dark clothing and seemed to be looking toward her as she stood in the hospital doorway. Lighting a cigarette? She was drawn to the figure but as she stared, he seemed to disappear.

She looked up and down the rows of cars outside. Nothing and no one. She pulled out her smartphone and tapped the magic numbers.

"Captain Smooth." Mary Margaret answered in her on-duty voice.

Neighbors since the age of six, Mary Margaret Smooth and Rita Mars were inseparable. Together they survived growing up and coming out. They'd been through Rita's father's suicide, Mary Margaret's mother's wrath over her refusal to become a nun, Mary Margaret's long-term relationship with Lola, and Rita's trail of failed matches— including the latest devastation wreaked by the seductive but faithless Diane Winter.

"Mary Margaret. He did not kill himself and I know it." The words flew out of Rita's mouth. "I'm going to find who did this." She pounded her fist on the wall.

"Rita?"

"I'm going to find them and I'm going to make them pay." With teeth clenched, Rita punched the wall again.

The admitting clerk stared at her, but she didn't care.

"Do you hear me?" She was yelling at Mary Margaret.

"Where are you, Slick? I'm coming to get you. Just tell me where you are," Mary Margaret said slowly.

"I'm . . ." But tears burst from her again and she couldn't tell Mary Margaret where she was. She closed her eyes and pulled a deep breath into her shaking body. In a moment, she could speak and she gave details to Mary Margaret.

"I'm ok," Rita said at the end. "I'm leaving now. Meet me at the usual spot?"

"I'll be there, Slick." Mary Margaret hung up.

ℳ

It was well past 1 a.m. when Rita pulled into Baltimore City. The top still down on the Jeep, she had the heater on full blast against the long cold ride from West Virginia. She'd found an old sweatshirt she'd left in the back seat and pulled that over her polo shirt, but it was a thin comfort on a deepening October night.

Rita trundled past the food and shopping pavilions along the Inner Harbor—all the shops were closed and dark. She wound her way down Eastern Avenue toward Fells Point. The bars were still in full swing, jack-o-lanterns in the windows and jukeboxes blaring from the open doors. Loud drunks staggered in gangs along the sidewalks or leaned against brick walls toward an alley as they peed into the darkness.

She arrived at the *Sip N Bite*, open twenty-four hours and serving breakfast any time of day. In younger days, she and Mary Margaret had come here after hours of drinking and dancing in the nearby women's bars on Lombard Street.

Rita found a parking space in front and chained the wheel of the open Jeep. Inside was a mixed crowd of partied-out college kids and off-duty policemen. The kids, sitting at the long Formica counter, were trying to bring food to their mouths without spilling it in their laps. The policemen kept a silent corner of booths to themselves, sipping coffee and scraping up every morsel of fried egg with forks and shreds of toast. The place smelled of old beer and bacon with a hint of onion and Lysol. Every time she came in here, Rita felt like she was walking into an Edward Hopper painting.

"Hey, haven't seen you long time." Nick, *Sip N Bite's* owner and chief cook, called out to her. "You fren' comin' in too?"

Rita nodded. Nick motioned to a harried waitress to take coffee to her table.

The woman was young, but she had deep lines around her grey eyes. Her pulled back hair straggled from its rubber band and her thin hands were roped with veins that made them seem older than the rest of her body. Her pink uniform was clean, but the apron was stained with coffee and ketchup. She poured Rita's coffee, left two menus, and shuffled off toward the kitchen.

The door to the cafe opened. The drunks struggled to sit up straighter and the beat cops finished their plates and paid. Captain Mary Margaret Smooth in her starched black uniform, Glock on her right hip, stepped inside.

She was the tallest 5'6" cop in the city. With her dark hair and eyes, she could easily have been Rita's older—and taller—sister. Mary Margaret had perfect Catholic school posture that gave her height and presence and an unwavering gaze she had plagiarized from the Mother Superior at St. Frank's. When she entered a room, people cleared a path.

"Slick," she whispered when she took off her hat and sat down, "what the hell is going on?"

The story rushed from Rita's mouth. At several points Mary Margaret had to slow her down and get her to repeat.

As Rita concluded, the waitress slipped their bacon and eggs in front of them.

"And I'm telling you, Smooth, Bobbie Ellis did not kill himself." Rita leaned across the table. "He was meeting somebody that weekend—a source. He was on to something. He knew too much and somebody killed him."

Mary Margaret sipped her coffee. "But you said he was found hanged. That's a mighty tough act to pull off as a murder."

Rita chomped into a strip of bacon. "Are you saying you don't believe me?"

"No, I'm not saying that at all. But having done a turn in homicide, I say it's not a likely murder method." Captain Smooth now headed a vice unit.

"I agree," Rita said. "Though if this was the work of some government spook group, they could have carried it off. The last series of articles he was working on was a government expose."

"Slick, you sound like talk radio. You were an investigative reporter too long."

"Tell me it's impossible."

"I can't," Mary Margaret said.

"You're looking at me with that Sister Mary Holy Water face of disdain," Rita said.

"I am not."

"Smooth, this was a great guy. He helped me so many times, and even though he was headed down the tubes, he fought his way back. He was not about to end it all. I can't let this go."

"And you want me to . . ." Mary Margaret set down her coffee cup and waited.

"Help me find the killer," Rita said.

Mary Margaret nodded and sighed. "I have no choice."

"What's that supposed to mean?"

"Shall we count the times I've posted bail, pulled you out of close encounters of the assault kind, and . . ."

"Never mind," Rita said. "I got it."

♏

Rita's office was in the labyrinth of narrow side streets surrounding the Baltimore City courthouse. The worn brick Homer building on Lafayette was the headquarters for bail bondsmen, finance companies, a collections agency, and RM Security Services. Rita could have afforded better, but she decided that the location provided greater anonymity than high-class suburban office buildings. Clients did not like to be recognized visiting a private investigator.

As a frosty sun gilded the city streets, Rita wheeled her Jeep off the Jones Falls Expressway in the direction of that office. She still had on the jeans, cowboy boots, and polo shirt, she'd worn to West Virginia. She could brush her teeth and comb her hair when she got to the office.

The light was on in her reception area where her admin, Beverly, was already at work. Rita hoped he had brought some doughnuts. She'd had no sleep since her late night meeting with Mary Margaret and she had a craving for the twin foundations of improved focus: sugar and caffeine.

Today Beverly wore six-inch imitation crocodile heels, a black leather mini skirt, and a white angora sweater with a plunging neckline—the white accented his clear chocolate skin. His makeup was textbook exceptional, as were his accessories, and he'd had a fresh nail job, plain red this time instead of the orange and black he'd sported in honor of Halloween.

Beverly Hills was Rita's administrative assistant. Her real name was Charles Tyrell Wheatly. When she'd first met Charles, she called herself Helen Wheels, but having matured over time, she felt that the new name conveyed a greater sense of class and sophistication.

She'd first met Bev when she was working on a story about a serial killer stalking transgender individuals in the Baltimore-Washington community. Four dead and the police didn't seem to take notice. Rita's angle was to bring attention to this fact and force authorities to step up the pace before others were murdered. The story turned sensational and lit a fire under police after a prominent—and closeted—banker fell victim.

A close friend of Beverly's was one of the murdered. She came forth then and offered, through Rita's liaison between the community and the police, to act as bait. Rita had advised against it, unsure that the police would give her real protection.

"I have to," Beverly said. "That was my friend."

Rita never forgot those words and they remained close long after the killer was put away.

"Morning." Rita grunted and shuffled to the coffee pot to pour herself a cup.

"Doughnuts?"

"Well, aren't we the cheery one today?" Beverly took a white bakery box out of her desk. "Your favorites, my dear. I picked these out myself." She handed over the box.

Rita extracted a chocolate frosted and wandered off to her desk in the adjoining room. She plopped into her big leather swivel chair, sat and stared.

Beverly followed close behind. "And I'm welcome, I'm sure."

Rita set down the coffee and her doughnut on the blotter.

"Honey, what is the matter? You didn't run into that Diane girl again, did you?" Beverly stood with hands on his hips.

Rita shook her head and took a deep breath. "I'm sorry, Bev. A good friend of mine died yesterday."

Beverly rushed over to stoop beside the chair. "Honey, I'm sorry."

"Bev, I think he was murdered."

"Oh, my. Is it somebody I knew?"

"I don't think you ever got to meet him. He'd just called me last week. I went to see him in Harper's Ferry and—he was dead." A lump rose in her throat and she squeezed back tears.

Beverly scooted into the bathroom just off Rita's office and returned with a handful of tissues. "Here you go, honey."

"Bev, cancel my afternoon appointments, will you? I've got to think about how to handle this situation."

"Honey, I can cancel those afternoon appointments, but you've got a woman's gonna be in here in about five minutes. Called last thing Friday as I was leaving."

Rita blew her nose and tossed the tissue into her wastebasket. "Tell her I'm not here. Tell her I'm sick, tell her—"

The main door opened then and through her office doorway, Rita could see a well-dressed blonde woman. The woman nodded and took a seat in the outer office.

"Dammit." Rita walked into the bathroom and started running cold water. "Stall her until I can wash my face and brush my teeth at least."

The woman was petite, Rita's size, but with ash blonde hair and pale hazel eyes. Rita stopped breathing. It was the reaction she'd had the first time she'd seen Diane—like being terrified and wildly happy at the same time.

Her visitor wore a tailored navy suit with a leather folio under her arm. She carried herself with confidence and a businesslike demeanor, though she did do a subtle double take as Beverly welcomed her into the office.

"Karin VanDreem," she said as she extended her hand. She had such elegant fingers, a lapis pinky ring on her left hand, a diamond band on the right.

Rita popped on her bifocals, hoping the lenses would obstruct the red puffiness around her eyes. Karin sat in the wingback chair in front of Rita's desk. She stole a last glance as Beverly exited.

"I'm sorry, but I didn't get a chance to ask my assistant about the reason for your visit. Will you fill me in?" Rita opened her notepad and picked a pen from her top drawer. When she glanced up, Karin's soft hazel eyes caught her attention.

"I know your name from your journalism career," Karin said.

"Thank you."

"Particularly the series you did on domestic violence and stalking."

Rita nodded. She couldn't keep away from those hazel eyes.

"That's why I came to ask for your assistance." Karin paused and took a breath.

"You need advice about—"

"I need to hire someone for security." Karin shifted in her seat.

"That's not the usual kind of thing I do." Rita looked up.

The hazel eyes were waiting. They sent shivers through her.

"Your advertisement says Investigative and Security Services." VanDreem stiffened.

"It does," Rita agreed. "But the kind of security I do is providing people for events or background checks or short-term chaperoning for visiting celebrities or executives."

"Look, you know from the articles you wrote what a woman's options are when this kind of thing starts. The police are useless. They're only going to come to my house when they get the 911 call after someone's found my body."

"Exactly who is stalking you?" Rita asked.

"My ex-husband. We were divorced a year ago. It started three months ago with my coming home from work and finding things taken from the house or rearranged or small dead animals in strange places."

"And it escalated?"

VanDreem nodded. "Phone calls in the middle of the night from untraceable numbers. Scary laborers who showed up at the house asking for work."

"But you have proof it was him?"

"None that the police will accept."

Rita leaned toward her. "Then how do you know it was him?"

"He has played on every fear he knows I have. It's too perfect, too pat, to have been anyone else." VanDreem pressed her hand against her forehead for a moment. "I'm sorry. I'm about at the end of my rope with this and I don't know what else to do." She looked around the room. "Do you happen to have any coffee?"

Rita jumped up and went to the door to the reception area and motioned Beverly for another cup of coffee.

"Oooh, ain't she sweet," Beverly whispered in Rita's ear as she brought in a tray with coffee and the remaining doughnut arranged on a silver plate. VanDreem tried to hide another quick appraisal of the black Amazon who was Rita's secretary.

Rita poked him in the ribs as he walked by.

With Beverly safely back at the reception desk, Rita sat again across from Karin VanDreem. She took a sip of fresh coffee and watched as her client poured in the cream and sugar.

Perfect nails, short, cared for, unpainted. Slim fingers sloping from a small hand and delicate wrist. Rita followed the coffee cup to Karin's lips which were also unpainted and delineated a tender mouth around which hovered smile lines. VanDreem said something.

"I didn't catch that," Rita said.

"Will you help me?" Karin asked.

"What did you have in mind, Ms. VanDreem? Body guard duty twenty-four hours a day is not a possibility." Rita took too big a gulp of coffee and burned her tongue.

"Please, just call me Karin. I don't need someone to be glued to me. I was thinking more along the lines of random checks of the house. Checking out the source of phone calls. I need a case to put in front of him and his attorney that will be conclusive enough to threaten his livelihood if I take it public."

"And what does he do that publicity would hurt him?" Rita asked.

"Dr. Douglas Sevier."

"The child psychiatrist?"

"Author of Parental Direction, Families and Bonding, etc."

"The guy with the talk show," Rita mused.

"His attorney is Steven Cushman."

Rita raised an eyebrow. "Cushman's the king of white-collar plea bargains."

"They went to the University of Virginia together." Karin set down her coffee. "And how did Douglas and I get together is the question rolling around in your head."

"Can't say that it didn't," Rita admitted.

"It's a long and dull story. Suffice it to say that I worked with him a long time ago. I'm a PR consultant. I let professional admiration get confused with emotional neediness." Karin looked away for a moment.

"It's happened to us all," Rita said, Diane Winter coming uninvited to her thoughts.

"Look," Karin said, "I know you were an investigative reporter for more than seventeen years. You were relentless in pursuit of your stories, and you frequently used some—shall we say—unorthodox methods to get what you wanted. But I also know, from the body of your work, that you have a deep sense of commitment about what's right."

Rita leaned forward. She could smell the perfume now. She smiled. "After that comment, how could I refuse to take this case."

"So what do I need to do now?" Karin asked.

"We have an agreement to sign. I'd like access to be able to do security checks at your house. Initial payment." Rita pulled a contract from her desk drawer and handed it across the desk. "And I need some information about your ex-husband."

Karin reached into her folio. "Here are an extra set of keys to my house—basement door is this little one." She slid them across the desk. Next she unfolded her checkbook.

With business complete, Rita followed Karin VanDreem into the reception area. She saw Beverly watching out of the corner of his eye as he typed on his computer.

"I have to comment on this," Rita said as she walked Karin to the door.

Karin raised her eyebrow.

"For a woman supposedly in danger, you seem pretty matter-of-fact."

"It's a trick I've learned over the years in business dealings. I can't reveal that I think my client's ideas are ridiculous or that I'm afraid to lose the account. I also teach at the woman's prison. In that setting, I don't want my students to see revulsion for their crimes and above all, I don't want them to see fear. I would be doomed." Karin swallowed hard. "But make no mistake, Ms. Mars—I am afraid for my life."

Their eyes met and Rita, for just a moment, saw that truth.

Then quickly Karin VanDreem extended her hand and Rita took it. She knew it would be a firm and warm handshake. For a second, when the ritual ended, Karin's hand lingered in hers. And the perfume—*Obsession.*

Rita took a deep breath.

The door closed and Karin VanDreem was gone.

"I see you didn't eat that doughnut I brought you. Must have been distracted." Beverly smiled and kept on typing.

"She's straight." Rita walked toward her office.

"Yeah, and so are some of my best friends," Beverly said.

Rita slammed the door behind her.

Behind her desk, she bit into her doughnut. She could still smell perfume. She glanced at the empty chair, then back to her notepad.

Quickly she scribbled a list, people connected to Bobby Ellis, people who might know more than she. Next of kin was his brother, Edmund, face doctor to the rich and shameless around the DC beltway. At least that's who the West Virginia hospital told her they had contacted about the death and transport of the body.

And there was Trisha, Bobby's ex-wife. They still had to be in touch. Even in the depths of his addiction, Bobby had talked about his son and made weekly pilgrimages to visit after the divorce. He had been so afraid he would never see that child again.

Then came the flashback. Rita saw her father in his resplendent Maryland trooper brown. He was starched and straight, and he looked like a prince. Over and over he would tell Rita and her brother, Kit, how much he loved them. She heard him say that to her mother many times. But the alcohol came before them all, and it was a master who demanded blood sacrifice. All she had left was his official police photograph, a Glock 22 and a banged-up chrome lighter with a doomsday warning.

This thought returned her to the task at hand. She jotted down more names and places. The newspaper where Bobby had last worked, and the place he was trying to get back to—
The Star.

Rita finished a long list and sighed. She'd been awake too many hours. Her eyes burned. Even with the sugar and caffeine overdose, she was fading.

"Bev, I've got to get some sleep. I'm dead on my feet." Rita paused at the reception desk.

"I'll be in early tomorrow," Bev responded.

"You're a doll," Rita said

"Honey, don't I know it." Bev gave her a wink.

♏

It was a forty-minute ride to Rita's house in the country. She had fallen in love with an old white farmhouse in Baltimore County north of the city in the heart of Maryland horse country.

It had been a tedious two-and-a-half-hour drive from there to The Star's DC office on L Street. She'd bought it two years before she left the paper. Unconsciously she must have known she was on her way out of the newspaper business.

The land out here was gently rolling, much like the West Virginia landscape she had just left. The difference was that the hills were softer. Though suburban warrens of townhouse communities threatened to swarm across the rich pastures, it was still a vista of wide-open space. Horses grazed here instead of dairy herds.

Rita punched down on the Jeep's accelerator and sped further out I-83 toward home and away from the city. The top was still down and she had the heater on full blast. She switched on the radio.

The tune was "Dancin' in the Dark" and Rita sang along.

Rita wheeled into the short uphill drive to her house. Near the top, she slammed on her brakes and honked the horn.

"Move it, buster."

A large yellow tabby lay sprawled across the asphalt. He raised his head at the screech of the brakes and stared at the vehicle looming over him. This was The Great White Hunter. Just after she'd moved in, he'd been dropped near the house and a few days later hit by a car. Rita had footed the vet bills and the rest was history.

Rita tapped the horn again. The Hunter leisurely pulled himself to his feet, stretched, sauntered to the edge of the drive.

"You're really playing this a little too close, bud." Rita emerged from the parked Jeep and walked over to scratch his head.

"Hellooooo." A frail, white-haired woman in a flower print dress and cardigan waved energetically from the front yard of the house next door.

"Loretta." Rita waved back and walked across her drive and the next one into her neighbor's front yard.

"How do you do." The woman said and extended a wavering hand freckled by years of gardening. "My name is Loretta Mondieu. My husband is Vernon—though he's not here right now. And you are?"

"Rita Mars. I'm pleased to meet you, Loretta."

"Mars. Unusual name, my dear. Very unusual." The woman cocked her head thoughtfully. "You know we've lived in this house for more than fifty years. My family's owned this land for more than a hundred."

Loretta had Alzheimer's. For the last two years, Rita had repeated this introduction at least once a month. "Isn't Scarsdale handsome?" Loretta gestured with pride at the stone goose still in his Halloween outfit. He wore a black cape and a black pointed witch's hat. Leaning across his left wing was a tiny homemade broom.

"He is striking," Rita agreed.

"Yes, striking."

"Well, it was a pleasure meeting you, Loretta. I hope you'll give my best to Vernon."

"Come again," Lorretta said. "And if you see Hodge, tell him we've been expecting him for dinner."

Hodge was Loretta's long deceased uncle and the former owner/occupant of Rita's home. Loretta concluded every meeting with Rita with a request to be remembered to him.

"I will certainly do that," Rita said.

When she walked through the back door into her kitchen, she shivered. She kept expecting to see the ghost of Hodge one of these days.

Right now she didn't want to see anyone, alive or dead. She craved sleep. The first day of November was near an end. The same sliver of moon that had hung over Harper's Ferry on Sunday night now rose above the rolling hills. A fox barked from the line of locust trees that ran along the ridge above her back pasture.

Rita locked the door behind her and trudged up the wooden stairway to her room. She stripped to nothing and snuggled under the down comforter on her king-size bed. She was going to sleep forever.

She woke around midnight and threw on a sweatshirt, socks and a worn pair of sweatpants. Armed with a Coke and a slapped together cheese sandwich, she slipped into her home office.

The office was small. On three walls were shelves of books. On the remaining wall was frame after frame of 5x7 photos of her favorite people. Her grandmother, Lily. Rita and her brother at the beach, governors, senators, law makers and law breakers. Two presidents and three Attorneys General. Her cocker spaniel, Huxley, friend and companion from fifth grade through freshman year at college. The gang from The Star at the Press Club Awards dinner, 1987—Bobby Ellis was in that picture. Her first lover, Tricia. There was a space where one frame had been recently removed.

Rita sat and turned on her PC. She immediately launched into her search to track down the stories Bobby Ellis had written for the Montgomery Monitor. The first was about violation and circumvention of procurement regulations. Boring. Mundane. He was still rusty here. Nothing new. Nothing different. The second was about pollution credits. The writing was crisper, but she recognized it as rehash of alternative press reporting. She shook her head.

"This is not what got you killed," she said to herself.

The third made her sit up and take notice. Bobby was into this story. It punched hard. It named names and catalogued a host of details that only an insider could know.

"This is where you picked up your source." Rita sat back in her chair.

The story was about the senior senator from Pennsylvania. It clearly outlined with facts, the money and the gifts and the trips from pharma lobby and how it compromised the senator's ability to render objectivity as chair of the committee advising oversight of the FDA.

Britt Hillman was up for election this year. The vote was scheduled for Tuesday. Rita clicked into another data source. The usually unbeatable senator was sweating out a neck-and-neck race in the polls.

"Did he kill you?" Rita took a swig of Coke. "Or did your source give you something too hot to handle by yourself?"

Chapter 4

The Star's newsroom had once been the home of a secret society of crusaders. It was dim then and sectioned into a warren of small, private offices. The air was thick with the hint of power and the endless search for inconvenient truths secreted by the rich and infamous.

Now it was a boiler room operation, lined row after row with long, open carrels. On every wall were huge monitors constantly streaming the news from channels around the world. There was a huge glass enclosed live shot arena for video interviews. It was open. It was bright lights, big city. It was not her newsroom any more.

And yet every story written, those of the doomed and those of the chosen, the beautiful and the bad, they all still lived here. Rita quivered with that high voltage rush brought on by the thrill and threat of deadlines.

Reflex, she said to herself. It's only the vestige of seventeen years of memory.

It was a quarter to four and the evening edition crew was on board. A few graying heads, but the rest looked like they should have been in high school. I can't be this old, she thought to herself.

Then she caught a glimpse of the person she was looking for. Huntley Shell sat at his computer where day and night news stories from across the universe appeared at the magical touch of a computer key.

Shell was tall and lean with a movie star jaw and dirty blond hair. He was the kind of guy you saw on the golf course with an easy swing and casual saunter—country club pretty. His eyes were blue, evasive with a prurient glaze. He was not the guy you wanted on night watch if you slept in enemy territory; he'd sell you in an instant for a hot story byline. Huntley Shell was lead man on the White House beat.

He looked up.

Rita took a deep breath and approached him.

"Hey, Rita. How's the detective biz?" he asked.

"You make it sound like Amway."

"I get an image from it, you know? Spying on errant husbands, sneaking around in rubber-soled shoes."

"Thanks for the vote of confidence." Rita rolled her eyes, then plunked heavily into a nearby chair.

"Hey, I'm only kidding." Huntley pushed back from his desk to face Rita.

"No, you're not, but I don't care. I came here for information."

"Ok, so what do you need?"

"Bobby Ellis. I heard he was bucking to get back here."

"Avery would never have taken him back," Huntley snorted. Bill Avery was *The Star's* managing editor.

"And why not?" Rita asked.

"The man was a loser. He couldn't write a bad check."

"According to who?" Rita snapped forward in her seat.

"I'm telling you. Bobby was a used-up cokehead who'd been through the rehab mill and was pretending to get it together. You know how he got the job at the *Montgomery Monitor*—working for less than scale. He wrote a lot of schlock. Then he came up with that over-hyped series on government influence buying," Huntley said.

"He was a good reporter." Rita could feel those nasty little furrows that scrunched between her eyebrows when she was mad. She massaged the bridge of her nose.

"Well, the *Monitor* material was better than his last stuff here. I will give him that, but not—if you will forgive the term—star quality." Huntley cocked his head at a snobbish angle.

"*Star* quality?"

"Come on. He was hacking at tired targets. You've got to get in tight with the big boys to make your name with a story."

"Damn it, Huntley. If you're doing an investigative piece, the 'big boys' aren't going to say diddly." Rita propelled herself from the chair.

"In this day and age, you've got to have high profile connections or you're nowhere. This is the age of celebrity," he said.

"This is not the age of celebrity," she said drawing herself up as tall as possible. "This is the age of proctology—which is why I left. I got tired of the view."

Huntley stared at her.

Rita closed her eyes. "I didn't come here to start a fight."

"I'm sorry. I know Bobby was a friend. I shouldn't have called him a loser," Huntley said. "But dammit, he pissed me off. He had it all. Besides his goddamned looks, he got the stories—the really good ones. Then one day he decided to suck his life up his nose."

"I don't think one day he decided that." Rita's voice was soft and sad.

"Well, it was a stupid move and it cost him everything," Huntley said.

"Yes, it did cost him everything."

Huntley Shell and Rita Mars looked away from one another.

"So, what do you need?" Huntley said at last.

Rita sat down. "What was going on with Bobby? Any rumors?"

"I know he was trying to get back here. He called Avery once a week. The 'influence' series was supposed to be his ticket in. Avery liked the series, but didn't promise anything. He wasn't sure about the coke cure."

"He burned a lot of bridges while he was snorting," Rita said.

"Damn right. I'm still surprised the *Monitor* picked him up."

"Anything else?"

"Avery said Bobby told him that the last in the series was the best. It was going to blow the hinges off some very big doors," Huntley said.

"Did he say what it was about?"

Huntley shook his head.

How foreign this newsroom had become. A cough here or there, silent heads staring at flickering screens. The only sound was the tapping of keyboards and the occasional ding of the breakroom microwave.

"Did any of Bobbie's stories draw any flak?" Rita asked.

"The fourth one—PAC money piece on Britt Hillman, the esteemed senator from Pennsylvania. Hillman got bent out of shape. Sent lots of letters. He and Bobby got into a shouting match at a press conference where Hillman denied the charges. I was there. Hillman gave Bobby a shove and said rumormongers like him should be shot. Bobby was in his glory, smiling—knew he'd drawn blood. He came up to me afterward and said he hoped he'd have a desk next to mine." Huntley turned away from Rita. "I didn't have much to say to him."

"Ok, so Hillman gets a knot in his knickers and mouths off. He pokes Bobby and lobs a cheap threat witnessed by a swarm of hungry reporters."

"Not exactly the performance of a hit man who means business," Huntley said.

"The story do much damage?"

Huntley shrugged. "Who's to say? Nothing seems to stop a longtime incumbent. Name recognition is everything."

"Yeah, put a face on TV enough and, bingo, sheep are gonna follow." Rita nodded.

"Other than that, I know nada."

Rita rose from her seat. "Thanks. I appreciate your help." She shook Huntley's hand.

"I'll keep my ears open. I hear anything, you'll be the first to know," he said.

"Here's my card."

Huntley stared at the card. "Rita, you were a damned good reporter. Come back."

"Got to do this, Huntley," she said, "but thanks."

Rita stepped outside onto L Street again. The predawn air was chill and melded with the scent of gasoline exhaust and sewer fumes. The capitol dome gleamed as a beacon of order above a conflicted city. Sirens howled in pursuit while sodium street lamps poured golden light across dark alleys and heroic statues, people of power and people of poverty.

Above Rita's head the *Star* sign glowed like a Broadway marquee. There were so many stories. She had written some of them. She took a backward glance at the door she'd just closed and walked away from temptation.

♏

It was just before six as Rita approached Baltimore from I-95. She decided that she would swing through Karin VanDreem's neighborhood instead of heading for home. She wanted to familiarize herself with the territory in the dark as well as the day.

Karin lived in Guilford. The community was characterized by huge old colonial and Victorian homes with expansive yards, well-tended gardens, thick stands of trees and shrubbery. As Rita thought about it, the place was perfect for predators with robbery in mind, easy cover for concealment and escape.

Over the last ten years the surrounding neighborhoods had gone to seed. Guilford was an island bounded on all sides by areas of high crime and transient residents. Rita wondered why this woman stayed here at all. The aging fortresses seemed like bulwarks against the unthinkable, but these venerable addresses were frequent notes in the police blotter.

Rita turned off St. Paul onto Stratford. The curbs were spotted here and there with Beemers and Mercedes and Volvo wagons, though all of the residents had garages and were off the street. At this hour most windows were dark.

Karin VanDreem lived at the end on the corner of Stratford and Underwood. It was a big brick colonial with thick English boxwood hedges that ran the perimeter of a wide yard. Rita could see the front door plainly, but that was all. Two oaks deepened the darkness in front.

Rita took a left on Underwood, drove down a block and turned around to scout the scene coming from the other direction. The house faced Stratford and doubling back this way gave her a better view of the east side of the house.

Movement in the hedge. Imagination or real? Did someone step back through the boxwood from the street into Karin's yard? Rita passed the front door once more. Nothing.

But the action out of the corner of her eye demanded attention. She neared the next intersection, slowed, cut the Jeep's lights and rolled to a stop. Now what, bright girl, she said to herself. She wasn't carrying her weapon and she wasn't about to stroll around a stalking victim's back yard in the dead of night without some kind of protection.

Rita looked in the glove box. No pepper spray. She thought of taking the jack handle under the back seat. Fat chance. By the time she dug that thing out the entire neighborhood would be on alert.

The bat, of course. Through the summer Rita pitched in an "over the hill" softball league. She kept her glove, her cleats, and her good luck bat in the Jeep. She reached back and clasped its worn rubber grip, then snapped off the dome light so that opening her door wouldn't draw attention.

Her breath quickened as she slid quietly out of the driver's side and left the door ajar in the interest of stealth. She had on a pair of Italian loafers. Not the best to run in, but what the hell, it beat six-inch heels. Too bad they made such a scratchy crunch on the sidewalk.

As she walked, she hoped no overly alert homeowner would spy a woman walking down his street with a baseball bat in hand. She moved closer to the hedgerows and fences and out of the light from the street lamps. The remnants of wood smoke hung in the chill air.

Rita halted at the entrance walk to Karin's. She couldn't see around or over the hedge so she stood still for a moment and listened. The morning was silent. Only her breathing made any sound.

But as she crept toward the end of the hedge, she heard the snap of a stick. Someone was walking on the other side. Rita held her breath. Whoever it was stopped moving.

Rita waited. Was it a footstep? But then, the soft swish of fabric on fabric. It was not imagination.

Rita crept to the end of the hedge. The dark was almost impenetrable. Karin VanDreem's house was between two streetlights, both blocked by trees still in full leaf, and the porch light was too weak to carry this far.

Rita took a chance and thrust her head around the corner for a quick peak. The streetlight cast just enough light to make out a silhouette. He had his back to her, looking at the house. He carried something in his right hand, maybe a magnum flashlight.

He was much taller than her, heavier, but that's all she could determine. She had no idea if he had a gun. She slipped quickly around the hedge again when she heard another twig crack. He was walking, slowly, toward the back of her house. She had one way to make this work.

Rita stole around the hedge to draw a bead on her target. Then she launched herself. Treading as lightly as possible, she sprinted to a spot at the man's left elbow. There she planted her feet, cocked the bat, and swung away across the back of the man's knees.

He fell like a chain-sawed pine. Rita was on him immediately. She held his upper arms down with her legs and yanked the bat under this throat in a chokehold.

"Who the hell are you?" Sweat trickled down her temple.

"You broke my knees."

"You'll recover. Now tell me who you are and what you're doing here."

At this point, he started to twist from his hips to try and throw Rita off. She tightened the grip on the bat. He lay still again.

"You don't want to do that."

"I can't breathe." His voice was muffled.

"Then tell me who you are."

"Guilford Community Security," the man gasped. "The association hired us to patrol the area. Too many robberies."

"What were you doing sneaking around this house?"

"I wasn't sneaking. I saw somebody and came to check it out. Hey, let up on this damned bat will you?"

"Gun?" Rita asked.

"Shoulder holster, left side."

He was correct.

A light went on in an upstairs room of Karin Van Dreem's house.

"Radio?" Rita said.

"Right hip. It's a cell phone."

Rita reached back quickly, grabbed the phone and dialed 911.

Robert Ruger was the security guard's name. He had a bruise under his chin and one on his ego, but was otherwise healthy when the police arrived. The security company's night manager pulled up shortly thereafter. He was as angry at Ruger as he was at Rita. She apologized, explained the situation, and promised she would notify the company if she did any more night surveillance. Karin, in a wine-colored robe, charged into the growing crowd in her yard to defend Rita. The police took a dim view, nevertheless, and muttered their usual comments about pulling Rita's license.

By now half of Karin VanDreem's neighbors hung out of windows or walked out onto their sidewalks to check out the commotion. Police reassured them, shooed them back inside, and then took off into the rising sun. Robert Ruger left to nurse his wounded pride, and Karin invited Rita in for a cup of coffee.

The warm yellow kitchen was homey and big, with utensils and appliances that Karin probably knew how to use. It smelled of homemade cookies. Karin set a mug of coffee and a plate of fresh chocolate chip cookies in front of Rita. She sat down beside her at the breakfast nook under a huge bay window. The first rays of morning spiked through.

"Well, that was pretty interesting," Karin's eyes sparkled with excitement.

"Yes, it isn't every day that I get to capture a real live security guard." Rita took another cookie.

"But I'm glad you were here and observant enough to see that something was going on." Karin's robe gapped at her throat and plunged a V straight to her breasts.

Rita turned away and stared hard at the cookie she was eating. "The one thing I'm concerned about is that he told me the reason he was wandering around in your yard is he saw someone here."

"Oh." Karin stiffened. She noticed her robe falling open and pulled it together.

Rita breathed a sigh of relief. "Now, I'm sure whoever it was is long gone. Between the police with their gumball lights and the neighbors spilling out into the streets, he probably got the hell out of Dodge."

"I'm sure." Karin stared into her coffee.

Rita brushed cookie crumbs off her hands with a napkin. "Before I leave, I want you to take my cell phone number. I never turn it off. If you get the least bit worried, if you see or hear something, call me. I can get someone here, even if I can't make it."

"Do you think you should spend the night?" She touched Rita's arm.

"You'll be fine. I promise."

Karin VanDreem nodded. She went to the counter and took up a pad and pencil to jot down the number.

Rita started to reach for another cookie, thought better of it and drew back her hand.

"Go on. I'll just end up eating these all myself." Karin pushed the plate toward Rita.

"These are great. Thanks." Rita bit into another. "For the next two days, I'll be in West Virginia. But I'll call you several times each day. Remember if anything looks weird, call me."

"I will," Karin said.

Rita stood to leave. "Keep the house locked. I'll have a friend of mine do a security check on the doors and windows to see how tamperable they are. And we need to get some motion sensor lights around here. It's a stalker's dream out there."

"I've resisted that idea. It seems so—paranoid," Karin said as she followed Rita to the back door.

"You know what they say—just because you're paranoid . . ."

"I've heard it a million times." Karin smiled.

"I'll come over when I get back in town." Rita said.

Karin touched her arm again. "Thanks for being so watchful." She took Rita's hand in both of hers. "It makes me feel safer already."

Rita could smell the perfume again.

Chapter 5

The ride to West Virginia was different this time. Rita drove hard, kept her eyes on the road, ignoring a glorious November sun. The radio was off. Time and miles passed swiftly. While Rita was out of town, Bev was in charge of Karin VanDreem's security and nothing was going to happen during Bev's watch. Bev had survived Iraq in the front line of "Desert Storm," so she was no amateur at vigilance and protective measures. At this point, it was the only sure thing Rita possessed.

She passed the general store in Bolivar. Two old men in flannel shirts lounged in rockers out front, smoking their pipes. They didn't look up as she sped by.

Three miles later she entered the town of Harper's Ferry. How convenient, she thought - the police station, post office, city hall and a liquor store were housed in the same brick building. Two houses down was the white-columned portico of Friendly and Sons mortuary. It could have been the veranda of Scarlett's Tara except for the bronze colored hearse parked in the circular drive.

Rita swung into the parking lot beside the liquor store and walked to the station house. Behind the counter were two metal desks and a radio dispatch console. At one desk sat a brown-uniformed officer. He was the goon who had grabbed her at the motel the day Bobby was found.

At the radio console sat a woman in uniform pants and a polo shirt; the radio was quiet and the woman was reading *People* magazine. To Rita's left was a glass enclosed private office for the sheriff. He wasn't in.

"Good morning." Rita's entrance occasioned a glance, but the officer didn't get up. The radio operator turned to stare.

"Morning." The deputy was tall, very thin with a slight paunch of skin that folded just at the top of his Sam Browne belt. His face was weathered and lined; ferret eyes glinted at her with suspicion.

"I'm Rita Mars. I called yesterday about getting information on the Bobby Ellis case."

The radio operator looked at the policeman who rose slowly then and took his time in getting to the counter. "The suicide. Yeah, I remember the chief saying something about that."

Rita waited for him to offer assistance. When none came, she said, "Yes, he said I could review the files."

The radio operator kept watching, but when the policeman glanced back at her with narrowed eyes, she swiveled to face the console again.

"Sheriff'll have to get those for you." The man's voice was slow and tight with resistance.

"I can't just see them now? It won't take long."

"No, ma'am. I have to get permission from the sheriff to take those out." He rested his spidery fingers on the counter.

"But he said it would be all right for me to look at them." Rita could feel the rise of heat and thunder in her chest.

The radio operator spun around in her chair. "He told me if she—"

The deputy turned on her. "This is police business, Margie. Sheriff said he'd let her look at the files, he'll have to be here."

"OK, then. Is he around?"

"He'll be back directly. Have a seat there if you want to." He pointed to a long wooden bench against the wall and went to his desk.

"Thank you." Clenching her teeth made Rita's head hurt. As she waited, the radio crackled with a static jittery voice. Rita could make out nothing of the call, but the deputy reached for his ranger hat, plopped it on his head and came around the counter.

"Margie, those files stay put 'til the sheriff gets back." With that he swung out the door without a glance at Rita.

"Charming man," Rita said.

The radio operator craned her neck to watch out the front window. When the tan police cruiser nosed out into the street, she spoke. "Lamar don't mean anything. He's just pissed because he didn't make chief deputy, so now he wants to make everybody else miserable."

The woman pointed to a coffee maker. "Want some?"

Rita smiled and nodded. "Thanks, it's a long drive from Baltimore. Do you know when Sheriff Carter will be back?"

The woman handed a Styrofoam cup over the counter. "Lunchtime."

It was a little after nine.

"Three hours?" Rita put her head in her hands. "Can't we call him? I'd like to get this done."

"Sheriff's out hunting today. Squirrel season."

"Great. I'm going to sit here until he bags his limit. Is he going to be as difficult as Captain America?"

"Shoot, no." The woman bustled toward a metal credenza. "Now what was the name on that suicide?"

Rita put down her coffee to pick up her leather portfolio. "Ellis. Robert Ellis."

"Sad thing for a family when somebody kills himself." She rooted through the hanging files. "Now you just go in the sheriff's office and sit down." She slipped a manila folder out of the drawer.

Rita glanced out the window. "What if the terminator comes back?"

She followed Margie into the office. A potent trail of Taboo wafted behind. Rita hadn't smelled that since high school.

"He's not gonna be back here for hours. That radio call was from his girlfriend in Ransom. Her trucker husband just hit the road."

"I don't want to get you in trouble." Rita eased into the pliant leather chair behind the desk.

"I'm the sheriff's niece. I'm not going to get in trouble. Besides I heard him talking to you on the phone when he said it was all right." Margie deposited the file on the desk. "You need anything, give me a holler. Copier's on the table over there."

Mary Margaret had told her that the police might not let her make copies; she'd have to take notes. Rita felt like jumping up and giving this woman a hug—except that her potent perfume might transfer. Margie closed the glass door to the office as she left.

Rita opened the file. On top were the sheriff and coroner reports; below she could see the black and white glossies. Without looking she pulled the reports out and closed the file on the photographs. She'd have to prepare herself before examining them.

At 11:30 a.m. on Sunday, September 10th, a call came in from the Overlook Inn. A body was found hanging in room 107 from the bathroom shower rod. Lamar Houston was the first officer on the scene.

Rita tapped the report with her pen. The prose was too articulate for Lamar. She flipped it over to see the signature of Justin P. Carter, Sheriff, Harper's Ferry. He had the orderly penmanship of a schoolboy. Was he really out shooting cute little squirrels?

Lamar phoned the chief and Dr. Eustace McClung, coroner for Ransom, Bolivar, and Harper's Ferry. He left the body in place until both arrived. He made the housekeeper, who had found Bobby, stay in the room until the Sheriff Carter arrived.

Black and white edges of the police photos caught her eye. Rita glanced down at the manila folder. She touched the tab and pulled back the cover.

A shot of the entrance to the room. The bed was still made. The curtains to the sliding glass door on the other side were closed.

Next shot. The bathroom from the doorway and a man at the faucet end of the tub. He seemed to be straddling the side, but he was slumped, asleep, tired. Rita closed the folder and looked out the glass toward the radio console. Margie had the mike in her hand; her lips moved.

Rita looked down at the folder again. She'd seen a million Viet Nam, Gulf War, Afghanistan pictures. Worse, they were far worse; children and charred bodies, IED victims, decapitations, field executions. But she had not known those people, read their stories, shared drinks with them, argued politics. She had not held their hands or wiped their tears.

Rita took a deep breath and reopened the folder.

Bobby Ellis had a tie around his neck, the wide end knotted at the shower rod. Rita squinted at the rod. Most of the hotels she'd been in recently had tension bars. They never would have held the weight of a grown man.

Look, Rita, she said to herself. Look for the piece that doesn't fit. Bobby Ellis was dressed in jeans and a long-sleeved shirt. He had on socks, but no shoes.

The next shot covered the body but from a distance. It showed the tiny vanity around the sink. On the Formica counter was a comb; an open tube of toothpaste; two plastic glasses, one shrink-wrapped, the other with water; a toothbrush with the foam of used toothpaste across the top of the bristles. The mirror over the sink was clean and clear, catching Lamar as the photographer.

After that was a headshot of Bobby Ellis. Rita stared at the closed eyes, the grim downturn of the darkened lips. From the angle of the photograph she could see the lividity of the ligature mark seeping above the tight noose of the tie.

He looked asleep. At any moment his eyes would open and he would be himself again. But in the last photo, Bobby Ellis remained strung from the tarnished shower rod of a bathroom alcove in a tiny mountainside town in West Virginia.

"Pretty sad pictures, aren't they?" A tall shadow fell across the sheriff's desk.

Rita jumped up. "Yes, yes, they are." She held out her hand, but braced herself for another Lamar-like encounter.

The sheriff was a big man, a mountain, but with a voice steady with kindness and deep-set brown eyes that understood suffering. He didn't appear quite the slayer of squirrels that she expected.

"Margie said it was all right and I . . ." Rita scooted out of the way in case Justin Carter wanted his desk back. He wore brown canvas hunting pants and a field jacket, topped by a florescent orange cap. He smelled of pipe tobacco and wood smoke.

"You take your time," he said. "Just came by to check and see how things are doing."

"I don't want to get in your way." Rita gathered the contents of the folder back inside. "I can look at these out there in the waiting room."

"Stay where you are. Go ahead." He pointed at the desk and then perched on the edge across from Rita. "Got what you need?"

"I think so." She looked at his eyes again.

"Found anything?"

"Not really." Rita sighed.

"Families hope, you know. They don't want it to be the way it is." He reached to touch the folder. "Suicide means they got to carry some of that guilt."

"I think that's true." Rita settled back into the chief's chair. "But are you completely sure it was suicide?"

"Yes, ma'am, I am."

Rita wasn't going to push it. "Well, I appreciate you're letting me look through the files."

Justin Carter slid off the desk to face her. "You find anything strange, you'll share it?"

"I'll do that."

The sheriff turned to leave, then stopped in his doorway. "Lamar gives you any trouble, you let me know."

Rita looked straight at him, but let his offer pass without acknowledgement.

Carter exchanged a few words with Margie then left. Now's the time, Rita thought. She slipped two photos from the file folder and snapped pictures of both. Then she gathered the sheriff's and the coroner's reports and went to the copy machine.

On her way out of the office, Rita asked Margie, "Where can I find Dr. McClung?"

Margie cackled. "Under the weather about now."

"What do you mean?"

"Too late in the day," Margie said. "It's way past lunchtime and Doc McClung's into his cups, but good. You need to sneak up on him first thing, before he gets too much hair of the dog in him."

"I see." Rita clutched her portfolio. "So where is it I need to sneak up on him first thing?"

McClung's home was one street over from the sheriff's office. Rita circled by on her way to the Overlook Inn. Every window in the shabby old Victorian had curtains securely draped to protect against light and prying eyes.

Rita eased her car back onto the main drag. A Harper's Ferry sheriff's car nosed beside her. Lamar glided along dangerously close and glared through police issue sunglasses with gold mirror lenses.

Rita rolled down Jeep's window. "Have a nice day," she called with a leer. Under her breath she added, "Asshole."

Lamar tapped the accelerator and turned toward the sheriff's office while Rita sped ahead. At the end of the street was a five-hundred-foot drop to the Potomac River and on the edge of that precipice was the Overlook Inn. Rita was going to sleep in the room where Bobby Ellis had spent his last night.

Chapter 6

Rita wheeled around the Overlook Inn's circular drive and its raised garden with the flagpole flapping the stars and stripes. At the base of this patriotic gesture was a dense mass of gold and burgundy chrysanthemums. She pulled up in front of the panoramic front porch. The day was as beautiful and crisp as the Sunday she'd driven here to meet Bobby.

"Rita Mars. I have a reservation."

The clerk was the same young woman as that fateful morning. She was thin and unsmiling; today she was dressed in a print shirtwaist dress. The flesh tearing nails still gleamed in blood red.

"One night?"

Rita nodded. She glanced around the parlor-like lobby as she drew her credit card from the wallet she carried inside her jacket. Though the sun blistered a cloudless foil sky outside, in here it was grey, the air thick.

This was a room designed for people built like sausages who wore too many clothes. Directly behind Rita was a scarlet horsehair sofa, its unyielding back stuffed in tight satin. Beyond were spindly straight wooden chairs, tense wingbacks, and two oversized upholstered creations, which promised little comfort. Potted palms in dull brass buckets added a funereal tone.

"If you'll just put your tag information here and sign." The clerk indicated two lines on the registration form, dropped the pen she had used as a pointer and immediately turned to fish a key from the honeycomb of key boxes on the wall behind her. She plunked one onto the worn marble counter.

Rita handed the registration form back. "This isn't the room I asked for."

The clerk stared.

"I asked for Room 107."

"107?" The woman took the key from Rita and inspected it.

"Yes, I'm the detective who phoned about the Robert Ellis case," Rita said.

"The guy who killed himself?"

"The man found hanged in that room a week ago," Rita corrected.

"Let me see if it's available."

"Your manager guaranteed me that room." Rita tapped her foot. An elderly couple toddled in, smiled at her and disappeared across the parlor.

"Let me get him." The young woman hurried to a narrow door at her left. A small metal sign displayed the title "Manager."

"Ms. Mars. I'm Gary Simpson. I remember your talking with me." Simpson wore a polyester, short-sleeved shirt and tie, carried a plastic pen clipped to his breast pocket.

Rita held out her hand. "I was explaining to your clerk about the room we agreed on."

"Of course." Simpson nodded. The young woman hung behind with downcast eyes as her boss seized control. He picked a key from a lower cubbyhole and pushed it across the counter.

"Thanks." Rita took the key. "And before I go to the room, I'd like to ask you both a few questions."

"Of course." Gary glowed with his best hospitality management enthusiasm.

The three of them settled in Simpson's closet of an office. Gary behind the Army surplus metal desk; Rita and the clerk, now identified as Eugenia Watkins, sitting in grey metal chairs on the other side.

"Do you remember seeing Robert Ellis during his stay here?"

"To tell you the truth, I don't think I ever saw him." Gary shook his head.

"I do. I remember him," Eugenia said, suddenly eager.

Rita reached into her portfolio and drew out a recent black and white proof Bobby had taken for his press pass. She handed it to Eugenia.

"Yep. That's him."

Gary shook his head again as he checked the picture and returned it to Rita.

"I remember him because he was by himself," Eugenia volunteered. "Men don't usually come here by themselves, you know. Their wives drag them to the outlet stores down the road, or they come here when the fall colors change. So I asked him was his wife coming up later and he said 'no' and I thought that was strange."

"Did he say why he was here?" Rita asked. Maybe the reluctant Eugenia would be a fount of information after all.

"Said he was working on a story for a newspaper. He seemed to want to talk and all. I checked to see if he had on a wedding ring. He didn't so I figured it was ok." Eugenia halted. "Some jealous husband didn't do him in, did they?"

"I don't think so." Rita decided her clerk was warming to the role of star witness. "So you checked him in?"

"I did—came in around five that Friday. I liked talking to him. He was friendly without being pushy the way some men are. Asked where was a good place to eat. Asked how far to the races."

"He asked about the races?" Rita asked.

"Charlestown. Flat track about ten miles from here. They put in slots and now it's a big casino with a hotel and all."

"I'm familiar with it." Rita responded.

New guests tapped the hand bell on the front desk and Gary excused himself to check them in.

"Is this going to be on *60 Minutes* or *20/20*?" Eugenia asked.

"Maybe," Rita answered. Great, this woman wants to be a TV star. "Did he mention any specifics about the newspaper story, what it was about, who?"

Eugenia rolled her eyes upward into her thoughts and squeezed her eyebrows together in contemplation. "No, nothing."

"Ok," Rita went on, "so you checked him in. What happened after that?"

"Uh, oh yeah." Eugenia resumed her narrative. "He got his key and went to his room. But he did say somebody might be looking for him and it was all right to just send him on to his room. We don't usually do that, you know. We call the room and get permission."

Rita pursued this. "Robert Ellis said he was expecting someone? Did he actually say that, Eugenia?"

"I said that, didn't I."

Can't afford to piss this woman off now, Rita thought, but she turned the question around from several angles for the clerk before she let it go. Eugenia Watkins was certain that Robert Ellis said he was expecting to meet someone at the Overlook Inn.

"Did he say who he was meeting?" Rita asked.

"No?"

"A friend, a relative, anything like that?"

"I said no." Eugenia slumped in her chair to pout.

"I'm sorry this is such a pain," Rita said, "but I need to get the facts straight in my head. And there could very well be a killer out there who made Bobby Ellis' death look like a suicide."

This perked Eugenia up. "Hey, like Claus Von Bulow." She leaned toward Rita. "*48 Hours.* Do you think we could end up on *48 Hours?*"

Play it as it lays, Rita said to herself. "Well, now, there's a possibility, Eugenia."

The woman's face lit up. "What else do you need to know?" She gripped her chair arms in excitement.

"Did you see Robert Ellis any more after he finished registering and went to his room? Did he phone the desk for anything?"

"Nope, but I did see him leave for dinner."

"You didn't see him return?"

"My shift's over at eleven and if he went to the races and stayed, he wouldn't be back 'til after then," Eugenia offered.

"Who comes in at eleven?" Rita slipped Bobby Ellis' picture off the desk and into her portfolio.

"Night guy, Sam Baker. Hey, is this it? We're done?" Eugenia frowned.

"For now. But I'd like to see the call detail report from Bobby's room that night." Rita stood.

"I'll run it." Eugenia headed out front with Rita trailing behind.

"You've been a big help." Rita took the call printout. "If you think of anything else, please let me know." She handed her business card to the clerk. "I believe the police report stated that a housekeeper found the body. Is that right?"

"Evie Pepper."

"Is she around?" Rita asked.

"Probably having a smoke out by the supply room on the other side." Eugenia smirked. "It's over by your room, lower floor, all the way to the end, nearest the drop-off."

"I'll check." Rita started for the front door.

"Around back."

"Thanks."

"Don't forget," Eugenia called, "let me know if we're going to be on *48 Hours*."

"Will do." Rita waved the room key.

♏

The front of the inn's annex was a small loose gravel parking lot that could accommodate only five cars. It was full. At the far end of the building, on the lower level was a tiny gift shop with windows all around that framed a breathless view of the valley and surrounding mountains. A narrow gravel footpath circled the building.

Rita thought of picking up her luggage, but decided to try and find the housekeeper first. Once she passed the parking area, the gravel path grew weedy. On her left was the inn, on the right, scrub trees; poplars and catalpa crowded an overgrown strip of lawn.

The trees were so close that branches extended across the path toward the building, almost touching the cement balcony on the second floor. It would be very dark back here at night, Rita thought to herself and she scanned the building for floodlights. One was mounted at each end. The only other light would come from individual fixtures over the door of each room.

Cigarette smoke wafted from behind an open door at the end. Unlike the others, it was a dull grey color and bore no identifying number.

"Evie Pepper?" Rita peered into the supply room.

A skinny little woman with an incredible map of wrinkles across her face, jumped and spun around. "Lord, you have about scared me to death." An unfiltered cigarette with a precariously dangling ash survived the fright.

"I'm sorry. I should have said something sooner." Rita extended her hand into which Evie let fall a leathered, but limp collection of fingers. "My name is Rita Mars. I'm investigating the death of Robert Ellis which occurred here."

"Hell, yes, I remember that." Evie snorted down a powerful dose of postnasal drip and exhaled a blue stream of smoke from the same passage. "You police?" Evie squinted.

"Uh, no, I'm a private investigator," Rita said.

"Like that *Murder She Wrote* woman?" The ash dropped from Evie's cigarette.

"Well, not exactly." Nobody's real anymore. We're all copies of TV characters Rita thought. "I was a friend of Bobby's."

"It was a terrible thing. I can tell you that." Evie took a last drag and flicked the depleted butt toward the woods.

"I would like you to tell me about it."

"I knocked on the door Sunday morning about eleven. Didn't hear no answer so I went in with my key. Air conditioning was going full blast in that room. Couldn't figure that since it being September and all up here, temperature at night drops real good." Evie leaned on the big stainless steel cleaning cart loaded with soaps and shampoos, toilet paper and cleaning supplies.

"Did you see the body right away?"

"Nope, couldn't see into the bathroom from the door."

"Did you notice anything unusual?" Rita asked.

"Well, I turned off that danged air conditioner," Evie said, "and went for my vacuum. There was these little tiny pieces of paper near the door. I picked up a bunch. Looked like money all tore up fine."

"Money?" Rita made a mental note to review the police report. She hadn't remembered that part.

"Yeah, so I got the vacuum and went over 'pert' near the whole floor 'til I got to the bathroom and then I seen him. He was hanging like a hog for slaughter." Evie lowered her head. "God rest his soul. He was a pretty man too."

"What did you do then?"

"Screamed." Evie reached into a dirty half apron pocket and pulled out a pack of Lucky Strikes. She lit up with a purple plastic lighter.

"I see, and then what?"

"Got on the phone there and called the desk, told them to get the police down here quick on account of somebody's hung hisself."

"Then the manager came over?"

"No, Gary, he was off that Sunday, took his family to Charleston to visit his in-laws. But the police come quick. Lamar was the one here first. They called the chief too."

"They called for the coroner?" Rita watched the ash on Evie's new cigarette bobbing as it elongated.

"Hmp, such as he is. Eustace McClung." Evie finally flicked the ash. "Wasn't staggering too bad either."

"And when he got here?"

"Didn't do much—walked in, went to the bathroom. Nodded his head. Said 'take him down, boys.' Friendly'll be here in a minute."

"Friendly?" Rita asked.

"Local undertakers, whole family of 'em. Do all the burying around here."

"He never mentioned an autopsy?"

"Nope."

"They let you stay in the room the whole time?"

"Yep."

"Tell me, Evie, since you were there the whole time, did you notice anything else, besides the paper, that seemed unusual to you?" Rita asked.

"Well, it was kinda unusual to find a man hanged hisself from the bathroom bar on a Sunday morning, I can tell you that."

"Anything around the room?"

"Found some race tickets in the trash can when I emptied it." The cigarette burned down to a point where the smoke rose directly into Evie's eyes. She squinted again.

"Save them?"

"Threw 'em out with the rest of the trash."

"Hmm. Do you think they were Bobby's?"

"They were from that night," Evie confessed. "I looked at the date and then checked the sports page to make sure he hadn't throwed away no winners."

"Evie, you have been a terrific help. Thank you so much." Rita extended her hand.

Evie shook it with her work worn leathery fingers. "Glad it helped. Gotta keep movin' to finish up here though. "

"Of course." Rita handed Evie a card. "If you think of anything else, give me a call."

"Will do, honey." Evie and her rickety housekeeping cart rolled to the next room.

Chapter 7

It wasn't as creepy as she thought it was going to be. Nothing in this impersonal little cell connected her to Bobby Ellis. Rita set her overnight bag on the bed. It was dim in here the way hotel rooms are, and the air was stale with the scent of machine pumped ventilation.

Her first impulse was to flick on the television. She hated that grey eye staring blankly at her, but she resisted. Instead she went into the bathroom. Being so short, she had to stand on the ledge of the tub in order to grasp the shower rod.

Rita grabbed tight with both hands and let her feet fall away. The rod gave a little; she heard the anchor screws tear at wood and drywall. A few grains of plaster trickled down the ceramic tile wall. The rod held however.

So this is what it would have been like. Only she knew from her buddy in Baltimore's medical examiner's office that it wasn't exactly. He had explained to her that the ligature would tighten and strangle the carotid. In seconds the brain would choke and black out. Death followed immediately.

Her arms ached from holding herself suspended. She pulled her feet back onto the tub ledge to support her weight and bounced to the floor. She gripped the wall as her head spun.

Her friend at the ME's office also told her that you didn't have to fully suspend yourself in order to achieve the deadly effect. The majority of suicides who hanged themselves did so from doorknobs. It was a common fallacy that a body had to drop completely. Death came from lack of oxygen to the brain, not from a broken neck due to the force of the fall.

Rita inspected the bathroom then went out to the table to review what she had so far. Out of her portfolio she pulled the copied police report. She read it again, line by line, to see if anything jumped out.

Then came the crime scene photo she had stolen. She hated staring at Bobby's limp body, but she made herself look. He had on a polo shirt and a pair of slacks, no shoes.

On the sink was his watch. Beside the watch was one of the plastic glasses supplied by the inn. It was half full of water. Then there was his toothbrush, bristles foamy with used paste. He hadn't put the cap back on the toothpaste tube. A man decides halfway through brushing his teeth that he doesn't want to live anymore?

Rita placed this picture on a pile separate from the police report and reached into the portfolio for the inn's telephone report. Bobby Ellis made two phone calls the night of his death. He called his voice mail and a number in DC. Rita made a note on the report to check with her contact at the phone factory and find out who in DC Bobby was calling.

Rita leaned back in her chair and propped her feet on the table. Evening swept an early hand across the mountains and here at the rear of a building crowded by trees, the tiny room faded to black like the end of a movie scene. Rita felt the familiar emptiness that opened within her as darkness fell.

She sat with that feeling for a moment, but when she could no longer endure, she reached for her smartphone on the night stand. On the other end, ringing. But like those exploratory radio signals to the universe, she got no answer. She listened again until voice mail kicked in. Finally she hung up. She'd try Mary Margaret again later.

Swinging her feet off the table, she pulled the chain on the hanging lamp. A glaring beam of yellow light splayed on her materials. But she didn't want to look at them anymore for now.

She glanced at her watch. Post time for the Charlestown races was seven o'clock; it was now six. She knew she could escape the emptiness with activity. She didn't have her running gear, but she could get in her car, go to the track and start grilling people.

m

A stream of cars and pickups bumped over the long dirt drives that radiated into the parking lots. Stadium lights blazed down on the grandstands and a billboard dazzled with floodlights proclaimed that this arena was the great and wonderful "Charlestown Races." It was carnival time.

Rita eased her Jeep next to a pickup from which four people emerged. They were young and laughing; two blue jeaned men with cowboy boots and hats, two women with heavy eye makeup and tight stretch pants. Rita followed the couples to the entrance.

Inside the grandstand area, the concrete floor was gritty with sand. Smells of grilling hot dogs mingled with beer and cigarettes and horse manure. Overhead electronic boards flashed odds and time and pools of money wagered. People milled about, some eating their concession food dinners, others studying racing forms and programs. The warehouse-like space buzzed with voices and the occasional announcement from the PA system.

Rita went to the management office and tapped on the door.

"Help you?" A man with a belly flopped over a huge silver belt buckle answered the door. He had on rumpled suit pants, short dress boots and a string tie.

Rita flipped her ID badge. "I'm Rita Mars, private detective. I'd like to ask you a few questions about . . ."

"Now, I'm tellin' you right here and now," the man said. "I ain't talking to nobody about who's runnin' with who. I've told you people before, and I mean it. I got a job to do here." He started to close the door on her.

"Wait, what are you talking about?" Rita put her hand to the door to keep it from closing.

"Divorce. That's what I'm talkin' about. I don't want no parts of gettin' involved. Last time I did, fella wanted a piece of my butt." The man pushed at the door again.

"It isn't that. I promise."

The man eyed her from her soft Italian loafers to the top of her silk turtleneck. "This better be quick."

Rita stepped inside. "I appreciate your help."

The man was already back at his desk, counting a wad of bills he had left there. "Keep talkin'."

Rita explained her investigation of Bobby Ellis' death. The man never looked up.

"What'd you want from me?" He licked his thumb as he went on counting.

"I want you to look at this photo and tell me if you remember seeing this man the night of his murder, and I'd like a list of people to see here about the same thing."

"You with the FBI?"

Rita shook her head.

"IRS?"

"Hardly."

"All right," the man said, "but I find out you're with the IRS, we're gonna have some words." He stood up and waggled a finger at her. "You understand me?"

Rita met with the teller supervisors who gathered their crews for a quick look at her picture. No one remembered Bobby Ellis.

She went to each concession stand. Nothing. She checked the program and tout sheet sellers. She drew a blank.

At last she went into the clubhouse dining room. It was a big, high room with an expanse of plate window that swept a wide-open view of the track and centered on the finish line. It was quieter in here; the white clothed tables were full of Saturday night couples and foursomes.

"Table for one?" A woman in a black dress with a white apron approached Rita.

"Actually I need to ask a few questions."

The woman sighed as she slipped the menus back under the maitre'd station and leaned heavily on it toward Rita. "Shoot," she said.

"Do you remember seeing this man here about two weeks ago on a Saturday night?"

"You the police?" The woman's eyes narrowed under a florescent blue shadow.

"Private investigator. This is not a divorce case. I'm working on a possible murder."

The woman kept an eye on Rita for a long time before she finally glanced down at the photograph.

"Yep. He was here." The woman smiled. "Nice guy. Another guy came in while he was eatin' dinner and sat down with him. Real jerk. Like I said, your friend was nice, kinda flirtin' with me, jokin'. Kind of guy leaves a good tip, kind I like waitin' on. Anyways, this other dude comes in, real expensive clothes. Starts bein' a pain, tells me to get him a cup of coffee and buzz off."

"What did he look like? Would you know him if you saw him again?" Rita asked.

"Might, but I might not. Assholes like that I pretend they're not there. Know what I mean? I got enough to pay attention to." The woman straightened up as she looked beyond Rita.

"'Scuse me honey, got some folks to seat here."

When she returned, Rita took her name and number.

♏

The next morning Rita stood at the edge of Dr. Eustace McClung's front yard. The stench of cat urine had smacked her in the face as soon as she got out of her Jeep. She looked for the culprits who had fouled the approach to the shabby wooden porch. Not a cat in sight.

But a flock of scrawny strays might be in keeping with this house. The lawn was a bad haircut of tall weeds and shaggy grass. Lots of slats were missing from the peeling picket fence. The wisteria at the front of the porch wound its way like an invading alien life form across the entire expanse of the railing.

Rita held her breath and approached the steps once more. The second one shifted with her weight. She tottered but caught her balance, making it quickly onto the porch.

The curtains at the front window were pulled shut even though it was nine o'clock and full morning sun streamed directly onto the house. Rita went to the door. The screen was locked and the window in the front door was obscured by a dingy set of sheers.

"Dr. McClung," she called as she rapped on the aluminum-screened frame.

After a minute, Rita rapped again. She pressed her nose to the screen and tried to peer through the door sheers. She saw a reflection of maybe a hall mirror but no movement. She walked to the window, put her hand to the side of her face to shield the glare and tried to look through the curtains.

"You a peeping tom, or what?" said a raspy, smoker's voice.

Rita jumped. "Dr. McClung?"

"Yeah." The front door had opened, but the screen remained locked.

"I'm Rita Mars, I phoned earlier about meeting with you." She walked to the front door.

McClung said nothing.

Rita could barely make out the troll who stood in the doorway, face far back from the invading sun. He had on a dingy white shirt and trousers with suspenders.

"May I come in?"

McClung unsnapped the aluminum door, then walked down the hall as Rita entered. The house was a mausoleum. She blinked her eyes to acclimate to the dim interior. The raw scent of cheap whiskey hung like a cloud.

In the kitchen McClung slumped into a chair at an enameled metal table. In front of him was a tumbler three quarters full of amber liquid. He picked it up for a sip as Rita took the chair across from him.

"You're here for what? I forget." McClung stared at her with pale rheumy eyes. The lower lids drooped so that the inner reddened linings shone like a fresh scratch.

"The Bobby Ellis case."

McClung picked up the glass again, but did not register recognition.

"Two weeks ago, at the Overlook Inn," Rita said. The smell of alcohol radiating from his pores shook her with a wave of nausea and memory. With that odor, she was immediately back in time with her father, during the later years surrounded by the day-after scent of sweat and metabolizing booze.

"Overlook?"

"The man who was found hanged," Rita prompted.

"Yeah, yeah, now I remember. Guy who hanged himself."

"I have reason to believe it may have been murder."

"Suicide." McClung gulped down a big swig from his glass.

"It could have been murder."

"I was there. I saw him. Open and shut." McClung banged the glass on the table for emphasis.

"He was in the middle of brushing his teeth when he was hanged."

"So?"

"So why didn't you ask for an autopsy?" Rita's jaw tightened.

"Like I said open and shut case. I'm the coroner. What I say goes. I've seen 'em all. No need for an autopsy." McClung scratched his unshaven cheeks.

"Were you in this kind of condition the night you were called to Bobby Ellis's room?" It was a threat and not a question.

"What the hell you trying to say?" McClung swayed to his feet. A little man, he was not much taller than Rita.

She stood up across the table from him. "You were too damned drunk to know what the hell you even saw, let alone order proper procedure."

"Get out of my house." McClung's body tensed for a fight, but the alcohol jellied his posture. He leaned his knuckles on the table for support.

"You're pathetic." Rita shouted.

"Get out of here you stupid little girl trying to act like you're so smart."

Rita halted at the open front door. "You're nothing but a damned drunk," she hurled back at him and was out in her car without waiting for his reply.

She hit the gas and shrieked off. She drove with one hand as she bit hard into her other fist. She was out of control, angry and sad about events that had nothing to do with Eustace McClung or even the death of Bobby Ellis. She almost drove by the Friendly Mortuary without stopping.

Chapter 8

Rita expected organ music as she stepped into the silent hallway of Friendly Funeral Home. On either side of the long narrow passageway were viewing rooms. Most were open; one at the far end was sealed by a folding vinyl door.

The air was redolent of the waxy fragrance of greenhouse flowers. Rita took a few steps and glanced into the rooms to her left and right. One was empty; the other was lined with folding chairs.

"Hello?" Rita kept on walking, checking rooms as she went by.

Finally she encountered a dead end where another hallway crossed the first like a T. She heard loud music behind the metal door to her left, so she chose the other end of the corridor where she was rewarded with a door marked Office.

She had gone with her mother to Phillips and Sons when her father died. They entered such an office and sat with a nicely groomed young man who assumed they were grieving. Rita brought her father's blue suit and a shirt and tie, her mother having decided not to bury him in his state trooper uniform.

They walked through the casket showroom. They went home and came back the next day with eyes as dry as they had left.

"Hello?" Rita tapped lightly on the door as she opened it.

A startled older woman with rinsed grey hair had been typing behind a shining wooden desk. She had on a rose brocade dress with fake diamond accessories. "I'm so sorry. I didn't hear you come in. There's an electric eye up front that rings a bell back here, but with this computer on, I don't hear it all the time."

"I'm Rita Mars. I called earlier today."

"Do you remember who you spoke to?" The woman flipped through the big ring bound calendar on her desk.

"Joe Friendly," Rita answered.

"Now which Joe would that have been?" The woman looked up. "Mr. Joe is the old man, the owner. And we've got Joe, Jr. and Uncle Joe—he's only kin by marriage—and Young Joe."

Rita stared back. "I have no idea. I was talking to him about the body he prepared for transportation to Maryland about two weeks ago, the suicide at the Overlook Inn."

The woman brightened. "That would be Young Joe." Immediately the smile dampened to appropriate concern. "Would you be family?"

"No, no, I'm not," Rita said. "I'm a private investigator and I wanted to ask Joe, uh, Young Joe, a few questions."

"Well, now we followed state procedure. We're real strict on that here. If somebody had a problem with that body, it surely happened at the receiving end." Now the woman drew herself up in defense, her rose brocade a stiff fabric of armor.

"Actually, there was no problem in that sense," Rita assured her. "I'm working on a murder investigation. So if you could call Joe for me, I won't take much of his time." She smiled as a conciliatory offering and hoped the woman would just get on with it.

The woman picked up the telephone on her desk, but kept a wary eye on Rita. She whispered into the mouthpiece and turned her back as she spoke.

"He says go on back." The woman stared pointedly at Rita's cuffed trousers, following them up to the turtleneck and cashmere jacket lapels.

"Thanks." Rita shook her head.

"Door at the end of the hall. It's a work room," the woman called after her.

Rita faced the door she had first rejected. Loud music pounded inside, muffled as it was by the thick metal. She could have sworn it was ZZ Top playing "Sharp Dressed Man."

Rita knocked. The music crashed on. She knocked again, reluctant to barge in on who knew what.

"Joe," she called. "Joe."

An older man in a black suit scurried out of one of the viewing rooms toward her with a disapproving scowl on his face. He opened the door and slid inside so that not much music could escape. In a few seconds the music halted, the older man returned and held the door open for her.

"Sorry." A man in his late twenties stood at the front of a metal gurney on which lay a white-sheeted figure covered from head to foot.

The room was completely concrete. Rita noticed the slope of the floor that led to a drainage grate at the center under the gurney. She swallowed hard and kept her eyes on the young man who was holding out his hand.

He was cheery with a sweet round face and the broad smile of an altar boy. Built like a runner, lanky but coordinated, he was sockless with a pair of loafers and jeans.

"I'm Young Joe Friendly," he said. "Sorry about the music. It kinda takes my mind off what I'm really doing in here."

Rita's hand suspended in mid-shake when he said this.

"Oh, don't worry. I wasn't doing anything like—you know—serious. I'm doing some cosmetic stuff." He pointed to a table against the wall. "And I took off my gloves already."

Rita was afraid to touch the hands of Doctor Death. But she pushed herself and shook his hand with a hearty, if abbreviated grasp. "Thank you for agreeing to see me," she said.

"Glad to. How can I help?" His eyes followed hers as they rested on the inert form behind him. "This make you nervous? We could step into the casket room."

"No thanks," Rita said. "This shouldn't take long. I said I was working on the Bobby Ellis case."

"Guy who was hanged." Young Joe nodded.

"Curious you say it in that way. Everybody I talk to says it like he hanged himself."

"That's how the doc called it."

"But you don't think so?"

"Didn't say that." Young Joe shifted his feet as he checked his loafers.

"But maybe Dr. McClung was mistaken." Rita chose her words carefully. She caught and held Young Joe's earnest eyes.

"Could have been."

"If he were mistaken," Rita posed for him, "what would have been the details he could have overlooked?"

Young Joe grew very interested in his loafers and jabbed his hands deep into his lab coat pockets.

"Joe, this is so important," Rita pleaded. "It's possible that Robert Ellis was murdered. We can't let a murderer go free if we can help it."

A long pause followed until Joe lifted his head to look Rita in the face. "Well, to tell you the truth, I was surprised how much hematoa—bruising—there was on the throat. I mean the guy was supposed to have hanged himself with a silk tie. Something like that doesn't leave that kind of damage."

"Anything else?" Rita waited.

"Petechial hemorrhaging was severe—that's the burst capillaries in the eyes. Seemed, now I say, 'seemed' to be too much for the way he supposedly hanged himself. And there was one other thing. He had a small scratch on his neck just under his ear. You know, like maybe from a fingernail."

"A fingernail," Rita said. "So what you've just described to me sounds like strangulation rather than hanging."

"It's what I told Lamar."

"And Lamar said what?"

"Don't worry about it. Said Doc's signed the death certificate and that's that. He told me to prep that body for transport to."

"And you did that?"

"Yes, ma'am, I did. There's rules around here that aren't written down, but you don't dare ignore them. One of those rules is not crossing Lamar." Young Joe stared into Rita's eyes with some expectation of understanding.

"I appreciate your help, Joe." Rita held out her hand. This time her grasp was warm and grateful.

"I don't want any trouble with Lamar," he warned. "And I will change my story."

"I hear you loud and clear," Rita promised as she left Young Joe Friendly.

"Sharp Dressed Man" blasted once again from behind the door.

♏

A lazy orange sun reclined just above the mountaintops. The temperature of the brightly lit autumn afternoon turned sharply into the deepening shadows. Rita could smell wood smoke on the chill air as she came out of the Overlook's lobby after checking out.

She had taken one last look around Bobby Ellis' hotel room before she left, but she had no sense of him. She cued in on neither tragedy nor despair in that impersonal space, envisioned no transaction of his death. She didn't have ESP— she'd have to do her work the regular way.

In the span of two minutes Rita traveled the length of the Harper's Ferry town center. She passed the combination police station-city hall-post office-liquor store and glided by Friendly Undertakers. No one was on the street at this late afternoon hour. She passed the little wooden Bolivar grocery. The door was wide open, but the interior was too dark to see inside.

When she visited small towns like this, she would suddenly be struck with a weariness and longing. Life seemed simpler here. But then the words of Young Joe about Lamar spoiled that happy illusion.

She sped up and turned on the state route that led back toward Interstate 70. She had a lot of work to do when she returned to Baltimore. As she wound around the narrow cliff and ravine lined road on which she arrived, a car behind caught her attention as its headlights switched on in the gathering twilight. A police car?

Young Joe had certainly given her some things to think about. She wondered if it might be possible to order an exhumation. Still, the coroner's death certificate said suicide and she'd have to come up with a lot more evidence in order to have a judge rule in her favor.

The car behind came up fast and close as if he was going to touch bumpers. As quickly, he dropped back.

"Asshole," Rita mumbled. The word transported her to her meeting with Eustace McClung. "Waste of human breath."

The road widened now, though traffic was sparser as she travelled through more open countryside away from the cluster of small towns behind her. Rita settled back in the Jeep and switched on the radio. Only a sliver of sun peeked over the mountains now.

A siren. Rita glanced at the speedometer though she knew full well she was cruising at the posted limit. In the rear view the blue gumball machine lights spun like pinwheels. She eased to the side of the road. Damn, it was Lamar.

A quick glance around told her she was in the middle of God's country. To her right was a rocky pasture with a scattering of grazing milk cows. Across the road was a harvested and stubbled cornfield. Not much traffic this time of night just outside of Harper's Ferry.

"Step out of the car, please." Lamar towered over her as she slid out from the wheel. His hard serpent eyes fastened on her.

"Officer, I . . ."

"Driver's license. Registration, please."

Rita reached for her wallet inside her jacket. Lamar slapped his hand to the .38 on his thigh. Rita threw her hands to the air.

"My wallet's in my jacket pocket," she said. Even in this chill mountain air, sweat beaded at her temples. She could feel her knees turn to mush.

Lamar kept his right hand on the handle of his gun while he patted first one side of Rita's jacket, then the other. He made sure to press against her breasts with a squeeze of his wide palms. Rita's reaction was to attack, but she knew it would be suicide. Instead she held her tongue and never let her eyes wander from his.

This is how it happens, she thought. My word against his. He could do anything out here.

What would she do? She could scream. She could fight. It would be useless. Later she would have to decide if enduring humiliation was worth the price of seeking justice for Lamar's liberties with speeder's rights.

Lamar slid her wallet out of her jacket. With a deft flick, he opened it and with a thumb he sorted through her credit cards and photographs even though her driver's license was clearly in the first of the card pockets. He edged out an old photo of Diane and looked toward her.

Rita said nothing, but kept her eyes fixed on him.

"I'll have to check this for outstanding warrants," he said. "You come on back to the car."

When Rita didn't move, Lamar grabbed her arm and pushed her ahead of him. She sat in the back seat while he radioed in her plate and driver's license numbers. The car smelled of sweat and cigarette smoke. The radio check came back negative, but Lamar took his time writing out her speeding ticket.

He walked her back to her car. "Speed limit's forty-five. This ain't the city where you can do whatever you want and get away with it. And we don't like people who come here and act like they can." He slipped her wallet back into her inside jacket pocket, again he squeezed against her breast.

When he was gone and Rita sat locked in her car, she shook. "God damn you," she screamed over and over and pounded her hands on the steering wheel. "God damn you."

Chapter 9

Rita's assistant, Beverly, lived in a restored Queen Anne town house in Baltimore's historic Mount Vernon. Her grey stone building faced a tiny urban park where the homeless and hookers occasionally took comfort on formal garden benches. In another time, the park bore the unappetizing, but appropriate tag of The Meat Market. Before the age of disease, it had served as a cruising ground. Now, after revitalization efforts by the city, the area drew a stable settled community of young professionals and wealthy gay men. The neighborhood was presided over by a lighted marble obelisk commemorating the contributions of George Washington.

Tonight Rita drove around the little park ten times before she could find a place to park. Each corner fueled the anger that Lamar had kindled.

"If I'd had a gun, I would have shot the son of a bitch," Rita said as Bev greeted her. Bev wore a turquoise and white velour lounging outfit. Diamond rings sparkled on each perfect chocolate hand.

"And a pleasant evening to you, Miss Thing." Bev shook her head as she held the door for Rita to enter.

The lower floors were perfectly appointed in contemporary furniture and Bev's collection of modern art—including several of the less provocative Maplethorpes. Rita had never been upstairs. Blue and orange flames danced in the gas fireplace.

"You won't believe what happened."

"With you, baby, I could believe anything happened." Bev followed Rita into the kitchen.

"No Cokes?" Rita shoved items around in Bev's refrigerator.

"Let me." Bev took charge, moved a bottle of seltzer and with a flourish produced a cold red and white can. "So tell me what you did in Harper's Ferry."

"Got any peanuts?"

"Do I look like the elephant man to you?" Bev asked, but she yanked a jar of dry roasts from her cupboard and handed it to Rita. "I'm getting a glass of wine. Go on in the living room."

Rita sat curled on Bev's beige and white sofa, shoes off and feet tucked under her. "I feel calmer already. Must be this quiet mind decor."

"That joke is getting old—and I happen to like it. So there." Bev came over and scooped a handful of peanuts from the jar. "Had enough noise, color and excitement in Iraq. Done with that."

Rita then launched into her tirade against the personal invasion by Lamar. She pounded the sofa arm with her fist for emphasis. Bev listened without interrupting.

"I ran into some slimy men when I worked for the *Star*. There were guys who thought because you weren't married you were part of open season. There were some who wanted to beat the hell out of me and would have if I hadn't been quick enough. But this—this was the worst." Rita squeezed the Coke can with her thumb so that it cracked under her pressure.

"When I started this business," she said, "I didn't want to carry a gun."

"You would have shot him?" Bev asked.

"On the spot."

"You would have pulled the gun, aimed it point blank and fired into his chest?" Bev asked.

Rita took a swallow of Coke. "Maybe."

"I thought so," Bev said.

"Damn it, you're not supposed to say things like that."

"Yes, I am. That's why you pay me the big bucks."

Rita's frown creased into a smile. They both laughed. "Ok, you win."

"Honey, I'm supposed to win."

"I hate that feeling of powerlessness." Rita said.

"I know." Bev touched Rita's hand as it clutched the sofa arm. "It's a scary thing. I've been there."

"Not you."

"Oh yeah. Ain't nobody gets to avoid that charming experience."

Rita bowed her head for a moment.

"So—did you learn anything?" Bev asked.

"I learned that a person's death is an inconvenience, a nuisance to be dealt with," Rita snapped.

"You know what I mean."

Rita pulled her feet from under her, placed them on the floor and turned to face Bev. "I talked with the mortician, a young guy—Young Joe as a matter of fact. He had the most solid evidence that Bobby didn't commit suicide." She explained that evidence to Bev.

"And he didn't tell the police or the coroner?" she asked.

"I told you about them."

"You think he had his facts straight?"

"Young Joe?" Rita asked. "I think he was right on."

Bev nodded.

"He seemed pretty honest to me. The other thing was he said he was afraid of going against Lamar. Gee, I wonder why? And that rang true to me, especially after tonight."

Bev leaned back in her chair. "But basically, you have nothing except this man's word—which conflicts with the county coroner and the investigating officer."

Rita sighed. "Good assessment. Joe said he'd change his story if he had to testify."

"You need more evidence." Bev offered the peanut jar to Rita who declined.

"I need eight by ten glossies of the crime in progress." Rita rubbed her neck. It was stiff from her long and angry drive home.

"You got no smoking gun proof out of this trip?" Bev rose and walked behind the sofa. She put her big, strong hands at the back of Rita's neck to massage her pain away.

"The things I got were vague and no one is going to testify to anything," Rita said. "I got a phone number from the room message report, a D.C. number, and when I went to the horse races with Bobby's picture, I found a waitress in the club house who remembered him being there with another man."

"Description?" Bev kneaded the muscles over Rita's shoulder blades.

"Well-dressed asshole."

"Now there's a break for you."

"Thanks." Rita leaned into Bev's hands.

"You know," Bev said. "I've been doing some thinking while you were away."

"Any ideas?"

"I was thinking about addicts in recovery."

"And?"

"Sometimes they don't make it because they get overwhelmed. Take the drug out of their system and it gets real clear how much they lost. They can get some serious blues," Bev said.

"Meaning?" Rita bent her head forward so that Bev could massage higher on the nape of her neck.

"Might be a good idea to talk to Bobby's counselor at the rehab he came from." Bev's thumbes gently worked the hairline.

Rita reached around and grabbed both her hands. "You don't think he was murdered, do you?"

"Didn't say that."

"You think he killed himself, just like everybody else." Rita twisted to face her friend.

"Baby, all I'm saying is I happen to know something about addicts—dated a few until I figured it out. I'm saying you got to get perspective instead of tunneling in." Bev's voice was stern.

"Like I usually do." Rita let go of Bev's hands and turned around again so that Bev continued her massage.

"Girlfriend, I didn't say that either." Bev stopped working.

"I know. I did," Rita said and then added. "And how was Ms. VanDreem while I was away.

"Safe and sound, just like you left her," Bev answered. "Safe and sound."

♏︎

Rita stole an appraising look at Edmund Ellis as he entered her office. In his Armani suit, he looked like the high-end plastic surgeon that he was. Women would put themselves in his hands, Rita thought. He was smooth and confident and his hands were steady with a gentle strength.

"Thank you for coming here." Rita pointed to the chair beside her desk.

"I had a meeting at Hopkins. It was no trouble." Edmund dropped an extra key to Bobby's apartment on her desk.

How different he was from Bobby who had bristled with adrenaline energy. Bobby paced and talked and gestured as he related to anybody and anything in a room. Edmund was completely unruffled.

"I need to ask you some questions," Rita began.

"Did you find anything concrete to justify continuing the investigation?" Edmund's calm steepled fingers degenerated to palm rubbing as he leaned toward Rita.

"I found a few things. I guess the most important of all is what the mortician at Harper's Ferry shared with me. He said the marks on Bobby's neck didn't match the tie he supposedly hanged himself with. There was too much bruising for a silk tie ligature. He said also there was a small scratch under the ear that could have been from a fingernail."

"My brother was strangled." Edmund spoke with the matter-of-fact monotone of the doctor.

"That was the assessment of the mortician." Rita watched Ellis, but he never flinched.

"Why didn't the coroner ask for an autopsy?"

"The coroner doubles as the town drunk."

Ellis nodded. "And the police?"

"Well, it may have been collusion, but lack of interest is a better guess."

Ellis steepled his fingers and stared past Rita to the window where morning light sifted in through the blinds.

"Everybody's too busy to do their job," Edmund said to the window.

Ellis shifted his focus back to Rita. He leaned an elbow on the desk as he spoke. "Bobby owed a lot of money to Skippy Lockerman. Lockerman is, was, Bobby's coke connection."

86

"What are you saying to me?" Rita's eyes widened.

Ellis answered hurriedly. "Bobby told me before he went into treatment that he borrowed a lot of money from Lockerman. He was really in debt. When he was getting back on his feet, he told me he was going to pay all that money back."

"To a drug dealer?" Rita's voice rose.

"To a drug dealer. It's a long, complicated thing, but he borrowed that money to support his son. And Bobby thought that getting honest with himself after rehab meant paying that money back. He was sending it in installments to Lockerman's mobile home business in Charlestown."

"Wait a minute." Rita waved a disapproving hand at Edmund Ellis' story. "You mean this coke dealer lives near Harper's Ferry. Bobby owed him big bucks, and you didn't tell the police that Lockerman could have killed your brother?" Rita ran her fingers through her hair.

"I don't think that he did," Ellis insisted.

"Why didn't you tell me this before?"

"It didn't seem important because I knew the story."

"What the hell else do you know that you haven't told me?" Rita said.

"Nothing." Edmund slunk into his seat. "I don't know. Bobby could make anything sound reasonable. I took him at his word about his relationship with Lockerman."

Rita shook her head. "Bev was right."

"I beg your pardon."

"I have a friend who told me that an addict can feel overwhelmed, maybe relapse, and that could generate suicidal feelings," Rita said.

Ellis stared at her for a long time. "You're giving up the case. You think Bobby killed himself?"

"I don't know what to think. I do know that what the mortician said pointed to murder. But I also know that I'm going to follow my friend's advice and check with Bobby's counselor at the rehab to make sure he wasn't a candidate." Rita shook her head again.

"I am sorry. I wasn't thinking. I've been so disoriented with all that's happened." Ellis leaned his elbows on his knees and bowed his head into his hands.

Rita watched the man fall apart in front of her. "Well, I hope you've been putting people's noses back in the right place."

"I haven't worked since his death." Ellis' voice choked with tears.

Rita felt the shame of her goading, but she wasn't going to let Ellis off the hook. "Ok, let me ask you this. Do you know of anybody else who had a grudge or score to settle with Bobby?"

Ellis shook his head, still burying his face in his palms.

"Did Bobby tell you anything at all about the last story he was working on?"

"Nothing."

"Well, I'm batting a thousand here." Rita leaned back in her chair and closed her eyes.

"I'm sorry." Ellis sat up at last, took a handkerchief from his jacket, wiped his eyes and blew his nose.

"Ok," Rita sighed. "Here's what you're going to do. I want you to go home and get a piece of paper and a pencil and write down anything, even if it seems insignificant, that Bobby told you during the last two weeks before his death."

Ellis nodded and blew his nose again.

"And I want you to tell me where the hell I can find Skippy Lockerman, the dealer with a heart of gold."

Chapter 10

In the winter Rita played basketball every Wednesday night at the Whitehurst Middle School gymnasium. Mary Margaret Smooth was captain of "The BeenGay Girls." Though Rita was the shortest member of the team, she compensated for this deficiency with the ferocity of her play.

Tonight Rita and Mary Margaret were battling the notorious Blizzard sisters and their "Hot Legs" team. The Blizzard sisters were twins, blondes. May was six feet even; June was a quarter inch taller. Born years too early for the WNBA,— and disinclined to be models—they were coveted team members in Baltimore County's "Just For Fun" recreational women's basketball league. They were coveted for more than their on-court skills.

At halftime, a sweaty, irritable Rita complained to the ref. "Can you watch those two a little more closely?" She pointed to May and June. "They're putting knots on my head out there."

The referee, a woman almost as short as Rita, laughed and walked away. "I should be so lucky."

May turned from the "Hot Legs" bench and winked at Rita.

"Come drink your Gatorade, Slick." Mary Margaret tossed her a squeeze bottle.

"I mean it." Rita sucked down a big gulp.

"The Blizzard sisters like you." Mary Margaret threw her arm around Rita's shoulder.

"They'd like to twist me into a pretzel." Rita took another drink.

"I think they have something more interesting in mind," Mary Margaret said. The rest of the team laughed. "You want to sit on the bench?"

"No," Rita answered.

"Then listen up." Mary Margaret delivered her second half strategy speech, which encompassed the impossible task of keeping the Blizzard sisters from under the basket.

The buzzer sounded and the BeenGay Girls marched onto the court. June Blizzard patted Rita on the butt.

"Hey," Rita said.

"Call me," June mouthed silently so that her sister couldn't see.

In the second half, Rita scored three baskets, a miracle since for most of the game she was the middle of a Blizzard sandwich and couldn't make a move without getting pressed between their bodies.

"I'm trying to play a game here," she snarled in frustration.

"Any time," May Blizzard responded with a smile.

Rita shook her head and dribbled rabidly in the opposite direction.

When the final buzzer sounded, Hot Legs once again was the victor. The teams lined up to shake hands. The Blizzard sisters were at the end of the line.

"Come on we'll buy you a beer," May said to Rita.

"Thanks," she answered peevishly, "but I'm dropping Smooth off at home."

May looked at June. The twin telepathy thing went into gear and after a minute, May said. "We'll buy you and Smooth a beer."

"Well, ladies, that sounds just wonderful." Mary Margaret said before Rita could answer.

"I don't drink," Rita said lamely.

June put a chummy arm around her and pulled her close. She whispered in her ear. "I'll buy you a Coke." She punctuated her offer with a peck on the cheek.

Outside in the car, Rita stabbed her key into the Jeep's ignition. "Dammit, Smooth. What are you trying to get me into?"

Smooth laughed and wiped the windows that had clouded when their steamy bodies were enclosed in the chilly car. "Hell, no worse than the stuff you've gotten yourself into—without any assistance from me, thank you very much."

"I'm not interested." Rita swung her Jeep out of the gymnasium parking lot.

Mary Margaret glanced out the window. "No one is asking you to pick out china and a silver pattern."

"I don't have the heart—or the stomach—for it anymore."

"Any more? Forever? Never?"

"Maybe." Rita switched on the defroster. The windshield

was steaming up again.

"Don't let Diane Winter have the last word."

"What the hell's that supposed to mean?"

"Just what I said. Don't let her dictate your life long after she's walked out."

Rita cocked her head. "Is that what you think?"

"I think you took a near fatal hit. I think it scared you good, and you don't ever want that kind of pain again."

Rita eased onto the Jones Falls Expressway behind the Blizzard sisters in their black Camaro.

"I'm a survivor and . . ."

Mary Margaret cut her off. "I know all that. But surviving isn't enough. In this life, we need to find a way to flourish and thrive, to savor the essence of our very existence."

"Did you get that from the Pope's book?"

"No," Mary Margaret answered, "I got it from myself."

"The seat of all wisdom," Rita said.

"Of course."

"I'm still not ready."

"You don't have to be ready. You just have to be willing."

"And able?" Rita watched the taillights of the Blizzards' Camaro duck into the parking lot of the Blue Heaven Lounge. They were in the heart of blue collar Baltimore.

"Just willing," Mary Margaret said.

ᕬ

The interior of the Blue Heaven was dark. Dark, scuffed vinyl flooring; dark paneling, back-to-back deep oak bars. Even the mirrors were dingy from decades of cigarette smoke. The usual suspects slumped on their barstools and never turned their heads to the new arrivals. It was the typical working-class bar aside from its all female cast of characters.

The Blizzard sisters made straight for the bar in the second room. Here there was a tiny dance floor surrounded by patron less Formica topped tables and a makeshift stage where a homegrown country and western band played on Friday nights. The bartender, Mickey, wore a Melissa Ethridge T-shirt, jeans, and a city's worth of locksmithing on a chain attached to her belt. She nodded without speaking to May and June. Mary Margaret and Rita sauntered in after the twins and captured one of the tables.

"You know, Smooth, some of these people look like they've been here for years."

"Probably have been."

May and June arrived then. They handed Mary Margaret a Coors Lite and Rita a Coke.

"I'll put something in the jukebox," May said.

"Make sure it's good," said June and followed her across the room.

S"Am I going to be sorry I did this?" Rita asked Smooth.

"I certainly hope so."

They took turns dancing: Rita with June and May with Smooth. Then May with Rita and so on for an hour.

94

"I'm dead." Rita held up her hands. "I need another Coke and then I've got to go to bed."

June, whose turn it was to dance with Rita, responded with a glowing smile.

"To sleep," said Rita, though for just a moment, she considered an invitation.

"Your loss," June said.

"Yes. It is." Rita whispered so no one else heard.

Outside, the November night was raw and windy. Rita pulled the collar of her fleece pullover to her flushed cheeks as she and Mary Margaret walked along Lombard Street to her Jeep. The East Baltimore brick row houses were shut tight and dark. A skinny cat ducked into an alley. No one else was about.

"Was it so bad?" Mary Margaret asked.

"No," Rita answered. "No, it wasn't so bad. I laughed. I danced. I forgot about everything but the moment."

"Where we all should live," Mary Margaret said.

"Where we all should indeed," Rita echoed.

♏

It was after twelve. Rita's body ached from the rigors of the basketball game and then the dancing. She envisioned a pillow, her comforter pulled over her tired body. But she was in the city. She had promised to watch over Karin VanDreem and had taken back the responsibility from Bev. She drove to the more affluent side of Baltimore.

The house was dark when Rita made a first pass and circled the block. As she came back around, another car, a champagne-colored Lexus, drove slowly by Karin's in the opposite direction. Community watch, Rita thought immediately.

She pulled her Jeep into the heavy shadow of a massive oak just down from the house. She'd sit there for ten minutes, make sure nothing was going on and then head home. She was afraid to lean her head on the car seat. She might fall asleep.

The car came around again.

Rita sat up. She noted the license number and when the car had passed, rummaged in the glove box for her notepad and a pen.

The car made another pass, but this time sped up when it reached the corner.

"Ok, dude." Rita started the Jeep and maintained safe distance as she kept her quarry in sight.

The suspicious car shot up the off ramp to the Jones Falls Expressway, the same route Rita would have taken to go to her house. She slowed as reached her exit and the car ahead wheeled onto the exit just north of hers.

"Who the hell are you?"

The Lexus made a right onto a winding country road. Rita waited and then made her turn. She glanced up the lanes to the big houses that nestled in among the sprawling horse pastures and sparse groves of locust trees. Nothing.

"I wasn't that far behind." Rita glanced in the rearview mirror.

The lights went on then. She could see them glimmer through a hedgerow of English boxwood that lined an unpaved barn entrance. The Lexus zoomed onto the road in the other direction. A trail of dust rose from the sandy lane as he went.

"Dammit." Rita jammed the Jeep into reverse and backed into a driveway. But the turning radius and maneuverability of her car was no match.

She arrived at the end of the road in time to see the Lexus shoot toward the Expressway exit. Rita watched the taillights and saw that he was heading back to the city.

She rested her head on her steering wheel for a moment. It was late. She was tired and this little excursion proved her thinking suffered from the fatigue. She was five minutes from home. She drove there.

The mercury light over the barn cast its comforting but unearthly blue glow over the parking pad behind the house. Rita glanced at the Mondieu household. The night-light was on in Lorretta's bedroom as it was every night.

But as she glided in toward the carport, she saw a small furry body in the middle of the asphalt.

"Hunter." Rita slammed on the breaks and ripped the keys from the ignition. The lights shone on the lifeless body.

"No, no, this can't be." Tears were hot in her eyes as she knelt beside the dead cat.

"What happened? What happened to you?" She touched the yellow fur as she looked for some sign of cause. The limp hanging head indicated a broken neck.

"Meow."

Rita stopped. The cat in front of her was dead. Was she hearing things?

"Meow." On the fence post nearest the house perched a solemn yellow tabby with a white face and white paws.

"Hunter?" Rita looked at the fence and then down at the body at her feet.

The Great White Hunter floated softly to the cold grass and meandered in her direction.

"What the . . ." Rita grabbed her cat and hugged him close.

The Great White Hunter, never one for public displays, wriggled violently until she returned him to earth. He sniffed at the unfortunate lookalike and walked away.

"I can't leave this poor guy out here like this," Rita said to herself and dragged off to the barn for a shovel.

♏

In the morning, when her alarm beeped, Rita reached over, switched it off and rolled back over.

When the phone rang, she was half asleep and punched the clock again, mistaking the jangle for the alarm.

"Hello," she managed to say after she had figured it out.

"I'm not interrupting anything, am I, honey?"

"Dammit it, Bev." Rita jerked upright and stared at the time.

"Well, your girl, Miss Smooth called here this morning and said you'd been out dancing with those evil Blizzard sisters last night. Just checking to see if you got lucky," Bev said.

"I'm lucky they didn't kill me."

"Um hm. Well, honey, you need to get on down the road. You have some appointments you're gonna be late for."

Rita was already out of bed and rummaging in a drawer for underwear.

"Thanks for calling, Bev. Listen, I have a license I need to run down. Will you call DMV for me so I can have it when I get in?" Rita read off the numbers.

"Sure thing, sweetie."

"Don't call me sweetie. You know it reminds me of my mom telling me to play nice."

"Yes, ma'am. Sorry." Bev hung up after she took the license number.

Rita brushed her teeth, showered and dressed in black flannel slacks with a black turtleneck. Downstairs in the kitchen, she phoned Karin VanDreem while she made coffee.

"Hi, this is Rita."

"Rita." The name wasn't registering.

"Great. How quickly they forget." Just a tinge of sarcasm in Rita's voice.

"Rita Mars. I'm so sorry, it's been a terrible morning already."

"In continuance of my terrible night."

"I'm sorry. What happened to you?"

"Came home and found a dead cat in my drive. It looked almost exactly like my own cat. But anyway, I didn't call to talk about that. I called because of a car that I chased out of your neighborhood last night."

Silence on the other end. Then. "A Lexus?"

"Yes, a light gold color."

"Douglas."

"I'm running the tag today. I followed him up the Expressway. We ended up about two miles from my house when he gave me the slip. But as he did, he was pretty blatant in letting me know that he'd beaten me at the game."

"Definitely Doug. And I'll tell you something else. It wasn't a coincidence, that cat in your drive. He killed it and put it there. Jesus, this is worse than I thought."

Rita stretched the phone cord as far as it would reach so that she could pour a cup of coffee.

"Now wait a minute. Let's not get carried away here. That seems like a bit of leap."

"I'm telling you I know him. This is what he does."

Rita burned her lip. "Ok. Ok. But how would he even know about me?"

"I don't know."

There was another silence.

"I'm giving up. I can't deal with this. Letting him win is far easier than living like this. I'm going to move to Delaware to live with my sister until I get a job there."

"You're not serious."

"As I can be. This guerilla war of wills has me on edge all the time. I can't take it." There was a tremor in Karin's voice.

"Give me a chance to work. You hired me because you thought I could help. I can, but not if you run off. You have my word. I will take care of this."

"I don't know."

"Tell me what you need to feel safe until I can set this straight."

"I don't want to be alone, especially at night." Karin paused. "I'm afraid. I can't even sleep. I'm worn down."

"I understand that." Rita took another sip of coffee. "My proposal is this: I'll spend the nights at your house. Would you be comfortable with that?"

"And what if you have to be out of town?" Karin asked.

"I'll send Bev."

"And what is he going to do? Call the fashion police?"

Rita bristled. "Beverly Hills, real name Charles Jamal Wheatley, is a former Navy seal. You're probably in better hands with her than with me."

"I'm sorry. That was a mean thing to say and I'm not as bigoted as that sounded."

"No offense taken," Rita said. "And you're comfortable with my sleeping in the same house?"

"Same house," Karin said, "different rooms."

"Absolutely."

Rita hung up the phone. She poured the remainder of the coffee in a travel mug and was out the door. The Great White Hunter was nowhere to be seen.

Lorretta, however, was in her front yard. She was preparing the stone goose, Scarsdale, for a new day. His outfit was a blue and gold football jersey and a matching helmet. She waved when she saw Rita.

"Lovely young man, my dear. Do tell him to come back." Lorretta returned to her task of dressing Scarsdale .

Rita walked over. "Young man?"

"I chose blue and gold for the Navy football team," Lorretta said. "They play Army this Saturday, you know."

"Uh, yes, but you mentioned a man?"

"Your young man who came calling last night. He was very nice. But you weren't home, dear. He said he'd left you a surprise."

The hair stood up on Rita's neck. What was she up against?

Chapter 11

This morning Bev had on a navy Dolce & Gabbana suit with coordinated pearl choker and earrings. On the nail polish inspection, Rita noticed she had opted for the ultra-conservative clear finish with French detail. Bev sauntered through the office on open toe six-inch heels, a perfect navy compliment to the suit.

"My God," Rita said when she walked in, "aren't you afraid you'll fall to your death off those things?"

"Oh, ye of little chic." Bev marched back from the filing cabinet without so much as a wobble and seated herself demurely at her desk.

"They don't hurt your feet?" Rita headed for the coffee pot.

"Never."

"Don't make your calves ache?" Rita took a sip and slid onto the edge of Bev's desk.

"I have never once addressed you as the Queen of Converse, miss." Bev crossed one smooth leg over the other as she started to type on her computer.

"Ok, ok. Hey, just asking." Rita removed herself from the desk and started into her office. "Did you get a chance to run that license number?"

Bev halted and tapped her keyboard.

"Dr. Douglas Sevier," Rita said before Bev could respond.

Bev rolled her eyes. "A Mrs. Cornell Chesteron, eighty. Vehicle is GM's version of the Nile river barge, Huntington blue Olds 98, model year 1996."

"No," Rita said.

"Yes."

"Are you sure?"

"My, we are irritable this morning, aren't we? Things not go well with the twins last night?"

"Dammit, Bev. I had nothing to do with those two and you know it."

"And maybe that's why you're so testy, sugar." Bev said.

"DFM 708?"

Bev beckoned for Rita to come and observe the screen. "SAR 526. You are more than welcome to search the Motor Vehicles database yourself."

"He's a smart bastard. He ripped off those plates, let me see him on purpose, knowing that I couldn't prove a damned thing."

"Is this the husband of Ms. VanDreem you're talking about?"

Rita then recounted the story about the lookalike cat and the man who had visited Loretta.

Bev looked at Rita. "This is a scary boy, honey. Are you sure you want to go on with this? Maybe VanDreem should go to the police."

Rita cradled her coffee cup in her hands. "Bev," she said, "you know as well as I do that the police can't help her."

"True, but my concern is you. Karin VanDreem's ex is crazy-dangerous." A furrow creased Bev's brow.

"Hey, you'll give yourself wrinkles." Rita started into her office.

"I brought you some doughnuts, sweet cheeks," Bev called after her. "But don't you eat too many of them now or those Blizzard girls are gonna look someplace else."

"Very funny." Rita went over to Bev's desk and picked up Mrs. Cornell Chesteron's address. She punched Karin VanDreem's number into her phone as she entered her office.

"And you have no idea who this woman is?" Rita asked.

"Never heard of her."

"How about 17120 Charles Street?"

"Sounds familiar."

"There's an apartment number too. I'm guessing it's one of the luxury high rises near the Hopkins campus."

"Calvert Towers."

"Is that where Douglas moved?" Rita punched the address into the crisscross directory on her computer.

"Yes."

"Well, so it is," Rita said. "So it is. My guess is they have an underground garage and good ole' Doug went down and did a quick switch on the nearest car. At that hour, not many people would be out touring."

"Are you sure you want to get involved in this?" Karin asked. "The more I see, I know the more scared I am. I thought I'd seen his dark side, but I'm discovering it has a depth I could never have predicted."

"I'm coming over tonight, remember?" Rita said. She brushed a flake of sugar off her desk.

"I had not forgotten."

"You'll be perfectly safe."

"And what about you?" Karin VanDreem asked.

The question caught Rita off guard. "Me? If the bogeyman hasn't gotten me yet, then he's never gonna catch me."

"It's not the bogeyman I'm worried about," Karin said. "It's Douglas Sevier."

Karin's words sent a chill through Rita. She shook it off with a laugh. "Then I guess he should be the worried one."

"What time?" Karin asked.

"I'll be there half an hour before you arrive."

"Seven."

"Seven it is." Rita said. She hung up the phone and reached for her second doughnut. Nothing like a high dose of sugar to pump up her courage. And then there was Bobby's case; she'd have to engage Bev to cover some of the immediacy of the VanDreem problem.

"The Hunter will be hanging by the back door when you get there," Rita said to Bev. "Now that it's getting cold at night, he'll stay in until around six am. Then he'll come in and meow to go out."

"Don't worry about a thing, baby. Me and the Hunter's gonna be fine. I'm picking him up a fine can of tuna so he won't miss his mama so much." Bev slipped into a sleek black cashmere coat with a gleaming gold serpent lapel pin.

"Well, I'm going to miss him." Rita reached for her pea jacket.

"Where's your weapon?"

Normally Bev's voice was sweet and smooth like a song. When she was deadly serious though the masculine qualities dominated. It always surprised Rita when that happened.

"Trunk of the car."

"Strap it on, baby," Bev said. "Check the magazine. Prepare for the unexpected."

"I will, Bev, I will."

"Don't wanna be comin' in here with a half dozen doughnuts some mornin' and have 'em go to waste. I ain't playin'. You hear what I'm sayin'?"

"Loud and clear, gorgeous." Rita flicked off the light in the office and held the door for her.

"Baby, I love it when you talk like that." In an instant, Bev was herself again.

♏

"You can put your things in here." Karin VanDreem held open the door to a guest bedroom just off hers.

The room, like all those in this Guilford mansion, was expansive, probably drafty in the winter. Inside was a cherry four-poster with matching chest of drawers. An expansive window, covered with white draperies hid the view to the darkened side yard. There was a small closet and a blanket chest at the end of the bed. The original 1940's lighting was cheerless, but Karin switched on the bedside lamps, which brightened the area considerably.

Rita tossed her suitcase on the bed. "Nice room."

"Thanks, and I'm just next door." Karin pointed to the west wall where a bucolic landscape was the featured decoration.

Rita went to the curtains and peeked out. "Plenty dark out there. We need to get the electrician here to put in the motion sensor floods."

"I'm going to feel like I'm living in a used car lot." Karin turned down the bed as Rita came back to unpack.

Rita picked up her suitcase and moved it to the top of the blanket chest.

"The drawers are empty." Karin went to the closest set and opened the top one as Rita approached with clean underwear.

"Thanks." Rita dropped in her things and went back immediately.

"Have you eaten?" Karin asked.

"Not yet." Rita stayed away from the chest until Karin moved.

"I can call in Chinese."

"Sounds great," said Rita. "I'm going to unpack and then do a perimeter run. By then the food should be here."

"Oh, certainly." Karin left and Rita could hear her on the steps downstairs.

Later, while they ate, Rita went over a list of things that needed to be done to secure the house.

"You have an electrician. He can do the lighting stuff. Your locks were changed?"

"Yes," Karin answered. "Are you going to eat the last of that shrimp?"

Rita pushed a carton across the kitchen table. "All of the locks?"

Karin's mouth was full. She nodded.

"Even the padlock on the bilko to the basement."

Karin stopped in mid chew.

"I'll pick one up tomorrow." Rita set a reminder on her phone.

Karin bent her head. "This is starting to wear me down. What have I forgotten to do to keep myself safe? Where is the next threat going to pop up?"

"It changes your perspective."

"In an unpleasant way, in a way that invites distortion of the world and life in general." Karin pushed her plate away.

Rita nodded. There were other things that distorted one's take on the world as well—tight shoes and women who left you.

"Rita?"

"I'm sorry," Rita said. "I was off somewhere. What were you saying?"

"I said I didn't mean to get so down. I have known people in similar situations. For all these years, I have blithely handed out directions. It's time to heed my own advice."

"I like that," Rita said.

"I don't like it, but I can do it," Karin said.

♏︎

The Seth Thomas clock over the mantle ticked ominously in the quiet den. Karin VanDreem sat on one side of the fireplace reading patient notes. Rita sprawled in an armchair on the other side, reading Stephen King. Seth Thomas boomed the eleventh hour.

"Geez." Rita sat up.

"It is pretty loud." Karin stood. "I think it's time to turn in." She glanced around the room quickly. "What should I do?"

"Get down on your hands and knees and crawl to the steps."

Karin stared at her.

"Joke. Just a joke." Rita stuck a slip of paper into her book and also stood up.

"I'm already paranoid enough. Don't play games." Karin waited for Rita to lead the way.

"I apologize. It isn't funny."

At the top of the stairs, Karin followed Rita into her room. "Do you need anything?"

Rita's hand brushed again the sleeve of her thick Ragg cardigan.

"I'm fine," Rita said.

"I'm right next door," Karin said.

"Hey, that's my line."

They laughed together.

Chapter 12

It was lunchtime and Bev was out of the office. She exercised religiously at the Downtown Athletic Club. Rita frowned. Bev's legs were better looking than hers, and it had been a week since she'd had time to get on the North Central Railroad Trail for a run.

She sat with her feet propped up on her desk and watched the screen saver marquee float across the screen. *Fortune Favors The Brave.* Rita snorted and lurched forward to the telephone.

"Captain Smooth," said the voice on the other end.

"Do me a favor."

"Sorry, I gave up killing people for Lent," Mary Margaret said.

"Well, I guess I'm in luck. We're heading for Thanksgiving instead of Easter," Rita responded.

"You're pretty clever for a heathen girl. What's the favor?"

"I need some dirt."

"On?"

"Dr. Douglas Sevier," Rita said.

"Define 'dirt'."

"Anything legal you can suck out of the criminal justice network. Parking tickets, assault, jaywalking, petty theft."

"I'm on it."

"Anything you can find, ok? I'm going to dig around for the unofficial stuff—at the university, the studio where he tapes his show. I found out he had a female mentor who started him down the TV trail to fame and fortune. They don't speak anymore."

"Very interesting," said Mary Margaret. "Coming to basketball tonight?"

"I'm still baby-sitting," Rita answered. "I'm going to take off early though and run, stop by and check on my house, say 'hi' to Lorretta."

"Homesick?"

"Bored."

There was a long pause.

"I saw your favorite queen of mean, Diane, yesterday afternoon. She asked how you were doing," Mary Margaret said.

"I'm shocked that she spoke to you," Rita said.

"Me too. I just shrugged."

"Good answer."

"I'll get on this Dr. Demento thing right now. As soon as I get through, I'll e-mail you what I find."

"Good deal."

"Have fun," Mary Margaret said.

"Oh yeah, it's a toss-up between the hilarity of this stake out and the antic humor of rusting pipes."

♏

The door to the office opened and Bev waltzed in. She wore majestically white cross-trainer sneakers, red sweatpants and a black velour pullover. Her lipstick and nail polish were a perfect match for the sweats. She carried a black gym bag.

"I have to admit. You keep those shoes as beautifully as mine," Rita said.

"It's as important to look good as to feel good." Bev disappeared into the bathroom.

"Ah, timeless wisdom from the cosmetics counter." Rita pulled on her navy pea coat and tugged her white polo shirt collar back up around her throat.

Bev emerged from the bathroom in a Valentino miniskirt with a pearly silk open neck blouse. She tossed in a dash of color with a demure lapis choker and matching earrings.

"Half a day?" Bev asked.

"I'm securing the VanDreem premises—locks on the bilko door and meeting the electrician to set up the motion sensor floods. I'm going to take a run on the trail out by my house, shower, and pick up some more clothes." Rita opened the office door.

"What's happening on the front?" Bev sat on the edge of her desk so that she could see into Rita's face.

"Nothing."

"Nothing?" Bev said.

Rita shook her head.

"Eyes open, girl."

"Always, Bev, always," Rita said.

♏

It was a clear, sharp November night. A solitary star glistened in the cutaway curve of a crisp quarter moon. The air was still and scented with the pungent streak of wood smoke. Rita could see wisps trailing from the huge brick chimney on the north side of Karin's house.

Rita pulled her Jeep into the driveway and closed the door softly. After her five-mile run and after she'd paid the electrician, she'd spent two hours at Johns Hopkins University where Douglas Sevier taught clinical psychology. She asked a lot of questions and still had nothing. Karin had beaten her home.

Rita decided she would test her handiwork. She walked slowly and deliberately toward the front door. The front floods popped on. Rita veered toward the oaks on the south end; more light. Rita approached the basement entrance. Bingo. And then to the north end. Another blaze.

"My God." Karin stood in the kitchen doorway shielding her eyes. "Where are the band and the elephants?"

"You gotta admit. No one is going to sneak up on this house." Rita said.

"Karin? Everything all right over there?" The voice was that of an older man, loud, but quivery.

"Yes, Dr. Preston. I'm fine. The lights will be off in a minute." Karin looked at Rita.

She nodded and as she did, darkness fell around the big old white colonial.

"Well, you call me if you need anything." The old man closed his door.

"I will, Dr. Preston. Thank you."

"An admirer?" Rita asked as they went inside.

"An eighty-seven-year-old widower."

"It's never too late," Rita said.

Karin rolled her eyes and locked the back door behind her.

Dinner was angel hair pasta with fresh homemade sauce, salad, and hot bread. The kitchen was fragrant with the scent of tomato and Romano. Rita was starving.

"This is fantastic," she said as she polished off her second helping.

"Thanks," Karin said. "I took some Italian cooking classes last year and this is the first time I've gotten to try anything out. Coffee?"

"Cooking classes," Rita said.

Karin poured boiling water into a French press. "Something wrong with that?"

"I would like coffee, please," Rita answered. "No, there's nothing wrong with that. It's just a foreign concept to me."

"How about a cannoli with your coffee?"

"I wish I'd known about that before I wolfed down all that pasta."

"Sorry—but you can have a bite of mine." Karin smiled.

"Deal," Rita said. "I went to Hopkins today."

"See Douglas?" Karin took mugs out of the cupboard.

"No, he was at a taping of his weekly show out at *Public Broadcasting*. Under the guise of writing an article for *Maryland* magazine, I talked to all kinds of people he works with, people he's written articles with, done research with."

"And they all said he was 'brilliant, a leader in his field, an asset to the university' and breathed nothing more." Karin smiled as she opened the refrigerator for the cream.

"How do you know this?"

"I've seen it. My guess is that half of them know only the professional side that the majority sees and the other half, the ones who have caught a glimpse of the dark side, are afraid to say anything. He has a lot of clout."

The coffee was ready and Karin poured into the two mugs she had placed on the table. She removed one cannoli from a small white bakery box, put it on a dessert plate and took two forks from a drawer. She handed one of the forks to Rita as she sat beside her.

"An accomplished hostage taker," Rita said.

Karin nodded as she stabbed a small bite from her cannoli. "I've seen him in action."

Rita reached over and broke off a piece of the ricotta filled shell. "When we have the stalking evidence, it's going to be important that there was a pattern."

"Good luck."

"Well, you were married to him for five years. You must know something or someone."

"I know a few names from the past, people who I no longer have contact with."

"That's a start," Rita sipped her coffee. "What about a first wife?"

"I only have a name. According to Doug, she drowned on a snorkeling trip a year before we met. He was supposedly deeply affected and didn't want to talk about it."

Karin and Rita looked at each other.

"I've never thought of it other than as an accident," Karin said.

"Give me all the details you have. I'll track it down tomorrow." Rita took a sip of coffee. "And what about Laura Quick?"

"Ah, the infamous Dr. Quick."

"Infamous?" Rita broke off more cannoli.

"According to Douglas, she turned into an obsessive, stalking bitch who wanted to control his life," Karin said. "Of course, all this occurred after she had master minded the launch of his career."

"I see a pattern here," said Rita.

"Absolutely. I believed his side in the beginning, but now . . ." Karin paused, fork in mid reach. "And you ate all the cannoli."

"Geez, another pattern. I'm sorry. It was so good."

"That's why I bought extra." She brought the box to the table.

"I think I need to chat with this ex-girlfriend, and check the police report on his first wife's death."

"Are you going to 'help' me with this one too?" Karin smiled as she placed the shell on the plate.

"I am not only too embarrassed, I'm too full." Rita saluted with her coffee cup. "Bon appétit."

That night Rita tossed and turned as she wrestled sleep. Was that a whiff of cigarette smoke? She kept getting up and looking out the picture window that faced the dark south end of the house. By the time she was sleepy, the crescent wafer of moon had set and a thousand stars glittered in the deep November sky.

Now Rita dreamed. In the ethereal story playing, she walked farther and farther into a wood. The trees were dense evergreens. They stood close, and it was difficult to pass. A ground mist rose higher and thicker as she walked. Suddenly Rita heard the shrill call of a strange bird.

The bird was persistent. Approaching. It was the clock alarm. No, the phone.

Rita sat up. The room had disappeared.

"Jesus." She dropped to the floor.

The shrill bird was the smoke alarm in the hallway.

Rita, shoeless and in her pajamas, crawled across the room on her elbows and knees.

"Karin," she yelled as loud as she could.

No answer.

"Karin."

Rita stopped at her bedroom door. "Karin."

No answer.

Rita could not remember the layout of the room, and she could see nothing. At floor level she had just enough oxygen, but she knew she had to get to Karin immediately.

Coughing.

"Karin."

"Rita?" More coughing.

"Get on the floor. The smoke rises. You can breathe down here." Rita, still on elbows and knees, rushed toward Karin's voice.

Rita looked around her. She had no idea where the door was. They were on the second floor, and she had no way of knowing where the fire might be.

Karin bumped into her. She was gasping.

"Stay close to the floor. Breathe. Stay low. We've got to get out of this house."

"Can't breathe," Karin choked.

"Keep moving. Stay low. Can you lead us out of here?" Neither woman could see the other. Rita put her hand out to Karin's face. Karin nodded.

"We can't lose touch. Get closer. Shoulder to shoulder as we move. Ok?"

Karin nodded again.

"Let's go."

Quickly they were in the hallway. The smoke seemed thicker and more acrid.

"I'm turned around." Karin sounded like she was going to cry. "I can't see anything. I don't know where the stairs are."

"It's all right." Rita put an arm around her. "Is there a balcony, a widow's walk on this house?"

"No." Karin was crying.

"Ok," Rita said. "How about an outside window railing or a trellis?"

Rita gagged. She pressed her lips close to the oriental carpet to suck in as much oxygen as she could.

"Nothing that reaches to the second floor."

Rita put an arm out around Karin. "Your room. Quick!"

They elbowed their way back.

"To the window."

Rita did not follow.

Karin halted. "Where are you going?"

"I'm going to close your door and stuff the sill. Just go to the window." Rita pushed her.

"I can't see." Karin started to jump to her feet. Rita wrenched her to the floor.

"Stay down." Rita's voice was raspy. She tried to sound calm. "You can't breathe up there."

Karin coughed violently. Rita put an arm around her again to reassure her.

The smoke was thicker, black. It left an acid taste on Rita's tongue. The thin air layer at floor level was getting thinner.

"Go to the window. Now," Rita said. She couldn't see her, but Karin crawled away into her bedroom. Rita followed.

She reached the bed and yanked the comforter back to the doorway. She slammed the door and stuffed the bed covering as tight to the sill as she could.

"Karin?"

"I'm at the window."

"Open it. Stick your head out and breathe."

Rita heard the creak of the knob as Karin rolled the crank on the windows. She felt a sharp blast of November air. The smoke turned toward the draft.

Karin coughed again. Rita's lungs were stinging as she hustled toward the cold breeze. She banged into Karin's feet.

"Open them all. Vent the room," Rita wheezed.

In a moment the three-bedroom windows were wide to the night. The smoke crowded the frames and rushed toward the sky.

Karin reached out a hand and pulled Rita up. "I can get some air here," she said. "But now what?"

"Do you have shoes on, socks?"

"No."

"Catch your breath." Rita made a grab for the bed and pulled off the top sheet, then the fitted. She knotted them together and tied one end of her makeshift rope to a leg of Karin's four-poster.

"We're over the kitchen porch. From there we can jump to the ground." Rita tied the sheet around Karin's waist.

"My arms aren't strong enough."

"I'll lower you. The drop isn't that steep. Get on the sill."

Karin perched tentatively on the frame. "I can't do this. I'm acrophobic."

"Afraid to leave the house?"

"Heights, dammit. I'm afraid of heights."

The smoke still billowed from the open windows.

"Trust me. Look at me. Watch me the whole way until your feet touch the porch. Then stand back from the sheet so I can climb down."

Karin started to look behind her at the ground.

Rita reached for her chin and gently positioned her face forward. "Look at me," she said. "It's the only way." With that she helped Karin ease downward from the window until only her hands were visible clutching the sill.

"Let go. I've got you."

Karin tried to let go with one hand, but didn't have enough strength to hold with just one. The sudden dropping weight of her body jolted Rita and banged her into the window cutting her lip.

"Grab the sheet," she called to Karin. "Hold onto it. I've got you."

In seconds, Karin was on the porch roof. She untied the sheet and tugged it to let Rita know it was free. Rita slid down the sheet, the cotton burning her hands as she fell.

Karin held her face in her hands and cried.

"It's ok." Rita held Karin so that her head rested on her shoulder. She could feel the tears through her nightshirt. "We're safe," Rita said as she tried to calm her own trembling hands.

♏

The fire department stampeded through the house like buffalo in hip boots. They vented the roof with axes and were perplexed by the lack of dense heat and flames.

"They can't find a source," the battalion chief told Rita. Karin was sitting in a warm squad car.

Rita had commandeered a fire coat to ward off the cold, and she stood with Chief Juarez by the hose truck.

"Magic flames?" Rita asked.

"No, but it's strange," the chief said.

A fireman approached from the house. He was shaking his head.

"Arson," he said. "Rags soaked with accelerant in the heating ducts. It's a good thing you ladies had a smoke detector. We need to get the cops involved in this."

"Rags in the heat ducts?" Rita asked

"Yes, ma'am. Soaked with a mix of detergent and black powder."

"Homemade napalm," said the battalion chief. "Nasty business." He turned to Rita. "You've got somebody who's taken a serious dislike to you."

Rita nodded.

"I've got to report this."

Rita nodded again as he walked off to his car and radio to call in the report.

She shivered as she looked around her, beyond the smoky house, beyond the busy firemen. She was looking for Douglas Sevier.

"Ok, you bastard," she said. "No more Ms. Nice Girl."

Chapter 13

The night clerk at the Inner Harbor Hyatt gave them only a passing glance. Two women; one in a fur coat and bed slippers. The other wore baggy sweats and running shoes without socks. They both smelled of smoke.

The one in the fur coat was nervous. Karin kept changing her overnight bag from hand to hand. She shuffled her feet as if she were trying to hide the fact that she was wearing bedroom shoes.

"Just the one night?" the clerk asked.

"That's right, Jim." Rita stared the clerk in the eye and dared him to comment further.

"Luggage?"

"We had a fire."

"Sorry," said the young man. He handed the plastic key card to Rita.

As she and Karin turned to the elevators in the empty lobby, the clerk called out to them. "Need anything? Toothbrushes, toothpaste?"

"No, thanks," Rita called back.

"If you think of anything . . ."

"Thanks. I appreciate the thought." Rita held the open elevator for Karin who ducked in and stood in the corner.

The door closed.

"Do you think he thought you and I . . ." Karin said.

"We don't care what he thought. Do we?"

"No."

The doors slid open on the eleventh floor. The corridors were empty. It was well after midnight. Rita led the way to the room.

"Hey, look." Rita went to the window. "He gave us a great view. Guy can't be all bad." She stood with her arms on her hips overlooking the lights of the city that sparkled on the dark shiny harbor waters.

Karin came up behind her.

"We could have been dead," she said.

"Yeah, but we're not." Rita was smiling when she turned around. "And we're not going to be."

"If you hadn't been there, I wouldn't have gotten out." Karin slapped her arms against her sides in her frustration. "I was scared. I was turned around in my own house. I . . ."

"Hey." Rita reached for Karin's wrists. "We are fine. We are here. The night is beautiful—and trust me, I was as scared as you were."

"You got us out." Karin looked into Rita's face. Tears pooled in her eyes.

"We got us out," Rita pulled Karin toward the window and gently turned her to the view.

Karin leaned back and rested against Rita, who took a deep breath.

"It's good to be alive," Karin said.

"Yes, and I think we need to get some sleep now." Rita grasped Karin's shoulders and eased away.

She stood staring at the king-sized bed. "Well, I guess I'll ask for a room change."

Karin continued to enjoy the view. "What's wrong with this one?"

"You didn't see the bed I take it." Rita hit the Front Desk button on the phone.

Karin rushed to the night table and punched down on the switch hook. "I saw it as soon as I walked in."

Rita stared.

Karin went over to her overnight bag. "I'm going to brush my teeth again," she said and went into the bathroom.

Rita placed the receiver back in its cradle. "I'm going to brush my teeth again," she whispered her exaggerated imitation of Karin.

"Did you say something?" Karin called from the bathroom.

"Not me," Rita said. "Far be it from me to say anything."

At breakfast Rita and Karin sat near the window in the Hyatt coffee shop. Rita's eyes were red. Karin looked as if she'd been on vacation.

"Coffee?" asked the waitress.

Rita shoved her cup toward the woman without a word.

"Thank you." Karin smiled and took a sip. "Look at the sunlight on the water."

Rita pulled her sunglasses out of her jacket pocket and glanced toward the harbor. "Nice day."

"You didn't sleep well?" Karin asked.

"No." Rita left her sunglasses on. "I'm not used to . . ."

Another waitress appeared at the table to take their order. Karin ordered fruit and a bagel. Rita ordered bacon, a croissant, and fresh orange juice.

"Not used to what?" Karin asked when the waitress left.

"Excuse me?" Rita burned her lip on the hot coffee.

"You started to tell me about why you didn't sleep well."

A long pause followed.

"I'm not used to sleeping with anyone." Rita looked over at the harbor again.

"I'm sorry. I really didn't mean to pry," Karin replied.

Rita shrugged.

Karin reached forward and gently removed Rita's sunglasses. "Are—are you crying?"

Rita dabbed her eyes with the linen napkin from her lap. "Of course not. The smoke last night irritated my eyes. That's all."

"I see."

The waitress arrived with their food then. Rita slathered butter and strawberry preserves on her croissant.

Karin carefully divided her bagel into quarters and picked up the first morsel to spread with cream cheese.

"It must have been very painful," Karin said.

Rita bit into the croissant. "What?"

"The end of your relationship. "

"It had been dead a long time. It was a matter of proper burial."

"Doesn't mean it wasn't painful. You must have cared about this person very much."

"I did." Rita took another sip of coffee. "Past tense."

"What was she like?" Karin asked as she put down her bagel.

For a moment, Rita said nothing. Then with a deep breath she said," She was the best of times, the worst of times."

The waitress drifted by with the coffee pot. Karin waved her on. "You're right. It's none of my business."

Rita's voice softened. "I wasn't implying that. She was like that. She could be incredibly kind, caring about people in one moment, slashing their throats with verbal razors the next."

"You fought?" Karin asked.

"No, not often. The anger wasn't directed at me, mostly at others. She had no skill in dealing with other people's feelings. She was traumatized by the careless nannies her mother hired. She grew up shy and afraid of Mom's judging. Sadly, frightened people are always the most dangerous."

"I agree with you there."

"She was exceptionally bright, but had no sense of humor. Sometimes that was maddening." Rita sipped her coffee.

"For you that would have been deadly."

"She had focus and vision and purpose, the likes of which I have never seen and which I certainly have never been close to achieving." Rita stuck the sunglasses back on her face. She turned to the glass wall that overlooked Baltimore Harbor.

"I'm sorry," Karin said.

Rita shrugged. "Some things work and some things don't. This didn't."

"Then I'm sorry that it didn't," Karin offered.

"Maybe there's nothing to be sorry about," Rita said. "I hung on way too long. She was a woman compelled to view everyone as a conquest. I got tired of stitching the fabric of the relationship back together, even when it became a worthless rag. It was not an endeavor to my credit."

"I understand that," Karin said.

The waitress drifted past again. This time Rita waved her over to warm both cups on the table.

When the waitress left, Karin asked. "So, what do we do now? I mean, I need to hire somebody to repair the damage to the house and . . ."

"Not until the arson boys get finished with it," Rita interrupted, "and I'm calling in a friend of mine who retired from the FBI arson squad to help me with this. And after I've made that little phone call, I'm going to visit Dr. Douglas Sevier, put him on notice. This failure to confront the guy is starting to get on my nerves." Rita snatched up the remainder of her croissant and took a fierce bite.

"Do you think that's a good idea?" Karin put down her bagel and shot a worried look across the table.

"Oh, he might get mad and try to kill us?"

"And I've got to find a place to stay," Karin said.

"You have one." Rita motioned for the waitress and stood up.

Karin gulped a last swallow of coffee and grabbed her purse. "I do?"

"You're moving to the country. You'll love it." Rita scribbled her name across the bottom of the check and marched toward the hotel lobby. Karin hustled after her.

♏

Dr. Douglas Sevier taught Clinical Psychology 401: Weirdness Personified on Monday, Wednesday, and Friday at 1 p.m. in Maryland Hall. Rita wore jeans, her pea jacket and a pair of boots and clutched a notebook to her chest. She was doing her best imitation of a graduate student and keeping an eye out for Sevier on his way to class from his office.

She blended in well. Students passed without giving her a second look. She kept wondering if that was a good or bad sign.

The classroom was small, down the narrow corridor on the left. Rita hung around the main entrance that opened out on the quadrangle. She expected Sevier to come through this door; his office was directly opposite the quad.

The hallway grew less and less crowded. Classroom doors closed. She could hear the murmur of lectures through the walls. Sevier could not have passed without her seeing.

Rita pretended to study the notes on the bulletin board at the door for a moment and then sauntered toward the room where he was supposed to be teaching. All the doors had windows and Rita casually glanced in as she passed. A young woman was sitting at the professor's desk up front. Before her was a jumble of desks with ten students scribbling madly in blue test books.

"Damn," Rita said to herself. The woman was probably his teaching assistant. There was no need for him to present himself for something as lowly as a mid-term exam.

Rita pulled up the collar of her coat and went outside. A fierce November breeze rattled the limbs of the naked oaks and made her wish she had remembered to bring gloves.

The office building was silent. She saw only one other person on the first floor, and he was locking his office to leave. Rita headed for the marble steps and the third floor where Sevier's office was located.

Her boot heels echoed through the dimly lit corridor where most of the doors were closed, offices dark. She was looking for 327. A door was open at the far end and a light was on. Rita heard classical music; baroque set her teeth on edge.

Douglas Sevier sat at his desk, peering over half glasses at his computer screen. He did not look up as Rita walked just inside his doorway.

He was taller than she estimated from the pictures Karin had shown her, 6'2" maybe. He had little grey in his hair and was obviously athletic. Karin had said that he was a cyclist. In a quick glance, Rita could picture Karin attracted to this man, but in lingering, she noticed there was something about his eyes. They were grey and cold and penetrating, like a raptor's.

"I've been expecting you." Douglas Sevier looked up from his computer and locked onto to Rita's eyes.

She never blinked. "I'm so glad. I aim to please."

For a moment they continued the stare-down. When Sevier saw that she wasn't going to move, he eased back in his chair. "And now that you're here—what?" His lips curled in a taunting smile.

Rita approached the desk, placed her hands square on top and leaned in to face him. "You are not going to get away with your nasty little game. I'm going to catch you. It's a matter of time."

"It's personal for you now, isn't it?" Sevier studied her face.

Rita could think only of Hannibal Lechter in Jody Foster's movie.

"It's always personal when somebody tries to kill you." It was her turn to watch for reaction.

Sevier raised his eyebrows. "I have no idea what you're talking about."

Rita wanted to leap across the desk for his throat. She thought the vein in her temple might explode. "You are despicable." She had any number of more appropriate terms flying around in her head and it was all she could do to keep herself from just screaming at the man.

"I believe you are becoming hostile, Ms. Mars." Sevier reached for the phone on his desk.

Rita's teeth were clenched as she managed to say, "I will stop you. I will expose you. I will show everyone who has ever seen you what a psychopath you truly are."

Sevier was cool. He picked up the receiver and punched a button. Rita grabbed for the phone, but Sevier was quicker.

"Security, room 327, hurry."

Rita ripped the line out of the jack. "You won't be able to blow your nose or eat your lunch or sleep without my knowing what the hell you're doing."

"Stalking me?" Sevier stood up and brushed the papers around on his desk. A few fell on the floor. He flattened himself to the wall behind his desk chair.

Rita understood his plan. She stood up straight, but not before two uniformed campus police rushed the room. They instantly gripped Rita by each arm. She did not resist.

"This woman has been threatening me, gentlemen," Sevier said.

Rita's instinct was to kick both of these men and then hammer Sevier, but she knew she would only succeed in making it worse on herself. With brute force, she willed herself calm as the guards dragged her from the office.

"I intend to press charges," Sevier called after them.

m

The Baltimore City Booking Center was touted as a high tech, state-of-the-art holding facility. But for all the PCs and the sunshine yellow walls, it was a jail after all. Rita had been in more than a few, though usually on the other side of the bars, but the smell was unmistakable.

She sat on a wooden bench with Vonzella, who had been snatched off the streets while soliciting an undercover vice agent. She chewed gum incessantly and reeked of sweat and cheap perfume. Rita suspected Vonzella also harbored a hundred dollar a day heroin jones. She sat on the floor at the back of the cell in the corner, rocking back and forth. Her eyes had rolled back in her head.

The clang of opening gates caught Rita's attention. She heard approaching footsteps and the accompanying jeers and catcalls from the other prisoners.

In the lead was an overweight guard whose blue uniformed belly preceded him. Behind was a police captain in demure pumps. Beside her was an elderly man in a seven-hundred-dollar Armani suit. He had beautiful white hair and fierce blue eyes that kept their fire in spite of his age.

The jailer stopped in front of Rita's cell. Vonzella was singing to herself now, still rocking and oblivious to the rest of the world.

"Well, well, well," said Mary Margaret. "You and the working girls. What a lovely way to spend an afternoon."

"Mars," the guard said and unlocked the cell door. "Step out."

The elderly man's eyes twinkled as a smile wavered across his thin lips.

Rita sighed and walked out of the cell as the guard secured the world from the threat of Vonzella.

"I was just—" Rita started.

"Can it, Slick, until we get finished with the arraignment."
Smooth marched ahead to join the guard.

"Not to worry, my dear." The elderly man patted Rita's
arm. "I have it well in hand."

Rita stood on her toes to peck his cheek.

♏

Mary Margaret Smooth lived in a twenty-story high rise on St.
Paul Street. On the eleventh floor, she had a perfect view of the
harbor. Her place was packed on the Fourth of July and New
Year's Eve; she had a ringside seat at the city fireworks displays.

She and Rita stood in the elevator with a widow and her
poodle, a maintenance man, and a Jamaican cleaning lady. Mary
Margaret carried two double cafe mochas. Rita clutched the bag
of macaroons from Kline's bakery.

"You can't just waltz in and start threatening people,"
Mary Margaret said.

"I didn't do anything," Rita said.

The widow with the poodle looked at Rita, picked up her
dog, and edged away.

"And the guy's going to accuse you of stealing his wife,"
Mary Margaret said.

"I never laid a hand on her," Rita countered.

The Jamaican cleaning lady took a step toward the widow.

"You wound up in the cooler with the street walkers, for
God's sake."

"Like I had some choice in that."

At this point the elevator stopped, and the maintenance man took an appraising look at Rita as she and Mary Margaret got off.

Mary Margaret's apartment was open and airy, a beneficiary of bygone and more generous times in real estate. Rita went straight for the window.

"I love this view."

Mary Margaret deposited the coffees on the breakfast bar in the small kitchen and went into the bedroom to change.

"Places available here," she called.

"Not on your life." Rita watched a man in a shabby overcoat rummage through a dumpster in the alley behind the building.

"Yeah, I forgot, you might actually have to live next to somebody."

"Very funny," Rita said. "I just like peace and quiet—and space."

Mary Margaret quickly emerged in navy blue sweats with Baltimore Police Academy in gold down the left leg of the pants. "Ready?"

She handed one of the cafe mochas to Rita and they sat on the sofa, which faced a gas fireplace. Rita opened the white bakery bag of macaroons and pointed it toward Mary Margaret.

"And how the hell did you get the most famous criminal attorney in Baltimore history out of retirement?" Mary Margaret sipped her coffee.

"Holt Howard is a buddy of mine. We go way back. I ended up finding some evidence in one of his old cases that helped clear his client."

"Well, aren't you special?" Mary Margaret took a bite of macaroon and leaned back into the sofa.

"Yes, I am as a matter of fact. But the truth is we've worked on a bunch of stuff together—some very interesting city graft cases in '03 and '07."

"And speaking of the city's legal establishment. You are in big trouble." Mary Margaret sat up straight. "You could end up losing your license over this. What the hell were you thinking?"

"I was thinking how much fun it would be to be dragged off the Hopkins campus by two growth hormone experiments." Rita bit into her cookie. "For God's sake, Smooth, it was time to confront this guy. He almost killed me—and his wife."

"I don't know which is worse, this Dr. Demento chasing you or the State of Maryland ripping up your investigator license."

Rita gulped down more macaroons with her coffee. "The license, definitely. That's why I called in Holt. I told him about this psycho, Sevier. He told me not to worry. Said we'd never get in front of a judge. According to him, Sevier would not want to call attention to his misbehavior."

Mary Margaret leaned back again into the sofa. "Girl, I never saw anybody who could get into trouble like you."

"I always get out," Rita said.

"Gotta hand it to you," Mary Margaret agreed.

For a while they sat quietly eating cookies and drinking coffee with the sun setting across the city. It cast purple shadows at the fireplace and illuminated the photographs on the mantle. The picture in the middle was that of a woman about Mary Margaret's age. She had shoulder length dark hair, smiling dark eyes that crinkled at the corners as a sign that she laughed often. She wore a polo shirt and held a golf trophy.

Rita glanced at Mary Margaret. "It doesn't seem possible that she's gone."

"Two years. Some nights I sit here and feel like she's going to walk through that door." Mary Margaret drank her coffee.

In the two years before, her lover, Lola Garcia, had died of breast cancer.

"I miss her," Rita said.

"Me too." Mary Margaret got up, went to the stereo and turned on the radio. The oldies station.

"We're gonna end up old maids," Rita said.

"Could be," Mary Margaret said. "Hey, turn that up."

Freddie "Boom Boom" Cannon was belting out "Palisades Park."

"Come on, old lady," said Mary Margaret. "Can you still rock and roll?"

"Who you callin' old?"

Rita grabbed Mary Margaret's hand and twirled her around. She sang along with Freddie Cannon.

Mary Margaret chimed in.

"The two shouted the chorus together.

And for a few minutes, they danced back and forth across the living room floor and sang and did not remember they were alone in the world.

Chapter 14

It was after six when Rita left Mary Margaret's apartment. She wove through the downtown streets, up I-83, and into the countryside. She passed several malls where the parking lots were still lighted hives of activity. She had bought exactly zero Christmas gifts. Rita turned on the radio to try and forget the usual last minute buying frenzy she faced.

Every station had holiday tunes, except for one. Madonna sang "Take a Bow."

"You've got that right, honey." Rita sighed. Even the non-Christmas songs were haunting her tonight. The ghost of Christmas past was not giving up so easy.

Rita had no strength for the memories that song brought back. Snippets played in her head, happier holidays with Diane. Rita had loved Christmas then. She marveled at the dread and loneliness with which she now approached the season.

She pulled into her driveway. She had phoned Bev earlier to ask her to stay at the house that night because she was going to be late. She also called Karin to assure her that she would be indeed safe in the house and not to be concerned that Rita wasn't there when she arrived.

When she entered, the Great White Hunter curled on the hearth beside the wood stove on which Bev had placed a pot of simmering potpourri. The Christmassy scents made Rita even sadder.

Bev was upstairs on Rita's treadmill. Karin was in the kitchen brewing a pot of coffee for after dinner.

"Your dearly beloved had me carted to the big house today," Rita told her.

"My God, what happened?" Karin asked.

Rita told her the story.

"He'll never follow through," Karin said. "Revenge is always personal for him and he would never trust the courts to get it right. I think for him exacting a penalty is pleasure. It validates his sense of control."

"Very interesting," Rita replied. "My attorney had a similar assessment."

"But it worries me."

"I'm not worried," Rita said.

"His focus now is as much on you as me."

"I can take care of myself," Rita told Karin.

"I don't trust him. The more I see, the more I believe he's capable of anything."

"I've never thought of him any other way," Rita said.

The phone rang.

"Ms. Mars?" The voice was quivery.

"Yes?" Rita was tentative and the response made Karin turn to her with a worried expression. Rita shook her head to indicate it had nothing to do with Dr. Demento.

"What should I do? I can't find her anywhere and I'm afraid she's walked off. She did this once last summer but my nephew was here . . ."

"Whoa. Leonard?" Rita asked. Karin came over to stand near the phone.

"Yes, from next door."

Leonard was seventy-five, spry and healthy, but frail nonetheless. From seven in the morning until six at night, he had a visiting nurse or a relative to help him with Loretta. For the remainder of the night he was on his own.

"Loretta's missing?" A knot clenched Rita's throat. The temperature had fallen quickly in the last hour and the wind chill had the mercury hovering at 20. The weatherman had mentioned the "S" word.

"Have you called 911? Have you called the people at the next farm over? Did you call your nephew to get him over here?"

"Ms. Mars, I called you first. I thought she might have walked over to your place. You know she thinks her Uncle Hodge is still in that house."

Rita heard tears in his voice.

"Hang on, Leonard," Rita placed her hand over the phone and yelled. "Bev, come down. I need you." She went back to Leonard. "Call your nephew. Tell him to come directly down Belfast Road. She might just be walking straight. I'll call 911 and the Stevens folks down the road. I'll get him and his two girls to start driving around."

"I'll go with you." Karin ran to the closet for her coat.

"What the hell are you yelling about?" Bev appeared in the kitchen in her sweats. Perspiration streamed down her face.

Karin did a double take at this unaccessorized Bev.

"Loretta's missing." Rita said. "We have to find her."

Bev turned immediately and ran back upstairs to get ready. "Just give me a minute."

Rita once more returned to Leonard. "Can you do that, Leonard? Can you call him and let me take care of the rest?"

"We got to find her, Ms. Mars. She'll freeze to death in this night. It's my fault. I should have watched her better, but she never ran off in the dark. She's afraid of the dark," Leonard sobbed.

"We can't waste time, Leonard. Will you call your nephew now? Turn on all the lights in the house. Stay there in case she's just around there and she turns up while we're looking. Ok?"

Leonard sobbed some more.

"Can you do that?"

"Yes."

Rita flashed Leonard off the line and called 911. Then she phoned the Stevens family who lived a quarter of a mile away on a road that ended across the street from Rita and Loretta's driveway. He and his two daughters would scout the roads that Rita told him. She gave him her cell number in case Loretta turned up.

"I'm ready." Bev had put on dry sweats and a watch cap. Rita asked her to search around Leonard's property and hers, then move on to the adjoining fields and pastures.

"She can't get too far into the woods around here because of the underbrush, but she might have wandered into my pasture or the guy's behind us."

Bev pulled on thick, lined gloves and went to her car to get her high-powered flashlight.

"You coming with me?" Rita asked as she was tugging at her own gloves.

Karin nodded.

Rita glanced at her watch as they headed for the Jeep. "It's seven thirty. We don't have much time."

"Do you want to take my car?" Karin asked as she pulled mittens over chilled fingers.

"Mine. I have the spotlight."

Rita put the Jeep in gear and rolled down the driveway. In her rearview mirror she could see the powerful beam of Bev's flashlight slice the darkness in the back pasture.

"We'll go to the end of Western Run first. You keep an eye out on that side. When we get to the pastures, I'll get out and run the spotlight."

Karin nodded.

Rita eased the Jeep along the shoulder of Western Run Road.

"See anything?" she asked.

"No," Karin said.

Rita drove three miles to the end of the road, turned and came back down the opposite lane. At each of the open stretches of field, Rita stopped and swept the dark land with the spotlight attached to the driver's side of the hood. With its extension cord, Rita could freely direct the beam in any direction.

She and Karin spotted deer and fox, a startled Labrador retriever, and a stalking barn cat. They saw no trace of Loretta.

Rita called Bev on his cell phone. "Anything?"

"I have seen jack shit," Bev said. "I'm on Wilder's farm behind you. The cows are a little restless and they are sure as hell makin' me nervous. I keep seein' myself stampeded into the ground."

Rita got an update from the family further down the road as well—nothing. She had seen no policemen and she was careening back and forth between panic about not finding Loretta and fury in seeing no police response. Rita pulled over on the non-existent shoulder. She rested her forehead on her steering wheel.

"You're doing everything possible." Karin touched her arm.

"I have to find her." Rita raised her head. She got back on the road and waited at the stop sign for the lone car to pass.

Karin sighed. "It may be that we don't find her."

"We will. I will. I will drive all night and all day tomorrow if I have to, but I am going to find Loretta."

"Rita, you can't take on that responsibility." Karin said quietly.

"I already have."

Rita pulled into the parking lot of the local convenience store.

"Coffee?" Rita asked.

"I'll come with you."

Inside Rita went first to talk with Buck, the young man behind the counter. He worked there a few nights; during the day he was a mechanic at the gas station. Buck knew everyone in the community. He had seen no trace of Loretta, but volunteered to ask those who came in until he left at eleven. Rita gave him her cell phone number.

"She may have approached a house, gotten confused and wandered up a lane, gone into a barn or an open garage," Karin said when they got back in the Jeep.

"Jesus," Rita said. "I never thought of that. We need to go back along my road and the lanes to the houses."

For another hour, Rita and Karin drove up the winding farm lanes, some paved, some mere dirt paths. They went to each front door and inquired. They looked in barns and run-in sheds and garages and playhouses, and they found nothing. When they had completed this search, they were once again at the little local store. Rita went in for more coffee.

Karin poured half and half into her steaming cup. "Are you crying?" she asked Rita.

"The cold is making my eyes tear." Rita turned away and snatched a handful of napkins after she had snapped the lid on her coffee cup.

Buck called after them as they approached the counter. "Hey, you don't owe me nothin'. You just find Mz. Mondieu. I'm still askin' anybody who comes in if they saw her."

"I appreciate it."

In the car, she flipped open the coffee cup lid then dialed on her cell phone again and phoned the Mondieu house. Loretta's nephew, Pete, answered.

The police had finally arrived, one patrol car. The officer was going to drive around the roads and look. Pete had not seen or heard from him in over an hour. The Stevens family was still out there: they were trying some of the closer roads that ran off Western Run. The black man who said his name was Bev had stopped by also, and said to tell Rita that he was going to scout through the thin tree line that separated the Wilder farm from Rita's. Bev hadn't seen anything either.

Rita pushed the end button. "Two hours. She's been out there for two goddamned hours." She pounded the dash with her fist.

"We'll find her." Karin put her own hand over Rita's.

"I don't know." Rita shook her head. "I just don't know."

"What's our next plan of attack?" Karin asked.

"The only thing I can think of is that she might be wandering around Steady Eddie's."

"Steady Eddie?"

"Eddie Rosen, surgeon extraordinaire. His house is less than a mile away from ours, off Tanbark Lane. The last time Loretta disappeared, we found her there. Loretta thought she'd arrived at Scarlett O'Hara's *Tara*. Eddie's a good guy, but he does have an ego and a house to match."

"To *Tara*." Karin sat back in her seat as Rita throttled the Jeep into gear.

The ride was swift and rough. Rita slammed on her brakes in front of Eddie Rosen's. Two massive brick pillars shouldered a black iron gate between. Buried flood lights played on the surrounding shrubs and a brass plate that proclaimed this was Rosewood Farm. A small metal box at the edge of the driveway sprang from the ground on a black iron standard.

Rita inched the Jeep close and rolled down the window. She pushed a button and waited.

"Can I help you?" A man's voice came back.

"Eddie, it's me, Rita, from down the road. Remember when my neighbor, Loretta Mondieu got confused and came down to your house?"

The iron entrance gate was already opening.

"This is a mighty cold night for her to be out. I haven't heard my dogs barking or anything."

"Can I just look around?"

"Take your time. I 'm getting ready to go out, or I'd help. There's a button to open the gate near the barn—you've seen it. Use that to get out."

"Thanks, Eddie."

"Rita, good luck in finding her."

Rita drove the Jeep inside Rosewood. Indeed, Eddie's was very much a *Tara*, big white columns and a huge brass chandelier hung from the second-floor porch that jutted over the front of the house. The principal difference lay in that Vivien Leigh had no battery of floodlights to show off her architecture once the sun went down.

"My God," Karin said as she and Rita passed the house and headed for the barns.

"The good news is that we get a real clear view of the house. The bad news is that Loretta isn't there."

Behind the house was a long low barn, closed for the night. Inside were seven polo ponies. Eddie, besides being an accomplished plastic surgeon, was captain of the Maryland Polo Club.

Rita and Karin got out of the Jeep. "Let's look through the barn." Rita rolled back the sliding door and was greeted with a few snorts, some stamping hooves and a long, low whinny. She switched on the light.

The barn was spotless with scrubbed rubber grid flooring. Each stall had its own brass name plaque and brass fixtures.

"These horses live better than some people," Karin said.

"Yep, and they have life insurance policies to match."

The two women checked every stall, the tack room, the feed room, and the groom's office. Nothing.

"Let's check the field." Rita closed the sliding door as she and Karin stepped outside.

"This way." Rita walked behind the barn. When she reached the back of the building, motion sensor lights bathed the area in light. She found the electric panel she wanted and reached in. Stadium lighting blazed across a perfectly manicured and beautifully striped playing field. "I don't believe this," Karin shielded her eyes with her hand.

Rita ran to the bleachers on the other side of the field, checked behind the scoreboard, and rattled the handle of the locked refreshment stand. Loretta was not here.

At the south end of the field, at the frame for the goal, Rita stopped. "Loretta," she cried into the still night air. "Loretta."

Karin rushed to her. "It's not your fault." She put an arm around Rita.

"It's not about fault," Rita sobbed. "It's not about that at all." For a moment she bowed her head and hid her eyes with a gloved hand.

Rita took a deep breath and brushed away the evidence of tears. "I'm ok," she said to Karin. "Thanks."

Karin left her arm around Rita's shoulders as they walked to the barn and shut off the lights. In the darkness they got into the Jeep and drove to Rita's house.

"You haven't even had any dinner," Rita said as she turned into the drive that she shared with the Mondieu house. "Do you want me to drop you off before I go see Leonard?"

"I'll go with you," Karin said.

At Loretta's house, her nephew, Pete, greeted them at the door. There was another young man there in cords and parka preparing to leave.

"Leonard's doctor, Dave Roberts," Pete said. Karin and Rita nodded as he exited. "Leonard was in a state. I was afraid he'd have a heart attack. Doc came over to check him out and give him a sedative."

"Any word?" Rita asked as she followed Pete into the kitchen. Pete just shook his head.

"The Stevens had to give up. School night. Coffee?" asked Pete.

Rita and Karin took the offered mugs and the cookies.

"Finally I got more police to respond. Had to call our county councilman. There's also a search team with dogs out there. Your friend, Bev, is still out there too. Got a call from him just before you came in."

"I know we'll find her," Rita said as she wrapped her cold hands around the hot coffee cup.

"It doesn't look good. I'd say she's been gone a good three hours now. With the wind chill, temperature's way below freezing. I know she doesn't have her coat. I checked the closet." Pete slumped into a kitchen chair and leaned his weary head back to stare at the ceiling.

Headlights from the driveway swung across the kitchen. More headlights. More.

Rita rushed ahead of everyone to the door. A police cruiser idled in the driveway. Behind it sat a gold Lexus with another cruiser easing up to its bumper.

A tall policeman, officer Brunell stamped on his badge, unfolded from the first car. He had a broad smile as he walked toward the house.

"We found her." The policeman gestured with his thumb toward the gold Lexus. "Actually, a passerby spotted her. Thank God, he realized the situation and picked her up."

The policeman led Loretta's nephew, Rita and Karin toward the car. He tapped on the window. Already the door on the passenger side opened and Loretta emerged. She looked no more distraught than if she'd been out for a Sunday drive.

"Hey, Doc, roll down your window for a minute." said Officer Brunell.

Karin froze.

Douglas Sevier leaned a smiling face to the group gathered around. His breath was dragon smoke in the chill night air.

"You son of a bitch," Rita snarled in a growl so low no one else could hear. She ran around the car to gather Loretta into her arms. "Are you all right? Are you hurt? Did he do anything to you?"

Oblivious, Pete and Officer Brunell grinned and thanked the good doctor, who explained how he had "found" Loretta on Western Run Road and then spent the next hour trying to follow her directions home. When he realized she couldn't help him, he had called police.

Karin was still as a statue on the other side of the car. Sevier winked at her.

The rear police cruiser started backing out of the drive. Brunell and Pete shook hands and Brunell reinserted himself behind the wheel of his own car.

Rita turned Loretta over to her nephew and rushed back to catch Sevier before he could escape. He was in no hurry. He hadn't even rolled up his window against the cold.

Rita grabbed the bottom of the window frame and thrust her face close to the doctor's. "If you hurt her . . ."

"Why I would never do such a thing. You're so, so paranoid. You really should get help with that."

"Doug, leave these people alone. It's me you're angry with," Karin said, but she moved no closer to the car.

"My dear, I'm way past that. And I really must be going. I'm holding up the officer." He gestured toward the police car ahead of him. Then he pushed the window button and Rita yanked her hands to safety.

Sevier halted the window midway. "It was just a reminder really, this little ride. You will remember, won't you?"

Bev walked up behind Rita and Karin then.

"I have a very long memory." Rita charged the Lexus, but Bev with one powerful arm swept her up.

"Don't do it, baby," she whispered.

"And do get some professional help. They're doing wonders for anger management these days." Sevier rolled up the window the rest of the way and dropped the car into gear. Rita, Karin and Bev watched him drift down the drive, followed by the police car.

Pete came out of the kitchen to thank the searchers for their help. He was shaking his head. "Damnedest thing. All Loretta will say is that she expected the devil's car to be red."

Chapter 15

The heart of night in the Belfast Valley was deep and black, and it made the silvery stars all the more bright in the clear December sky. A fox barked from far away. And beyond the tree line south, the muffled bumps and grinds of big rigs on the Interstate carried through the crisp air.

Bev trailed behind Karin and Rita as the three wearily tramped across the yards and drive. Breath steamed from their lips and every step crunched on frozen grass and twigs. Guided by the cool blue of the mercury lamp on Rita's barn, they didn't even bother to turn on their flashlights.

"Bev, just stay the night. It's after three," Rita said as they reached her back door.

"Baby, I have to be at the gym in three hours."

"Skip it for one day, for heaven's sake."

"You know I intend to be Miss Christmas Wish this year at the Hippo. And I can't be skippin' no rounds at the gym. Got to keep my girlish figure." Bev popped the hatch of her black Land Rover and threw in her flashlight.

"I can't thank you enough." Rita threw her arms around her.

"Oh, you'll be able to thank me," Bev said as she closed the trunk and hugged her back. "You—and you," she pointed at Karin, "are going to be in the audience clapping your hands off when I strut down that catwalk for the Christmas Wish title."

"Absolutely," Karin said. "I would not miss it."

"Nor would I," said Rita.

The Great White Hunter, sleeping by the woodstove in the living room, didn't raise his head as Karin and Rita came in. Both flopped into convenient kitchen chairs and sat staring.

"Long night," Rita said.

"I'm so glad we found Loretta." Karin fidgeted in her seat. "But I can't help but feel guilty that my being here brought on this whole ugly incident."

Rita leaned across the table toward her. "You can't do that. The bad guys are going to do the bad things, no matter what. If you're afraid to stand up to them because of what they might do, you're finished."

"My head knows that," Karin said. "But I shudder when I think of what could have happened to Loretta."

"Nothing." Rita got up and went to the refrigerator.

"What do you mean—nothing?" Karin followed her to stand behind and check the contents.

Rita took out a half gallon of milk. Karin pulled glasses out of the cupboard.

Rita turned to face her. "It's a game. Your dearly beloved had no intention of hurting Loretta. His intention was to scare you and me with the possibilities. He wants us to comprehend his apparent freedom of access and fear it."

Rita then handed Karin a loaf of bread, peanut butter, and strawberry preserves. Karin started preparing the sandwiches.

"There's another part of that game though," Karin said, "and I need to make sure that you understand that clearly." She poised a knife over a slice of bread.

"You mean the part where he might actually kill one of us?" Rita handed Karin two plates.

"Yes," Karin said, "yes, that's what I mean." She turned to Rita with her face drained of color.

"That is very clear to me."

Karin lowered her head and Rita put an arm around her. "I've known that from the beginning."

"I've put so many people in danger with my foolish decisions." Karin put down the knife and went to sit at the table.

Rita finished making the sandwiches quickly and put one in front of her.

"I don't feel hungry," said Karin.

"Who said you had to be hungry to eat?" Rita picked up half of Karin's peanut butter and jelly and held it to her lips. "This is medicine. Peanut butter heals the troubled mind."

Karin smiled and took a tiny bite. Then she took the sandwich from Rita. Rita picked up her own and snapped off a hunk.

"Peanut butter instead of therapy?" Karin said.

"Costs less. Tastes good." Rita took a big gulp of milk.

"Every day I look back and every day is filled with 'should haves' and 'what ifs.' I've caused myself so much grief and I'm trailing it after me as I'm trying to escape." Karin put down her sandwich.

"Stay with the peanut butter now. Don't give up."

"It's not going to help."

"Au contraire." Rita put down her own sandwich. "What you just said is everybody's dilemma. You know that deep in your heart of hearts."

"Maybe." Karin sighed.

"Every day we step up to our courage and strap it on like armor. And courage is getting up in the morning and going to work. Courage is taking the trash out and filling the car with gas, talking to other people—like we're doing now—and eating our lunch. It's about taking what life dishes out and, in spite of the bad, embracing the journey and keeping on."

Karin looked at her for a moment. She picked up her sandwich. "Well said."

"You would have told me the same thing."

"I hope so."

"I know it.

"Still, I find myself wondering how I came to fall in love with and marry someone like Doug."

Rita started on the second half of her sandwich. "Everybody gets to that question at least once in their life. After I broke up with Diane, I wondered how people survived love."

♏

Three days later Rita was driving to work as light snow danced in her headlights. It was 5:30 a.m., and she was beating the mad exodus of office commuters who fled the northernmost suburbs each morning. As she passed the exit to the Western Run Mall, she turned her head. Only fifteen more shopping days until Christmas and she wasn't anywhere close to ready.

Rita shot down the Jones Falls Expressway into the city. If she played this right, she could swing by the mall in the afternoon and do a kamikaze gift run.

"*Silent night,*" sang the radio.

"Yeah, right." Rita switched if off and swung into her garage.

Bev, in a wine-colored velour work out suit, was already at her desk. The coffee was made.

"My God, didn't you go to sleep last night?" Rita headed for the coffee machine and the bag of doughnuts Bev had sitting beside it.

"Didn't seem much point and I got a hell of a lot done."

"I don't know how you do it." Rita grabbed a honey-glazed out of the bag.

"Clean living." Bev reached under the desk and pulled out a *Baltimore Sun.* "Check this out, baby."

Rita studied the front page of the Metro section. "Train Garden Draws Crowd in Rosedale?" She bit a hunk out of the doughnut.

"And you call yourself a journalist." Bev pointed a demure ivory frosted nail at a photo and story in the lower right corner.

Rita snatched up the paper. "What the hell is this?"

"Interesting, don't you think?"

"Dr. Douglas Sevier, professor of Clinical Psychology at Johns Hopkins University, has accepted the Heidegger Chair at Oxford University. Sevier's award of this prestigious appointment is part of a distinguished teaching and publishing career. Of late, he has had his own popular radio show, *Good Mental Health*, where he responded to questions from a call-in audience." Rita tossed the paper back on Bev's desk.

"According to the article, Sevier is leaving for England," Bev said.

"So, what was the Loretta thing all about?" Rita pulled a chair up to Bev's desk.

"Last show of force," Bev said. "Maybe a power play that didn't go the way he expected."

"You mean you think he was planning to hurt Loretta to scare his wife?"

"He was using Loretta as bait and somehow the police found them, and he had no choice but to return her."

Rita sipped her coffee. "How about another scenario?"

"And that would be?" Bev leaned back in her chair.

"What if this award is phony? What if it's intended to lull us into letting down our guard? I quit the case. Karin moves back home. All quiet on the western front. Then bang."

"That could work," Bev admitted. "He's the kind of guy who would wait for the right moment."

"But the newspaper story," Rita said. "Now that would take some real work."

"He's not a stupid man."

"True." Rita finished off the doughnut. "I wonder if Karin's seen this?"

"We need to check this out," said Bev.

"I'll use my sources at the *Sun*, and I have contacts on the other side of the water, too."

"I'll snoop around at the college and his apartment."

"I don't like this," Rita said. "I don't like this one damned bit."

♏

By afternoon the snow had given up and true to Baltimore winter, the sky was dull slate. Karin had no late appointments, and the two were going to discuss the sudden change in Karin's circumstance. They stopped in a coffee bar near her office.

"Ah," said Rita as they entered. "Now when you die and you've been good, this is what heaven will smell like."

"And all this time I thought it smelled like a summer night," Karin said.

"Well, you know, there are seasons in heaven. Smells like that in summer—like this in winter."

"I see." Karin smiled.

They sat at a small table near the back with cappuccinos and a raspberry scone that they shared.

"I saw the article myself this morning," Karin said. "For a minute I breathed a sigh of relief."

"And then?"

"I've become so paranoid that I immediately thought of it as a ruse."

"That's what I want to talk to you about." Rita stirred the whipped cream into the coffee. "I mean we've frequently discussed your husband's behavior, his motive, as a game. If we're right and we continue our reasoning, we have to know his goal. Paranoia or real pain."

Karin nodded.

Rita went on. "I've been traveling down this path where the good doctor had murder on his mind."

"Murder?" Karin put down her cup in surprise.

"You thought the fire was a house warming present?"

"No, I . . . You're right." Karin picked up her cappuccino. "So, what do we do now?"

"I'm not sure," Rita said. "I've spent the morning confirming this Oxford gig. I've talked to everybody from the head of the Hopkins Psych department, to Sevier's landlord, to airline security. Bev is doing some research as well, but so far, everything checks out."

"The best of all end games for Doug." Karin gave a small laugh.

"Meaning?"

"He leaves his presence, his threat. Tracking his coming and going will be infinitely harder. Paranoia to be punctuated at some point by pain. It could play forever."

For a moment, Rita and Karin sat without speaking.

"We'll think of a way around it." Rita put her hand on Karin's arm. "I promise you."

Karin sighed, closed her eyes and nodded her head slowly.

With Karin returned to her office, Rita's attention turned to her undone Christmas shopping. From her Jeep, she dialed Mary Margaret's home number on her cell phone as she drove away from the city on I-83.

Clouds thickened across the afternoon sky. The deep slate tint on the horizon promised snow. A few drivers already had headlights on.

"Hey, it's me," Rita said when she got an answer.

"No *comprende Inglés.*"

"Tres droll, Captain Smooth."

"It's my day off, girlie, and I need to relax."

"I haven't finished my shopping," Rita said.

"No, no way, not this again," Mary Margaret responded. "I promised myself last year was the end."

"I need you to help me."

"You need a pair of rollerblades. I'm embarrassed to go anywhere with you. It's like trailing the Tasmanian Devil," Mary Margaret said.

"I don't shop well."

"Now there's an understatement."

"Please, come on, what else do you have to do? I'll pick you up and bring you back."

"The way you drive?" said Mary Margaret. "You think that's inducement?"

"Besides I have to talk to you about my stalking case," said Rita. "I'm almost at your door."

"You are gonna owe me. Big time."

True to form, Rita tore through the mall's first anchor, Macy's. She picked up a Lancôme gift set for Bev, Chanel for her mother, perfume for herself.

Next stop was Record Masters where she snatched up CDs for her sister. Then it was Gymboree for her niece and nephew, Britches for her brother-in-law, and on it went for a whirlwind hour and a half. Mary Margaret was hard at her heels.

"Voila." Rita pivoted to face her friend when she had scribbled her name on the last charge of the afternoon.

Mary Margaret checked her watch. "Ladies and gentlemen, a new world record."

"See, it wasn't so bad." Rita led the way back to the parking garage.

"Uh, I would like to comment that I saw nothing purchased for your best pal of all time and the shining star of Baltimore City's finest," Mary Margaret said.

"I ordered yours from a catalog, smarty." Rita unlocked the Jeep.

"You'd better not send me any more of those hundred-pound boxes of brownies either."

"Hey, they were good." Rita deposited her gifts in the back seat.

"And how would I know? You visited every day after Christmas and I got to eat one."

"What a friend I am. Keeping you from gaining weight by sacrificing myself." Rita started the engine as Mary Margaret snapped her seat belt.

"And you drank all my special blend coffee."

"'Tis the season for sharing. I know what a good Catholic girl you are."

Rita jammed the Jeep into gear and rocked out of the parking lot.

"I see your good doctor is headed across the Atlantic," Mary Margaret said as they were on their way back to her condo.

"Something's not right about that," Rita said.

"You checked it out?"

"To the nth degree. The I's are dotted and the T's are crossed. Bev is tracking down where he's supposed to be living and we are going to call there for the last confirmation."

"He's a weird guy," Mary Margaret said.

"He's more than that," Rita said. "There's an otherworldliness of evil about him."

"After all my years in Catholic school, even I don't believe in the devil."

"Forget Catholic school, what about all your years on the force?"

"I tend to think of the devil as poverty or ignorance. Pretty horrific results from those two, but I can't say that I have ever met anyone who I thought personified Lucifer."

"Then I must introduce you to Douglas Sevier," Rita said. "You'll be able to hear Mick Jagger singing in the background." Rita turned at the exit to Mary Margaret's.

"And speaking of necessary evils . . ." Mary Margaret said.

"What a segue."

"I need to stop at Eddie's for a few things on our way back."

"Not the grocery store. Please lord, not that," Rita groaned.

"Hey, I went Christmas shopping with you," Mary Margaret said.

"My God, I have to be home before I collect social security."

"Oh, stop whining."

"The last time you spent an hour and a half in the cereal section."

"I'm a careful shopper—and you grossly exaggerate."

Rita rounded the corner on to Charles Street. "Ok, maybe a half hour in the cereal, another half hour in the salad dressings. I was dying in there."

Mary Margaret snorted. "The hell you did. You went around the store three times and scarfed up all the free samples they put out. You ate so much you weren't even hungry when we got back to my place."

Rita eased into Eddies' parking lot. The hub of gourmet purveyance, this small market was always busy and every space was occupied. Rita let Mary Margaret out at the door. She made the rounds three times before a woman deposited a holiday party tray in her Volvo and departed.

Rita found her friend in the frozen food section, studying the pizza selections.

"Go for the grease or pick out some kind of organic thing?"

"Smooth, this is a disease. Grab what tastes good for God's sake."

"I have to think about this a minute."

"A minute, yeah. I'm going on patrol," Rita said. "I certainly know where to find you."

"I'll be getting some coffee ground after here."

"In an hour."

"Just go eat something and raise your blood sugar, will you?" Mary Margaret commanded.

Rita made a face and headed for the deli counter. This was the premier territory in Eddie's. As encouragement for patrons to buy, they provided lavish trays of cheese assortments and crackers, chips and dip, tidbits of ham or turkey and an assortment of other delicacies that could be purchased and taken home to enjoy.

She spotted her favorites, the small thick Italian crackers that were a perfect foil to the Boursin and several other high flavor cheeses, which accompanied it on the plate. She helped herself to several of these, each—to be fair—with a different cheese selection.

The crackers had made her thirsty. Rita headed into the produce section where in the winter they handed out samples of fresh squeezed orange juice.

"Perfect," she said after she'd thanked the produce manager for her ration.

Rita checked back at the frozen foods. Mary Margaret was comparing ingredients lists from Mama Celeste and Healthy Choice pizza. She decided caffeine might be a good idea. Eddie's had a coffee bar near the front of the store.

"Hazelnut, please," she said to the smiling young woman behind the counter, "and throw in a dash of chocolate syrup."

"Rita."

The voice was quiet. Still it sent a chill through Rita and she felt her muscles tighten. Diane.

The woman at the deli handed a container to Rita who put three dollars on the counter. Without waiting for change, she turned away from the voice and started walking.

"Rita, don't do this."

Rita could feel the presence following, but she kept on walking. If she looked back now, she would turn into a pillar of salt.

"Please," Diane said.

Rita stopped. "Respect our agreement," she said still facing forward.

"I just want to talk."

Rita could feel the approach and her hands clenched the hot coffee container. She swallowed hard and imagined herself on a beach, alone, far away where she breathed deeply and evenly.

"We've said everything there is to say."

"But you don't understand," Diane pleaded.

"The problem is not that I don't, but that I do understand," she said carefully. "That's why we have an agreement not to see or speak to one another."

Rita started walking away. She knew Diane was not following her.

At the frozen foods, she made a sharp turn. Mary Margaret had put a large pizza in her basket. She'd moved on now to peruse other potential entrees.

"I'm going to the car." Rita shivered as she spoke.

"Come on, I ran that entire mall." Mary Margaret turned to her. "Are you all right?"

"I'm fine. I have to go to the car."

"You look like you've seen a ghost," Mary Margaret said.

"Maybe. The Jeep is parked near the back." Rita started away.

"What the hell is the matter with you?"

"I can't stay in here."

Mary Margaret grabbed her arm. "Diane. You saw her. She's in this store, isn't she?"

Rita nodded and rolled the hot coffee cup between her freezing palms.

"I can do this later." Mary Margaret plucked the pizza package from her basket and walked down the aisle to return it.

"No, don't. I'm fine. I'll wait in the car. Take your time."

Mary Margaret put her arm around Rita and hugged her tight for a long time. Shoppers stared or rolled their carts too quickly past.

"I'm ok. Honest."

"I won't be long," Mary Margaret said.

In the car, Rita sat with her coffee. The hazelnut flavor was weak and the woman hadn't put in much chocolate. It was getting cold. Rita opened the door and poured it under the Jeep. She turned the ignition so that she could have heat. Too dangerous to turn on the radio. Too many chances for memory invoking songs.

Chapter 16

Joggers were everywhere in D.C. Like errant flies at the end of the season, they threaded your field of vision, now and too many times again. Each new runner reminded Rita she had a five-miler ahead of her when she got home. Fat never slept; you had to be on your toes to outrun it.

"Hey, get in your own lane," she yelled out the window at a caroming taxi. God, how she hated driving in this town. Getting behind the wheel with other idiots on the road was bad enough, but inner-city Washington lay on a jigsaw traffic pattern designed in hell. The circles were the worst.

Dupont Circle, where Bobby had lived, was one of the five points of the Great Inverted Pentagram of Washington, DC. To the south-southeast, Connecticut Avenue runs directly into the back corner of Lafayette Park, across the street from the White House. To the north-northwest, Connecticut ran all of the way out into Montgomery County, Maryland, finally dead-ending in the overbuilt residential neighborhood of Aspen Hill. Massachusetts Avenue, better known as Embassy Row, was a long elegant boulevard, which ran from the District Line in far Northwest to slant all of the way down into Southeast Capitol Hill.

P Street between Dupont Circle and Rock Creek Park was prime cruising territory. The P Street Beach, at the southeastern part of the S-curve of Rock Creek, gained notoriety over the years as a hangout for gay body builders. To the west of Rock Creek Park was Georgetown. Walk a few blocks west and there stretched along R Street the Oak Hill Cemetery.

Rita steeled herself for a merry-go-round session on a parking tour. But as she rounded the circle, an aging Mercedes edged away from a curb packed tight with other vehicles.

The old Georgian brick front was painted white with rusted wrought iron railing across the porch and lining the tiny patch of front lawn. Rita fingered the extra keys Edmund Ellis had given her—Bobby's had not turned up in his returned personal items. She unlocked the outer door to the foyer; Ellis' apartment was the first door on the right.

Rita touched the key to the lock, took a deep breath, then plunged. Quickly she was in, the door closed behind her. She was shut in a dead man's house. She looked left and right. What did she think she was going to see?

She had rifled people's garbage, bribed gatekeepers for entrance, lied about invitations and connections, but this was different. She had to overcome her sense of intrusion.

Bus brakes screeched. The outside door opened and emitted a tenant from the floor above.

"Ok, get a grip here." From the door, Rita surveyed the small combined living room, dining room area.

To her right was a big airy space, brightened on the outside wall with a many-paned bay window. The sill was a repository for magazines and books. In front of the window, and arranged so the user could see out while he was working, was a PC on a desk constructed by laying a blank door across two metal file cabinets. Also on the door were a coffee cup full of pencils and pens, a legal pad, and a calendar open across a plastic typing easel.

Bobby apparently did not expect guests. He had no dining table. He had so sofa. He had a television, old and small, sitting on a cheap white five-drawer chest. For viewing, he probably watched from the red canvas director's chair at the PC or pulled that chair toward an old vinyl hassock to prop up his feet in front of the screen.

On the far wall was a fireplace, its mouth blackened with use, but probably never stoked over the last many years. It had no screen and the andirons were sooty and dusty. On the mantel were photographs, all of Bobby with Trisha and his son.

To the left of the door where Rita entered was a minuscule kitchen with barely enough room to turn from the stove to the refrigerator and doorways beyond to a bedroom and bathroom.

"Is there anything wrong with this picture?" Rita said. The file cabinets were closed, nothing sticking out. Still the wastebasket beside the desk had not been emptied. Satisfied that the big picture yielded no clue, Rita moved to the more detailed work.

At the PC desk, she lowered herself into Bobby's chair and flicked on his machine. It booted into a control screen with icons for word processing, communications and a game of solitaire. A smaller icon at the bottom provided only standard PC management programs.

Rita clicked to file information to scan the directories and individual files on Ellis' hard drive. Everything was a directory for a software program, no individual files. She looked in every directory—still no individual files. Either someone had erased all individual files or Bobby used the same system as she did. She maintained programs only on the hard drive and saved her special info on thumb drives for safety.

Rita looked under the makeshift desk. She pulled out the drawers of the file cabinets on either side. She went into the bedroom and methodically—so that she could search again without having disturbed things—went through every drawer and cubbyhole.

She checked the refrigerator, the freezer, the oven, under the sink. She patted the carpet for loose patches, tapped the walls at suspicious seams. Bobby Ellis had nothing in this apartment on which he had saved stories or data. Rita made a note that she would check his machine at the newspaper. She went back to the PC in the apartment.

Rita went through the file cabinets. She found notes and documentation for the first four stories in Bobby's series on government influence buying. They were in separate manila folders in a single hanging folder.

She flipped through everything else—nothing that fit into the series format or subject matter. One drawer was dedicated to personal papers: six months of bank statements and cancelled checks, insurance policies, payroll receipts. Rita picked through all of these, particularly the cancelled checks. She made note of two made to individuals rather than companies.

"My neck." Rita leaned back as best she could for support in the director's chair. "Bobby, how in the hell did you sit at this thing and work?"

Her eyes drifted across the room as she rested. This is what Bobby Ellis saw as he sat as his computer. Through the bay window was a sparse patch of yard hemmed by aging sidewalk and shaded today by the sweet yellow fullness of a silver maple. The walls in his house were bare; faded cream paint with picture holes from previous tenants. He could stare at the blank grey eye of his television.

Rita shivered. She got up and wandered back to the bedroom where she stood in the doorway a moment before entering. She felt like a thief.

This room at least conveyed some sense of the personal. On the dresser mirror, two photos stuck in the frame—Bobby and Trisha when they were first married and Bobby and Trisha just home from the hospital holding a new son. Rita touched the one of Bobby and his wife. It was much creased as if he had taken it from its place many times to hold it.

She had such photographs. She remembered those rare happy moments of childhood through these. Childhood was a faraway place for her, a no-man's land surrounded by a safety wall of forgetfulness. She removed her hand from Bobby's picture.

Rita searched every inch of the bedroom, went through clothes and bed coverings and around and behind every piece of furniture. Finding nothing, she went to the closet and groaned when she saw the packing boxes piled on top of one another.

In the first box were albums of Bobby's press clippings. She went through them all, from his days as a stringer for the *AP* to Gulf War correspondent to the *Washington Star* years. She had her own cache of writing memories in her attic. Who would someday find and open that private treasure and would it mean anything to them?

The next box contained books. On top were some Richard Bach, under that were expensive erotic picture books, a paperback on restoring hair loss with herbal medicines, a manual for picking up women, J.D. Salinger works. Rita felt a lump in her throat.

She sat at the edge of the closet pulling the boxes out into the bedroom for examination. She stopped for a moment and rested her head on this box. She didn't want to know the secrets of vulnerability and desire Bobby Ellis had packed away from prying curiosity.

After an hour Rita reached the last box, tucked far in the back corner of the closet. Though she was short, she had to stoop to retrieve this box. It was heavy and she struggled to get it out into the room.

The National Press Club Award. The Associated Press Award for Distinguished Writing. The nominating letter from the Pulitzer committee. Tarnished brass plaques, oversized crystal paperweights, letters from big names.

Rita slammed the box flaps and lay back on the floor. She bit hard on her lower lip and squeezed her eyes shut tight against a tide of loss.

"Bobby Ellis," she whispered to herself, "why did this happen to you?"

Rita took in a deep calming breath and opened her eyes. The ceiling bore a rippling brown watermark where maybe the tub from upstairs had overflowed. She turned from the ugly stain and lay with her cheek scratchy on the cheap worn carpet.

A dull gleam under the dresser caught her eye. She tilted her head to squint for a better look. Something metal. On hands and knees, she scrambled over.

With a sweep of her hand, she jerked a set of keys from beneath the bureau. Sitting up she inspected the aging leather tab with slots for rings at either end. One ring was missing; from the other dangled a car key, a house key, a deadbolt key, and two lockbox keys.

A quick poke in the deadbolt at the front door confirmed these were Bobby Ellis' keys. Why weren't they on him when he died, and how had they gotten under the dresser? Too late, Rita thought of fingerprints, but she dropped them into her jacket pocket. Maybe some trace could be salvaged.

She took a last look around the room, eyeing every piece of furniture and appliance to make sure she had been thorough. Her eyes fell on the wastebasket beside the homemade desk. Papers peeped just to the top.

Rita dumped the plastic can on the carpet. The contents were mostly paper, though a Coke can did roll out across the room. A form letter from a credit card company, Rita balled that up and threw it into the can. Scribbled grocery list, solicitation for a book club, more credit card offers. Rita jammed these back into the can too.

She picked up an envelope. It was empty and she started to toss it when she noticed it was addressed to a Miriam Blalock, no return address. It was an ordinary business sized white envelope with the name and address typed. Rita noticed two envelopes in the pile before her. Both belonged to this Miriam Blalock.

It could be another tenant. It could have been a girl friend of Bobby's. Maybe he had stolen the mail from somebody else's trash for one of his stories. Rita kept the envelopes.

m

Rita glanced at the Timex on her wrist. She liked expensive handsome watches, always had, but anymore the numbers were too little for her to see without glasses. At forty-six, she wasn't going to wear those damned bifocals yet. She dialed Mary Margaret's office.

"Captain Smooth."

"So, how's your day going?" Rita stood outside a McDonalds's in Laurel. No way could she make it six hours without eating.

"Found Jimmy Hoffa and made a positive ID on Jack the Ripper."

"Well, aren't you special."

"Yes, I am. So, how's 'bout you?" Smooth asked. "Find anything at Bobby's apartment?"

Rita let the straw slip from her lips. The throat lump came back, but she wouldn't let it become tears. Old habits grow to be strong habits.

"He had his whole life packed in boxes, Smooth. He had his whole life in boxes waiting to be taken out and lived again. The apartment was a holding cell, not a thing personal in it, except when I got into his closet and there it was. His family pictures and favorite books, his clippings, his awards. Everything that was him was crammed into those little cardboard holders."

The words spilled out fast and then she halted. Rita turned from the phone to watch cars and eighteen-wheelers flash by on I-95.

"I'm sorry. I didn't hear what you said," she said after a moment.

Smooth repeated. "I said I was sorry, that it must have been very hard to go into that apartment."

"Well, it's my job, you know. I signed on for this."

"Are you all right?"

"Yeah, sure. I'm fine. Anyway, I found some interesting things that need explaining." Rita tested the Coke straw and when nothing came through, shot the empty cup into a nearby trash barrel.

"Like what?"

"I found his keys. I still think it's weird that he didn't have his house keys on him when he died. They were under the dresser in his bedroom. And he didn't have any individual PC files—none. You know, with stories or information, just program files. And I found a bunch of envelopes addressed to some woman."

"There's obviously more to this story," said Mary Margaret.

"I'm going to talk to Edmund to see if he knows the woman and check some other places where Bobby might have stashed disks and the stuff on his PC at work." Rita glanced at the watch again. She needed to run tonight. It settled her head.

"If you need to talk," said Mary Margaret.

"Love you, Smooth."

"Love you, Slick."

Chapter 17

Rita had visions of shuffling bodies in shabby robes and loose scuffs. She knew it wasn't like that, but the term "rehab" flipped that image across her mind's big screen. Once she got to Maplewood Manor, that picture dissolved to an extreme opposite.

Maplewood was a name known in wealthy Baltimore-Washington society circles. In the dark ages before addiction treatment was enlightened and recovery was a celebrity badge of passage, "The Manor" was little more than a plush holding tank for drying out. Today a better-educated staff combined the stuff of psychology and spiritual rejuvenation with an aim toward no recycling of clients.

Rita slid her Jeep into the visitor's parking lot. The big brick colonial reminded her of a country club with its white Georgian columns and railed porch. She half-expected to see a foursome of golfers swing out of the handsome oak and glass paneled front door. Instead she watched a noisy game of volleyball in the side yard.

"Tim Parks?" Rita tapped on the open door to a small office whose window displayed the volleyball game.

"You must be Rita Mars." The man who stood bore the rounded hard physique of someone who worked out regularly with weights. But there was a slight aberration; one side of his mouth was rigid and un-alive. He held out his hand to shake and Rita noticed the serpent and globe of the Marine Corps tattoo. Tim Parks' eyes followed hers.

"Thanks for agreeing to see me," she said.

"I was very upset about Bobby's death. We got to be good friends." Parks gestured to a chair.

"I was a close friend of his and also very upset."

"He was a guy I thought could make it."

Rita frowned. "You sound like you believe the newspaper."

"I don't understand." Parks interlocked his strong fingers and rested them on his desk.

"Suicide," she responded with the frown deepening.

"The paper said he hanged himself."

"The paper says it was going to rain today," Rita said.

Parks glanced out the window at the sunny lawn where the volleyballers were taking a break. "Enlighten me."

"I didn't come here to enlighten you. In fact, I came for just the opposite."

"I take it you oppose the suicide theory?" Parks reached for a pack of Marlboros then dropped it.

"Go ahead," Rita said. "Secondary smoke is the least of my problems today."

"Thanks." Parks poked the cigarette into the working side of his lips and lit it with a battered silver Zippo.

"Vietnam?"

"How nice of you to notice." Parks blew out a long stream of smoke.

Rita blushed. She knew he thought she referred to his facial paralysis. "It was the lighter and tattoo. My father brought home a Zippo. He was infantry in '63 to '64."

"I was armored," he said. "'65 through '67"

"Lots of time there, "Rita said.

"Lots of crazy after that." Parks waved his cigarette hand to indicate the office where they sat. "That's why I'm here now. So, you're here for what—the family—to disprove suicide so they can collect insurance?" he asked.

"No, I'm here to get an honest objective appraisal. You think you can handle that or is the chip on your shoulder going to get in the way?"

They glared at one another.

"I loved Bobby Ellis," Rita said. "I came here for some truth and for that reason, I purposefully didn't tell you my side. I didn't want a nice story or an edited edition of where his head was when he left here."

"Then you came to the right place." Parks squashed the barely smoked Marlboro in a clean ashtray. "Tell me how you want it."

"I want it from the beginning, from the time he came in here until the last time you saw him. I want plain facts and I want your professional assessment." Rita leaned forward to take in the story.

"Bobby Ellis came in here about eighteen months ago. He was a loser."

Rita winced at that word.

"His brother dragged him in here, half dead, hadn't eaten in days, hadn't taken a bath. He looked like a POW. But like all good addicts, he had enough mouth and ego left to act like he was doing us a favor by dropping in. He didn't need us. He was just humoring his brother."

"I thought Bobby put himself in here," Rita said.

"It may well have been his own idea, but at the end, you've still got to keep up that pretense that you're doing just fine. You know what I mean?"

Rita nodded.

"So anyway, Bobby's in bad physical shape. He's lost his family, his job. It's the job going away that actually drives us in. No cash, no stash."

"Then it wasn't the loss of his family that drove him to help?" Rita eyed the photos behind Parks' desk. Buddy shots from the field of war. No wife and kids pictures in the lot.

"It's like this. You lose the job, you lose the wherewithal to medicate yourself. A little clean time makes you realize the really important stuff that cut you."

"You sound like the voice of experience," Rita said.

"Hey, I did those three tours of Nam with an endless supply of cheap heroin. I get back here and act like the possessed until jail time catches my attention with a round of cold turkey. I got lucky and my head found a lucid moment where I recognized I didn't want to be like that anymore."

"I didn't mean to pry," Rita said.

"It's ok, besides you can't con a con and that's what addiction is pretty much about." Parks reached for the Marlboros again.

"So, Bobby's brother dragged him in."

"Yeah. Bobby starts to perk up, put on weight. He's still got to be a smart ass to save face, but I could see we were making progress. The second week he was here, I even caught him in the chapel—down on his knees no less. I backed out of the room real quiet so he wouldn't know I saw him. That first encounter with God is as scary as a blind date for some people. They don't want you to know they need one, but they're desperate enough to try. Bobby was one of those."

Rita thought of her own encounter. At fourteen she'd done her own passionate turn with the church. But her father didn't stop drinking or terrorizing her family. Finally she'd told God to buzz off and not to call again. She'd tempered over time, but theirs was an uneasy relationship.

"He did his twenty-eight days. He got better?" Rita offered.

"He worked his time," Parks corrected. "He participated in group. He and I talked a lot. I liked the man. I saw him as honest and sincere. I thought he would make it."

"You thought he would make it?"

"Yes, I did." Parks blew smoke through his nostrils. Rita noticed the right side flare; the left never moved.

"But when I first came in here you seemed to be saying you agreed with the suicide theory."

"Stuff happens," Parks said.

"Forget that," Rita demanded. "Tell me what you thought about Bobby Ellis when he left here."

"Are you taking back your search for truth and looking to prove some personal equation?"

"No, I want you to tell me if you, first of all, thought Bobby Ellis would keep himself clean, and secondly, would you have picked him as a candidate for suicide?" Rita slapped the arm of the chair.

"Yes, I thought he would stay straight," Parks said. "No, I never saw him as a guy to do himself in." He paused. "You know there's two types who come in here. One's the fighter who's going to fight everything—even the things that work for him. The other kind is a type of fighter too, but there's that will to live, a survival instinct that'll keep him from fighting himself when it's life or death. Bobby was the last kind. He had that instinct."

Rita closed her eyes and sighed. "Thank you."

"But stuff happens," Parks reminded her.

"Yes, sometimes it does—like you know the wrong thing about some very right people." Rita stood. "Mr. Parks. Thanks for your time. You've been a big help."

"We're here if you need us." Parks slipped her a business card.

"I knew somebody who could've used this place," Rita said as he stood beside her at the office door.

"It's not too late," Parks said.

"Maybe for this lifetime it is."

Parks studied her eyes for a moment then nodded silently.

On the way out, Rita passed the double doors to the chapel. She looked up and down the hall then ducked in. It was dim and faintly blue from a stained-glass skylight. In the front pew was a young woman, a teenager with a fresh face and long blonde hair. She looked up as Rita entered and rose to leave as Rita stayed.

Rita looked at the small altar and the votives burning there. For an instant she thought of something to say, but quickly banished it from her mind. With a casual salute at the candles, she turned and left.

"Next time maybe," she whispered.

♏

Rita got the same image every time she walked into a police station. Late at night and the house reeks of beer. At sixteen, she, her mother, and her younger brother clutched one another in fear on the sofa. Their father stood over them unsteady; his eyes glazed. His service revolver wavered toward them. This would be the last moments of their lives.

"I'm gonna' get this over," her father said as he drew back to fix his aim.

The door burst open with a bang. A man as large as her father materialized into the room with a presence that seized her father.

"Put it down." Her father's captain spoke in a low, slow voice. "Put it down, Troy."

Her father stared at the blue metal gun as if he had never seen it before. In a moment, his shooting arm fell so that the revolver swung from his finger and dropped to the carpet.

Her mother wailed and Rita held her tight. Both her mother and her brother cried with shuddering sobs. Rita's eyes were dry and hard.

The police captain guided her father into the kitchen and started to shout. "You stupid son of a bitch. What do you think you were doing?"

Her father's answer was unintelligible.

It was up to Rita to gather her mother and brother into her bedroom. They fell together, weeping on the floor beside her bed. Rita left and went to the kitchen.

"You going to turn him in?" Rita asked.

"No, honey, I'm not." The captain towered over her father who sat bowed in a chair at the kitchen table, head in hands, tears streaming his reddened face. "He didn't mean it. He wouldn't have done it either. He's your father. He loves you a lot. He just gets out of hand from the liquor."

The captain took her father with him that night and kept him for three days. He never spoke to her or her mother, just swept the threat out of their lives for the time being. His words stayed with Rita, but somehow she could never reconcile that night of destruction and terror with her definition of love.

Now, Rita sat in a well-worn interview chair outside the shift commander's office in the Baltimore Street station. She leaned her head back against the smoked stained walls and closed her eyes.

"What is it I have to do to jeopardize my job this time?" Mary Margaret kicked Rita's foot and offered her a coffee as she jumped from the seat.

"You're mean, you know that?" Rita took the coffee container.

"I'm a cop, remember? We're all mean." Smooth pointed her coffee cup in the direction of her office. The two women sat down behind the glass-paneled walls where they could speak in private.

"I am more convinced than ever that Bobby was murdered," Rita said.

"How so?"

Rita explained the Harper's Ferry scenario, complete with Lamar, Eustace McClung, and Young Joe Friendly.

"Sloppy work or deliberately covered up? That's my first question."

"I have no idea." Rita sighed.

"So, what do you have?" Smooth's tone was suddenly official and questioning.

"I've got a mortician who'll swear I lied about his comments on the cause of death. I've got a mystery woman at a post office box, and I've got a drug dealer with a penchant for altruism." Rita frowned as she enumerated her slim list of possible leads.

"Sounds like a 'who-done-it' to me."

"Maybe, but I've got to try. Listen, I found a couple of envelopes addressed to some woman at Bobby Ellis' apartment. All it had was a P.O. box. Can I get you to run her name through some networks and see if anything pops up?"

"Will do."

Rita gave Mary Margaret a 3x5 card with Miriam Blalock's name written on it.

"And one other thing. It seems that Bobby Ellis was repaying a loan to a coke dealer by the name of Skippy Lockerman. Works out of Harper's Ferry. Can you run a rap sheet for me?"

"For you, my dear, anything," said Mary Margaret.

"I'll call back in a couple of days to see what you find." Rita stood up.

"You'll call if you get in a jam?"

"That's me."

"Yeah, right." Mary Margaret walked with her to the office door. She put her hand on the knob before Rita could turn it. "You don't have to be your father, you know."

"He had street smarts. He was a good cop."

"That he was," Smooth admitted.

"I miss him sometimes."

"I know you do." Mary Margaret took her hand away so that Rita could open the door. "In the immortal words of TV— be careful out there."

"Thanks for helping me, kiddo."

As Rita made her way through the squad room, more uninvited thoughts about her father rushed in. Absently her hand went to the battered chrome lighter in her jeans pocked. He had taught her so many things about human nature and observation. With all that knowledge about good and bad, she asked herself for the millionth time: why was he never able to put the equations together about himself?

Chapter 18

Rita's office reeked of garlic. A half-eaten Greek salad wilted in a plastic take out container, a plastic fork plunged into its heart. Weighing down the lid was the one last slice of greasy cold garlic bread. Two empty Coke cans guarded the remains.

Strewn across the desk were the pieces of the Bobby Ellis puzzle Rita worked on identifying. Right now, her attention focused on the Washington telephone number, which Bobby had called the night of his death. There was a woman she knew who worked in Security for the phone company, but she was out for the week on medical leave.

"Great." Rita slammed down the phone. "I'm here trying to solve a murder and she's having her navel rotored."

How to get this phone number. She could phone Smooth and ask for an additional favor. She shook her head and picked up the phone.

"Hi, this is Rita Mars." She gave her cell number. "I have a call on my bill and I don't recall who I made it to."

"I don't see this number on your current call detail. Was this on last month's billing?"

"No, it wasn't. But I gave you the number," Rita said.

"I'm sorry. We cannot provide information without verification that you actually made that call."

"Can't you tell me just the name?"

"I'm sorry we cannot provide that information."

"Now let me get this straight," Rita said. "I can't call and get the name associated with this phone number because it isn't on my bill. However, I could dial this number today, call you back in a month when I get my new bill, and as happy as a clam, you'd tell all."

There was a brief pause on the other end. "I'm sorry. The number must appear on your bill in order for us to provide that information."

"Never mind." Rita hung up. She eyed the greasy garlic bread slice. Frustration made her hungry. Instead she dialed the phone again.

"Hello," she said in a timid voice, then sniffed. "I was wondering if you'd help me with something."

"Yes ma'am. May I have your account number please?"

"Oh," Rita stopped, smiling at her own duplicity, "it isn't my account number."

"I'm sorry, but—" The woman was ending the conversation.

"Please, let me explain."

The woman allowed her the explanation.

"You see," Rita sniffed again, held her breath. "My husband was away a few weeks ago, in West Virginia and—"

"Ma'am, we don't handle West Virginia accounts in this office."

"Oh, I know that," Rita said hurriedly. "But a friend said you might be able to tell me where a call went to. And well, you see, I think my husband is having an affair and I need your help." At this Rita broke into her crying act.

"Mrs.?"

"Mars."

"Mrs. Mars, we're really not supposed to give out that information unless the number appears on your bill."

"Oh, I know that." Rita's voice rose with a sob. "But can't you just at least give me a name. I'm not asking for an address. I—I just need to know." Rita crossed her fingers with this last line of one of her finest performances.

"What's the number?"

Rita spoke clearly and distinctly.

The woman on the other end mumbled something under her breath and put Rita on hold. When she returned, she whispered, "Your husband was calling a Senate conference room."

"My husband was screwing his Congressman?" Rita blurted.

"Mrs. Mars."

"Sorry," Rita said and quickly resumed her act. "You've been so kind to help me."

Rita pulled her worn leather binder across the desk. Bobby Ellis had phoned a Senate conference room the night he died. It was clear to Rita that his investigation series played an integral part in his death.

And who the hell was Miriam Blalock? Was she the woman in Bobby's room that night? Rita picked up the envelope and inspected the address. It was time for legwork.

The post office noted on the envelope was Silver Spring. It was a short straight drive from Rita's downtown Baltimore office down I-95. That's how the original road designers planned anyhow. As usual, traffic generated opportunities for patience and creative driving.

She could see the jackknifed eighteen-wheeler with its sprung back doors. Cars in all three lanes idled with brake lights lit. Undaunted Rita veered onto the right shoulder and plowed toward the next exit. She waved as the politely stalled beeped horns and glared. She passed the crash site where a safe but disheveled driver stood with hands on hips as he explained to police how he came to dump a ton of frozen fish at the Laurel exit ramp.

A few minutes later Rita flipped her ID at the postal worker behind the counter. He was an older man, probably a minute or two from retirement from his acute lack of speed. He wore his half glasses at the end of his nose and peered over them with a squint as Rita spoke.

"Hi, I'm Rita Mars, private investigator."

"Got a warrant?"

"Actually no."

"Can't tell you a thing." The man waved up a woman customer in front of Rita. The woman bought a book of stamps, stared curiously at Rita, then left.

"I'm working on an inheritance case for an attorney." She flicked out the envelope with Miriam Blalock's name and address for the man to view.

He waved the next customer for a first class package. With his deliberate movements, he might have been weighing weapons grade plutonium.

When the customer left, he scrutinized Rita's envelope through his half glasses by peering down as if he were looking into a microscope. "She's not here."

"Well, I know she's not here right now, but—"

"I mean she's not here," the old man insisted. "Private mail place over on Georgia." He pointed to the zip code. "Different number."

Rita drove to the Mail Stop on Georgia Avenue where a pale and chubby young man wearing a tired, clip-on tie and dirty, white running shoes proudly held the title of manager.

"Can you give me any information on this box holder?" Rita asked.

"I'm not supposed to do that." The kid took two steps back.

"I'm not going to hit you." Rita flipped out her ID again. "I'm a private investigator working on a murder case."

"Wow, really?" The young man recovered his two steps. "What do you want to know?"

The "shooting fish in a barrel" light registered in Rita's head. "Do you have the application for this box?"

"Sure, wanna see it?"

The street address was downtown DC and very familiar, but unplaceable. The mailbox rental was paid for an entire year.

"Ever see this person in here?"

"Nope, I'm new."

"Is it possible to look in the box?"

"Only from the user side." The young man's hesitancy returned. He scooped up the application as if he suddenly realized he'd overstepped his authority with his enthusiasm.

"It's ok. I wouldn't ask you to do anything illegal." She marched in the direction the manager pointed as the location of the box. Inside were several envelopes.

She looked back at the young man, but he slunk into his office away from her imploring glance.

Back at the office she revved up her PC and produced a lovely authoritative letterhead on watermarked bond. She hummed as she composed the letter from R.S. Mars, Attorney at Law. It informed Ms. Miriam Blalock that the firm was investigating the possibility of her as an heir to a substantial estate. Inquiries could be made at the Baltimore office.

When that letter was addressed and stamped, she dialed the Senate conference room.

"Committee Room 27."

"Excuse me," Rita said. "Who am I speaking to?"

"We've got a meeting in session. Who the hell is this?" the man roared.

"Hilary Clinton."

The phone on the other end slammed.

♏

Trisha Ellis lived in a townhouse community a few blocks from the Washington beltway exit for White Oak. Officially the name of the neighborhood was Woodmoor, but if anyone were asked, it was Silver Spring. The area was a mix, packed with traffic and checkered by ethnic enclaves within a predominantly white middle class assortment of individual homes and townhouses. It reflected the typical Washington suburban lack of planning.

Rita pulled into the narrow lanes of the Springview community and immediately ducked to begin checking house numbers. Trisha had given directions, a cul-de-sac off the right past the entrance. As she cruised, Rita noticed a commotion at the bare patch of ground graced by a metal swing set and jungle gym.

"Hey." Rita flattened the brake and left her car in park in the middle of the road. She dashed toward the playground. It was slippery running in the soft loafers and she could feel gravel punching in on the soles.

"Get the hell out of here." Rita yanked the arm of one boy, about twelve, who, with two others, were pushing and taunting a little girl.

"You can't touch me," the boy yelled in defiance. Rita's appearance arrested the progress of the bullying while the little girl, an Indian child of around ten, stood shivering and crying in the center.

Now one of the other boys yelled at Rita. "Yeah, I'll tell my mother and she'll call the cops." Although the boys were younger, they had almost as much body weight and they started to gather around Rita as a target.

"I am a cop, you jerk." Rita reached inside her jacket and flipped her private investigator's ID, hoping they were too stupid to pay close attention. "Now beat it."

"Police brutality," shouted one of the boys, but all three took a step back.

"I'll show you police brutality if you don't get out of here," she said in a strong firm voice as she guided the sobbing girl behind her. "I'll pound your mushy little heads so hard you'll have to breathe out of your butts."

This idea must have captured their imaginations. The boys continued to glare, but took a few more retreating steps.

"Outta here," Rita said.

The boys went, though slowly and looking back more than once to mumble threats.

Rita gave the girl a tissue to blow her nose. The child murmured a shy thanks and then ran away to safety.

"Land of the free, home of the brave," Rita said to herself as she slid behind the wheel of her Jeep.

Trisha Ellis was a tired blonde who at one time had probably been the Homecoming Queen. She still had a good figure, but the blonde hair was limp and tied back haphazardly and her blue eyes had the deep crow's feet of too much to do and too much to bear. The old school enthusiasm was the single constant.

"Can I get you something to drink?" Trisha asked. "Coffee, soda?"

"No thanks," Rita said. "And I'll try to be brief. I appreciate your time."

"Please excuse the house, I just got off work and everything's a mess."

With a quick sweep, Rita noticed the entire room was not only color coordinated, but also each item seemed to have its own place and was securely in it. Trisha pointed to the sofa with its loose cushion back. Each pillow dovetailed evenly into the next.

Trisha sat on the edge of a matching casual chair at the end of the sofa. She touched the magazines lined down the cocktail table.

"Please let me get you something." Trisha stood as quickly as she had sat and ran into the kitchen.

Rita sighed. "Coke is fine, thanks." She'd be here all night if she didn't let Trisha Ellis fulfill her mission in life as the perfect hostess.

Trisha came back with two-soda glasses and a cheese board with a small wedge of Brie rimmed by water crackers. She offered some pre-cheesed rounds on the board to Rita.

"Uh, thanks." Rita smiled, ate her cracker and washed it down with the Coke.

"Bobby's brother told me you were looking into the possibility that Bobby was murdered." The tired but pretty face of Trisha Ellis quivered with a promise of tears.

"I think it's a possibility, yes," Rita said softly. She looked away as Trisha pulled herself together.

"You know, I stayed as long as I could," she said. "I loved him. We were so happy in the beginning. I don't know how things got the way they did." She stopped and took a deep breath.

Rita stared at the cocktail table and the copy of House and Garden that lay at the end of Trisha's orderly line of magazines.

"Do you know of anyone who would have had any reason to want to kill him?" she said at last.

"No." Trisha's voice still held a quaver of tears.

"Did he talk to you at all lately?"

"We talked once a week. Mostly he called to talk to Stevie, but we kept on friendly terms."

"Did he mention the series he was working on—anything concrete or specific?" Rita asked.

"Not really. Bobby was really excited about it though. He thought it would get him his old job back with the Star. That's what he talked about most when he mentioned that series." Trisha smoothed the lap of her skirt. "I'm sorry I don't know much."

"You can't think of anybody who might have been angry in the least with Bobby?" Rita said.

"Well, maybe Skippy Lockerman. At the end when Bobby was spending all our money on drugs, I found out he was buying his coke from this guy in West Virginia. Bobby had written a check to him and I discovered it. He lied at first, but then he admitted it." Trisha's eyes filled. "That was the end of it for me."

"I'm sorry to have to bring up these memories," Rita said.

"It's ok. You have to get over them sometime." Trisha excused herself, gathered some tissues from another room and returned.

"So why might this Lockerman be angry now?"

"Bobby told me when he got out of rehab that he still owed him a lot of money."

The front door opened then and a man entered the room. He eyed Rita as he approached Trisha Ellis. He walked with a quick suspicious gait as if he were on the alert for attack. He was a neat and plain man, the kind you would pass over in a group shot or crowd scene, yet there was a furtive energy in him. He was the dog who bit without warning.

"Honey, this is Rita Mars. She's the private investigator working on Bobby's death," Trisha said.

Rita held out her hand. Still maintaining his wariness, the man offered an unresponsive hand. "Ron Steele." He then went to stand guard beside Trisha.

"I was just asking about people who might have had reason to do Bobby Ellis harm," Rita said.

"Anybody who came in contact with him." Steele touched a protective hand to Trisha's shoulder. "The only person he cared about was himself and he left a path of destruction in his wake. Personally, I'm glad he's dead."

Trisha turned to him. "Ron."

"I don't care. The way he treated you, I could have killed him if he'd come into my path."

"And where were you that night he was murdered?" Rita asked.

"Oh, I have a perfect alibi," Steele answered. "I was heading up a system cutover at work. You're welcome to check my story."

"Thanks, I will." Rita added Steele to her list of potential suspects.

Chapter 19

Rita swung her Jeep onto the Rockville Pike exit as she was dialing *The Star*. She barely missed clipping the sharp curb of Beach Drive as she turned the wheel with one hand and held her Smartphone with the other.

"Huntley, this is Rita. Got anything for me?"

"Rita, you've been watching too many tough cop shows. You sound like bad TV dialogue."

"You got anything or not?" Rita glanced at the van beside her where a bag of groceries rested snugly in the child car seat.

"The only thing I've heard is that Bobby's story kicked up a lot of dust for Brett Hillman, the esteemed senator from Pennsylvania. Bobby caught him with his hand in the old PAC till and told all in that fourth part of the series. They mixed it up at a press conference where Hillman appeared to deny the charges."

"Anything else?" It was damned hard trying to shift the car with one hand.

"Nothing. But I'm telling you, a lot of people aren't buying your theory about murder," Huntley said. Rita imagined him primping in the mirror he kept on his desk.

"Yeah, well I'm not in sales." She spotted the entrance to the *Montgomery Monitor* parking lot.

"Rita, you're a lunatic. This is why you had such problems on the paper. You were so far out there with your stories, nobody could believe what you were saying."

"It wasn't a matter of no one believing, Huntley. Sometimes people much prefer being lied to than being overwhelmed by the truth."

"Whatever. Listen, I'm keeping my ears open, ok? Hey, did I tell you I got a book contract."

Rita eased into a freshly vacated parking spot at the door of the *Monitor*. "A book on what—personal promotion?"

"Funny. For the stuff I did on the FBI." Huntley's voice took on righteous indignation.

"Oh, the gratuitous piece on national law enforcement?" Rita said.

"You've got to fight everything, don't you? Everybody's an opponent with you."

"You take me too seriously, Huntley." Rita laughed. "It's only sour grapes. You got the book contract; I've got zip. Ok? Truce."

Huntley sighed. "Sure. Shit, I don't know why I talk to you. And I don't know why I'm going to invite you to the contract signing party."

"Because I'm so cute in pink taffeta," Rita said.

Huntley snorted with laughter. "Yeah, that must be it."

"And thanks for asking around," Rita added in a more serious voice.

♏

The offices of the *Montgomery Monitor* could have fit in the men's room of the *Washington Star*. It was a profitable local weekly, run on a tight budget. The pages were mostly ads and the news mostly congratulatory. Every once in a while, real stories found their way onto the sheets.

Joel Stone was the managing editor. He was a wiry little guy with rimless glasses, which made him look younger than he was. Joel skittered about like a nervous terrier.

"This was Bobby's?" Rita paused with Joel at a paper strewn metal desk. On the right hand side was a small computer whose screen was fuzzy with dust.

"Haven't touched it," Joel said. "Haven't replaced him. Haven't had time."

"Mind if I go through things here?" Rita asked as she watched Joel quick step around in front.

"Sure, sure. Go ahead. You find anything, you'll let me know?" Joel asked. Now he scampered behind Rita, peering over her shoulder as he went.

"Joel, are you all right?"

"Sure, sure. Just checking to see nothing important left on there."

"Before you go," Rita said. "I need to ask you a few things."

"Sure, sure." Joel pranced in front of the desk to face Rita.

"Any ideas on who had grudges against Bobby?"

"Uh, nope, nope. Can't think of anybody." Joel adjusted his glasses to help him concentrate. "Well, now I take that back. That series stirred some people up. Brett Hillman was really pissed. His aide sent a nasty note, then Hillman sent a nastier one—threatened to talk to our advertisers. Hillman and Bobby got into it at the press conference where the senator was denying the PAC money charges." Joel ran his fingers through his hair and gave out a short involuntary laugh.

"Something funny?" Rita scanned the desk.

"Actually, no." Joel frowned. "We make our money on advertising here. We're not after the Pulitzer Prize. We're here to stay in business. I let him talk me into that damned series and the whole time I was on the verge of getting an ulcer. Bobby was the kind of reporter who made me nervous."

Rita smiled. "Yes, he was. I think that's why I liked him so much. He was always making somebody nervous."

"So, is that all? Got lots of stuff to do. Deadline's Thursday, you know." Joel's body was already departing.

"One more thing." Rita said.

"Ok." Joel halted where he was, but did not come back to conversational range, staying poised for quick departure.

"Anything unusual in Bobby's last few weeks?"

Joel's abbreviated laugh emitted again. "Everything about him was unusual. But the most annoying thing—I don't know if it's important—he changed his mind at the last minute on the final piece in the series." Joel paused. "Never said why. Just came in and told me. We had a fight about getting this thing in on time. He said he'd have it after the weekend."

"The weekend he died?" Rita said.

Joel nodded.

"What was the new story?"

"Don't know. Don't know. Never said." Joel inched away.

"Did he say he was meeting somebody in West Virginia?"

"If you knew Bobby Ellis, you'd know he wouldn't tell you shit. Drove me crazy. My theory is he was meeting a source, but then after what happened, I just assumed . . ."

"Yeah, I know." Rita nodded. "But did you tell the police about your theory that he was meeting a source and died in the process?"

"What police? Who's to tell? Look, I've got to get some figures for the publisher's meeting this afternoon. Take your time with the desk, call me if you want to talk some more." The words trailed after as Joel hustled off.

"Sure, sure." Rita imitated Joel's quirky response.

She sat at the desk and went through the papers on top. Then she flicked on the computer and found it organized much as the one at Ellis' apartment—only on this machine individual files were stored at a high capacity serving computer connected to all the other PC's in the office. The latest was the story on Brett Hillman and his PAC money. Nothing came after that.

"So, what the hell was the last story?" Rita said to herself. "And what made it so important he had to switch from his original plan?"

In the hanging file drawer, Rita found folders with information on the four parts of the series. She found nothing on the fifth.

♏

Rita stood at her bedroom window. Morning again. Red splashed across the black horizon as hearty stars held fast and blinked their light-year fires to the sleeping earth. She had been dressed for an hour.

The Great White Hunter took his usual turn around her ankles and she leaned down to scratch his eager head. Then he scampered off and down the stairs as his signal he was ready for breakfast.

"How can you eat that stuff so early in the morning?" she asked as she forked dark tuna into his bowl.

The Great White Hunter buried his head into his meal as his answer.

"To each his own." Rita laughed and slid the covered tuna can into the refrigerator. For herself it was coffee and juice this morning. She really wanted a piece of chocolate cake, but it was better not to keep it in the house. She'd only eat it.

Karin had gone back home. All had been quiet on that front for days; nothing from the maniacal Dr. Demento. The silence was starting to make Rita twitchy.

The phone rang. She glanced at the clock. It was a little after six.

"This is your local police," said Mary Margaret.

"Something wrong?" Rita asked.

"Not a thing. But you know how wannabe nuns keep their habits. I get into the office early to do my paperwork and drink my coffee." She cleared her throat. "I wanted to catch you before you took off for Charlestown."

"Why? You find something?" Rita set down her coffee cup and slid a note pad in front her.

"Found a lot of things."

"You planning to tell me or tease me?" She tapped her pencil on the counter.

"You be careful when you go interview that Skippy Lockerman. Ok? He's got a rap sheet from here to eternity. Nothing light on there either. Everything from statutory rape to assault with a deadly weapon and of course, his main business, drugs."

"He sounds like a busy boy." Rita said.

There was a long pause.

"Rita, if you are going to go—and God knows I know the answer to that—you have to carry a weapon." Mary Margaret's voice was stern.

"I have one."

"You'd use it?"

"If I had to. In the work I've done so far, I've never felt the need to carry it."

"Carry it today."

"Smooth."

"I'm asking you to carry it, Rita." Mary Margaret paused. "I know how you feel about that and I know it has to do with your father—and that night. But I don't want to have to come and get your body. You hear me? I couldn't live with myself."

"I'll think about it," Rita promised.

"Thinking is not what this is about," Mary Margaret said. "Drawing that gun and using it is pure instinct, survival instinct."

"Ok, ok, I'll carry it. You sound like Beverly, you know that?" Rita closed her eyes as she hung up the phone.

The drive to West Virginia would have been easy and peaceful without the harness and weight of the 9mm Glock. It was a reminder of responsibility, a reminder of mortality and split-second decision making.

She remembered her father's holster. When she was little and ran to him when he came home from his shift, she would pat the oily blue-black revolver at this side. He would smack her hand then lift her to comfort the tears.

"No, no," he said then. "This is not for you. This will hurt you." And though he had not used it, the pain it caused remained.

And years later when alcohol had overcome him with unpredictable fits of rage or maudlin philosophizing, he would lecture through his crying jag. "Heavy destiny," he would say as he unstrapped the side holster and laid the revolver on the table for display. "When you draw it, you have to understand that everything changes—forever."

Deep in her memories, Rita almost missed Lockerman's Mobile Homes as she cruised West Virginia's Route 340 through Charlestown. It was a bare dirt lot with a trailer office and tattered red plastic flag bunting. Mobile homes and RV's lined the frontage and packed into an aisle between them and the office.

When Rita pulled in, a man and woman talked to another man in a baby blue Western style jacket with rhinestones on the front. He had on a white cowboy hat, high heeled snakeskin boots and looked like a rat dressed for Halloween.

"Be right with you, Miss," the rat called when Rita got out of the car.

From the office a huge animal slouched out the door. His face was blank as if nothing in the surrounding registered on his brain. He had hands like sledge hammer heads and a thick jaw stubbled with a day or two of beard. He wore a plaid jacket and a pair of baggy, double-knit, grey pants.

"He'll be right with you." This person said to Rita.

She walked over to inspect a used RV to get away from this man, but he shadowed her. There was that scent of cigarette smoke she'd noticed lately. No one here on the lot was smoking.

"Now how can I help you?" The rat had let the couple escape without signing any papers.

Rita explained who she was and why she was there. She held out her hand. The rat, who was Skippy Lockerman, eyed her then glanced and nodded at the behemoth standing behind Rita.

"This here's Big Earl. Shake her hand, Earl."

Earl crushed Rita's slender fingers until she grimaced. "Hey, Earl, I need these for later. Thanks," she said when he released her. She kept a wary eye on him while she addressed Skippy.

"So you think I done in ole Bobby?" Skippy drew out a cigar the size of a horse's leg. Big Earl lit it with a purple Bic.

"I don't know."

Earl's eyes narrowed and Rita took a step back.

"Well, I didn't. You see, me and Bobby was friends and he owed me some money. What's more, he was payin' it back. I weren't about to kill no golden goose, you know." He puffed the cigar and blew smoke at Rita.

"Do you know of anyone who might have wanted to kill him?" Rita asked. Earl edged closer.

"Nope, can't say as I do."

"Did Bobby mention anything or anybody unusual about a story he was working on?"

"Bobby and me, we had a different level of communication, you might say. He didn't talk to me about no stories or writin'."

Rita stared into Skippy Lockerman's glinting black eyes. "And where were you the night Bobby died?"

Earl's belly shoved against her arm, but Rita wasn't moving.

"I was over to the bingo hall. I run the games there of a Saturday night." Lockerman smiled at Earl. "You can ask Deputy Lamar if you want to, he was on duty there."

Rita stared up at Earl then back to Skippy. She took out a card and handed it to Lockerman. "If you think of anything that might help me catch the killer of your friend, give me a call."

"Now I'll surely do that," Lockerman grinned. "Always eager to help out the law." He pointed to Rita's car. "Earl, why don't you help the lady with her door there."

Earl lumbered to the Jeep and ripped the driver's side door open. Rita backed toward it so that she could keep both Skippy and Earl in clear view.

"Thanks," she said to Earl who maintained a death grip on the door handle. He slammed it shut when she was barely inside.

As she drove off the lot, she noticed the dent just at her side window. Earl's thumb had left an impression in the metal.

Chapter 20

"Hello?" Rita sat at her desk at home. For the first time that afternoon she looked up to realize how dark it was. The extension lamp had lulled her into a false sense of daylight. She hadn't noticed how chilly it was either.

"Hello?" Karin VanDreem's footsteps padded on the farmhouse wooden stairs.

"Up here." Rita pulled her wrist in front of her eyes to see her watch. "Damn." She had been going to have dinner ready at seven. It was ten after. She sprang out of the room, the Great White Hunter leaping out of her way.

She nearly collided with Karin at the top of the stairs. Rita grasped her by the shoulders as she tottered backwards.

"I'm sorry," Rita panted. "God, time got away from me. I was going over Bobby's last stories."

"It's ok," Karin laughed.

"I'm sorry." Rita repeated as she lowered her eyes.

"We'll call in Chinese. No big deal."

Later they sat in the kitchen with their Chinese picnic spread before them. Rita had built a fire in the ancient woodstove and the house was warming with the heat and scent of burning oak.

"Any noises from Dr. Demento?" Rita asked.

"Nothing," Karin said. "All quiet."

"It makes you nervous."

"It makes me nervous." Karin confirmed. "But I guess he really did go to England."

Rita swirled her chopsticks in the sesame noodles on her plate

"Can't make me happy, can you?" said Karin. "Afraid when he's up to something. Afraid when he isn't."

"Who says he isn't? Besides, I like having you for a house guest."

Karin tilted the teacup at her lips, her eyes set on Rita. "Let's switch topics. How's the Bobby Ellis case?"

Rita watched her chopsticks twine the noodles into knots. "I'm chasing my tail."

"Can you talk to me about it?" Karin set down the teacup.

"I have squat on this case." Rita stabbed the chopsticks into her pile of noodles.

"You said you spent the afternoon checking his last series of stories."

"I was looking for some hint at who might have been pissed off enough to kill him. Maybe a story where there could have been more than he reported or a reputation that was trashed and burned," Rita could feel that furrow of frustration cleaved into her forehead.

"And?" Karin asked.

"The first story was about the Pentagon's black budget, their secret treasury for covert activities they conveniently neglect to tell the public about. Bobby dredged up some weirdo projects straight out of *X-Files*. I think it went over the head of his readers. Reaction consisted of one form letter from some junior undersecretary at DOD. I wrote this off as a catalyst for nothing but a George Lukas movie."

"The stories were all the same?" Karin rested her chin in her hand in a thoughtful pose.

"The second was a little harder hitting and a little closer to home. That was about selling pollution credits."

"Ok," Karin said. "This one loses me."

"Oh, the Clean Air Act created this monster system that when one air polluting industry reduces its emissions below its designated standard, it can 'sell' those extra reductions to a heavier polluter."

"This doesn't make much sense to me," Karin said.

"Apparently not to anyone else. Another form letter of protest—this time from Potomac Edison. No heavy breathing here either."

"Third story?"

"News control by advertisers and major public radio and television supporters." Rita grasped the chopsticks and twirled the noodles again.

"Number four."

Rita looked up with shiny eyes. "A better possibility for getting under someone's skin. Bobby got some good information on funny money that's going to Brett Hillman. Hillman got pissed." Rita dropped the chopsticks and doubled her fist and feigned a right cross. "At the press conference, Hillman punched Bobby, called him names, threatened him. Not only that but Hillman's chief aide, Peter DeVane started growling at Bobby too. Lots of poison pen stuff on this story."

"That seems a promising start. Have you talked to them yet?" Karin asked.

"No, those two are next on my list." Rita stared past Karin. "But the interesting thing is the fifth story."

"Which was?"

"Don't know. I talked with Joel Stone at the *Monitor* and he said Bobby changed his mind just before deadline. He never told Stone what the story was about though. He said he'd have the story done right after the weekend—of course Bobby didn't make it through that weekend."

"Maybe there was something in that last story," Karin said.

"I'm going to check out Hillman and DeVane first." Rita reached for one of the paper Chinese food containers to snap it closed. "But I'm also going to do my damnedest to find out what that last story was about."

Karin gathered up the plates she and Rita had used. She put the dishes into the sink and started running water.

"I don't have a clue," Rita called from the refrigerator as she stuck the leftovers inside.

"Sure you do. Not the smoking gun, but they're the next ones in this round of questions. That's what it's all about, isn't it—process of elimination?"

Rita stood beside her as steamy clouds drifted up from a soapy pool of dishwater. "You're just so damned clever."

"Capitol Hill tomorrow?" Karin handed Rita a rinsed plate for drying.

"Yes, and more than that." A smug smile wavered on Rita's lips. "I have an idea that I hope will bring the killer to scope me out."

♏

Outside the Capitol, vans with microwave saucers clustered like covered wagons around a campfire. Technicians with headphones trailed serpents of black wire as they adjusted their dishes to the heavens and spun the dials on the interior transmission panels. Television reporters smoothed their hair and jotted script notes. Behind the media troops, roped off by bored policemen, stood herds of gawkers who awaited their opportunity for fleeting fame on the eleven o'clock news.

The national healthcare bill had emerged with a key change in coverage for prescription drugs. The bill's detractors had swarmed to the inception site screaming about Rosemary's baby, while staunch supporters in Congress forged a protective chain of government-speak to stave off the attack. The developing spectacle promised a field day for newsmongers.

Rita snapped her press pass onto her lapel and pulled her collar closer around her neck. When she'd left home, it appeared the November morning would spread into a temperate blue-sky afternoon. Now clouds curled over the sun; the wind kicked scrap paper across the sidewalks and damp cold settled like marsh fog.

"Now what was it you wanted to ask me?" Kate Harrigan asked. Harrigan and Rita had worked together in the past. She was covering today for *CNN*.

"I want to run a trial balloon," Rita answered as she swept her vision across the multitudes where she herself used to wait for battle.

"Don't you miss it?" Kate cupped a Styrofoam coffee container with red and ungloved hands.

Rita jammed her hands in her pockets. "Sometimes."

"Don't give me that. I know you as well as anybody. You're an excitement junkie, pure and simple."

"Ok, I miss it." Rita turned her head to study the television logo on the van behind which she and Kate took shelter from the wind.

"You could come back," Kate said.

"I'm not travelling backward anymore in my life."

"Hey, it was a detour, now you can get back on the straight and narrow."

Rita smiled and swung her arm as best she could around the woman who towered over her by a good eight inches. "Thanks for the vote of confidence. I need that every once in a while."

The news herd shifted to alert as the first entourage emerged from the Capitol to approach the cameras and microphones set up on the marble steps. Activity quickened as techs jumped back into trucks to make sure pictures were clear and cameramen positioned for rolling footage, flicked on their high beams and back pedaled to catch the speakers descending. Like an incoming tide, the media crowd surged forward.

Kate and Rita waited through the posture and appeal process at the news podium. Kate scribbled notes. In less than half an hour, the circus ended, the high wire performers disappeared into limousines, the news crews packed up for a return to home base.

"Now for the real stuff." Kate laughed as she tugged at Rita's sleeve. "Just another thirty minutes and I'll be able to sit down to talk about why you came over."

At least no wind whistled through the halls of the Capitol. Rita rubbed her hands together as she tagged after Kate. They headed down a corridor lined with office doors. Some opened onto to secretaries guarding the inner sanctum; some closed the power cells from prying eyes. Kate halted in front of Senator Charles Strutt's door.

"I'll be ten minutes. No more," she promised. "That's all he'll give me anyway."

Rita nodded as she followed Kate inside.

"Kate, you're right on time." Randy Wyman stood beside the secretary, looking over her shoulder at the PC. "Come in. And you must be Rita Mars." Wyman extended his hand.

Rita studied him. Strutt's chief of staff, when she covered this beat, had been a guy by the name of Donald Grimm of the Maryland banking Grimms. She shook Wyman's hand.

"I've read many of your stories."

Rita noted that he'd read them. He didn't say he liked them or agreed with them.

"Come in, please." Wyman ushered them into a tiny cubicle in an adjacent room where Kate and Rita sat in chairs stolen from another cubicle and had no room between their chair and Wyman's desk to cross their legs.

Kate proceeded with her questions for Wyman. He was the staffer in charge of the controversial bill as it struggled through committee. As such, Wyman was a more important source than any of the Congressmen who claimed sponsorship. They would be mouthpieces; it was the staffers who moved the mountains.

Rita sat back and took in this interview. She found herself instantly categorizing the young man in front of her. Law school definitely—Georgetown or UVA. He had his own political ambitions, looked like money was a driver for him. He was attractive, dark haired and dark eyed, but preoccupation with his role as courtier detracted and gave him a hardness. She smirked while Kate went on with her interview.

"So, do you think conservatives can kill the bill's chances?" Kate asked.

"I believe," Wyman said as he assumed his best earnest expression, "that the American public doesn't truly understand how significantly they will benefit from this agreement. They're driven by some kind of primitive emotional response that prevents objective assessment."

Oh My God, Rita said to herself, mumbo jumbo at its finest. She glanced at Kate who scribbled a note without so much as a sarcastic look, without a question as to what the hell he thought he was saying.

"We want to make it worthwhile for those who join with us in accomplishing this landmark legislation," Wyman said.

Ok, Rita said to herself once more. So now we're giving bribes to the fools who cross party lines.

"And furthermore, we feel that once this agreement is in place, its true worth and benefit will be apparent." Wyman smiled on this note.

Rita gritted her teeth. In other words, you're pushing this thing down the throats of the people and they'll have it whether they like it or not. Great, it's the American way of government.

Kate smiled and thanked Randy Wyman for his interview. They all stood, but before the two women left, Wyman spoke to Rita.

"And what brings you back to The Hill? Is it Bobby Ellis' death as I've heard?" Wyman's eyes held her.

"I am looking into his death as a possible murder." Rita met his probe without blinking.

"Oh really. Any solid leads?"

"Only enough to confirm it as murder," Rita answered.

"But no killer as yet?"

"Not yet."

"Well," Wyman said, "I hope you get to the bottom of it. It was very sad." He came around the desk to escort them to the office door.

"I'm working on one other thing for Bobby too." Rita didn't move.

Wyman halted. "And that is?"

"I'm going to finish the last story in his series." She scanned for response, but saw nothing.

"Which was?" Wyman shuffled his feet and looked off to his left.

"His secret—and now mine—until I go to press," Rita answered.

"Keep me in the loop?" Wyman asked.

"Absolutely," said Rita.

Chapter 21

The beer-bellied man in the VFW garrison cap kept staring at her. Every once in a while, he shifted in his seat and nudged one of the two boy scouts who sat on his left side. The older woman in the pink wool suit with the amazingly abundant bosom coughed frequently and blew her nose; she had a lipstick smudge on her teeth.

Rita felt like she was in the doctor's waiting room. People squeezed next to one another in the meager seating that lined the small stuffy reception area in Senator Hillman's office. A few people stood in the corridor; some had coffee in Styrofoam cups.

The secretary stared obliviously at her PC screen typing furiously. She seemed mindful of the supplicants only as the door to the senator's office opened and it was time to announce the next in line. That door opened at ten-minute intervals to expel an audience and allow a new group inside. During that opening, a young man in a starched shirt with gold adorned French cuffs would snake his way in to the senator and rush out as the next interview began.

The waiting room never emptied but continued to fill and overflow as Rita waited an hour for her exalted ten minutes. Calls chirped in loud and constantly on the secretary's desk. Sometimes she answered and sometimes an unseen force in another room intercepted the signal. People dropped in and left messages and packages. Staffers hustled in and out of their office area.

Rita squirmed in her seat. She hated sitting. She remembered that part of her former life that she'd hated so much. Waiting rooms of the important where she cooled her heels and thought about taking up smoking just to pass the time. She much preferred the clandestine meets in the bars or the back roads where the interaction was quick and intense— and then done with.

"I'm getting my picture taken with the Senator."

Rita turned to the woman who sat beside her. She had on a blue wool suit with an enameled American flag pin on her lapel. Her perm gave her a foreboding grey helmet, but her smile was something you had to return.

"Congratulations," Rita said.

"I was elected to the state central committee two weeks ago and I wrote him a letter and he told me to just come on over." The woman's electric smile beamed on again.

Rita smiled. "That's very special."

"I did a lot of work for him and he said he was very grateful. He signed the letter himself." The woman jostled her with an elbow. "Doesn't do that for everybody, you know."

Rita nodded. She refrained from telling the woman about signature machines and the other paraphernalia that Congressmen employed to offer the illusion of special and caring constituent concern.

"Rita Mars." The secretary didn't look up as she read off her list.

Brett Hillman greeted her with his hearty constituent handshake. "Ms. Mars. I'm so happy to meet you. I understand you wanted to see me about some information on that healthcare bill. Bad piece of legislation, ill thought out and detrimental to American families. I'm always happy to work with the press to explain my viewpoint."

Hillman sat behind his polished walnut desk. Flanking him were the flags of the United States of America and the flag of Pennsylvania. Behind him immediately were photographs of himself with Ronald Reagan and George Bush.

"Actually Senator, I'm here to ask a few questions about Bobby Ellis."

The welcome light shut down in Hillman's face. "You can get out of this office right now."

"I thought you were always happy to work with the press," Rita countered.

"To work with responsible, honest people, not lying panderers to scandal mongering." Hillman rose to a rigid military stance.

Rita continued to sit. "I'm asking for ten minutes, Senator. I'm not here to pry about donations. I'm here in my official capacity as a private investigator working on a murder case."

Hillman wavered. "What do you mean a murder case? And I thought you were with the press."

"I used to work with Bobby Ellis on the *Star*. I'm a private investigator now. There is reason to believe Ellis was murdered and the incident is reopening. If you don't cooperate with me, you will eventually have to speak to the police. If I can get enough information from you now, you may not have to face that."

Rita didn't let his eyes escape hers.

"What do you want to know?" Hillman's voice was weary as he slumped into his chair.

"I want to know about your interaction with Bobby."

Hillman sighed and shook his head. "I took some trips, ok? Everybody does it. But he made it into something unethical and distorted the facts when he wrote that fucking story."

"I don't care what your official line is," Rita said, "and I care even less if you were bought."

Hillman reddened and brought his fists to the desktop. "I did nothing wrong."

"As I said, that's unimportant to me." Rita studied his face as she spoke. "I want to know why you became his target, how he found out about the trips, and what happened between you and him."

"I don't know how I got to be his target." Hillman sat back. "There were a bunch of people who accepted those junkets from the drug lobby; guys who took the speaking engagements. But in that damned article he made it sound like I was the only one."

"He came here and confronted you?"

"Talked to my administrative assistant, Pete DeVane. Pete tried to talk some sense into Ellis, cooperated even until it was apparent this was a lynching. I tried to talk to Ellis myself, but he wasn't going to hear what I said."

"You were pissed," Rita prompted.

"I was pissed. Publish and be damned I said finally."

"Which he did."

"And that's when I held my press conference."

"Where you threatened him and then punched him in front of a roomful of reporters," Rita said.

Hillman reddened again. "Stupid. He knew he had me pinned to the mat, but he came there to gloat. My temper got the best of me. I started screaming at him after I made my statement and he got in my face. I'm not proud of it and I know it doesn't look good. But I didn't kill the guy."

"Why not?"

Hillman stared at her.

"What the hell do you mean?"

"Just what I said. He threw a monkey wrench into your campaign for re-election. I saw your polls just after the story broke. You could have lost your seat."

"I could have, but I didn't," Hillman said. "For one, I made a statement where I acknowledged the questionable nature of my accepting lobby gifts. The stuff about punching Ellis at the press conference never got out of the room, Pete DeVane took care of that. And then Pete launched a massive mail-out and ad blitz just before Election Day. I survived. Ellis didn't. I figured I was out of the woods."

"You didn't see him again after that press conference."

"Not once."

"No more letters?"

"None."

"Where were you on September 20, the Saturday night Bobby was killed?"

Hillman's fist pounded the desk. "I told you I didn't have anything to do with it."

"So, you'll be able to tell me where you were and substantiate it." Rita watched stubbornness grip his body. "You'll want to tell me instead of the police."

Hillman let out the angry breath he had been holding and flipped his desk calendar. "Dinner at Burning Tree Country Club."

"National Pharmaceutical Association?"

"God damn it, it was a fund raiser for the homeless."

"But they were the sponsor."

Hillman said nothing and Rita's interview was over.

♏

Five a.m. The internal alarm sounded and Rita Mars' eyes flipped open. It was always dark at this hour. It was the hour her father rose every morning of his tortured life. He got up at that time because that's when the booze from the night before wore off and he had to stumble to his stash to quell the shakes.

That hour of the morning haunted her even after she had been gone from her parents' home for over twenty years now. It was the reason she hated staying overnight with her mother and sleeping in her old room. It was her motive for jumping out of bed and hiding in the activity of the coming day.

"Hey, you." Rita stroked the silky head of the Great White Hunter who maintained his curled sleeping position without opening an eye.

Coffee was waiting. She had the machine on a timer. Rita gulped down her first cup along with a glass of orange juice. She hated that damned drive to Washington again. For an instant, a chilling thought streaked across her mind: maybe she'd quit the paper because she thought she was getting too old, couldn't keep up with the frenetic pace. No way, she said to herself.

Today was warmer and there were fewer people milling around the Capitol when she arrived. She skipped up the endless flight of marble steps to assure herself of her earlier assessment that she wasn't getting too old. Hell, she'd run five miles this morning.

Rita swung into the Senate cafeteria and chose a table for two near the back in the press section. Within seconds, her appointment appeared. He looked around for a moment until Rita waved.

Peter DeVane carried a leather binder under his arm. He was a clean-shaven blond with very smooth skin and a slight build. He was not handsome, but he would make a statesman like appearance when he grew into his political career. In his youth with his oversized tortoise rimmed glasses, he offered a solid and scholarly presentation.

"I have to be at a committee meeting in fifteen minutes," DeVane said when he sat.

"You'll be there," Rita assured him. "Want some coffee?" The aroma of fresh brew wafted through the room.

"Don't have time."

"Staffers never have time."

"What did you need to see me about?" DeVane asked.

"Ok, I need to ask you about Bobby Ellis. I want to know what kind of contact you had with him while he was working on that story about your boss." Rita's eyes never left DeVane as she looked for tells.

DeVane swallowed before he answered, but his voice was steady. "The usual. He said he had some information about senators accepting trips and favors from some high-powered lobbies. To tell you the truth, I thought he was working on Charles Strutt."

"Strutt?"

"Yeah, he's notorious for funny money. Christ, he has a war chest a third world dictator would envy. Anyway I thought Ellis was on a fishing expedition. He asked me about Hillman's contributions. I said they were a matter of public record."

"But they weren't all public records, were they?"

"No, but then neither is anyone else's"

"That seems the most prevalent rationale these days—everybody else does it."

"Look, do you want information on Ellis or did you come here to give an ethics lecture? Hillman told me to cooperate on the Ellis stuff, but I'm not about to help burn my senator."

Rita pursed her lips. "Is that how you felt? Ellis tricked you into betraying your boss?"

"In a way."

"You were angry with Ellis," Rita said.

"Furious."

"You patched up the initial damage, but Ellis held some additional cards. He could have come back and finished the job."

"No."

"You had to put the real fix in."

"No."

"You told him you had a story for him. You lured him to West Virginia and you killed him."

"I did not." DeVane flew up from his chair so that the table tipped toward Rita.

She jumped up to confront him, but even as she did, she knew that the slim young man in front of her probably didn't have the physical strength to strangle Bobby Ellis who was taller and outweighed him by a good forty pounds. "You hired somebody."

"I'm going to my meeting." DeVane turned.

"I'm not finished," Rita called after him. "And I know your boss doesn't want his name linked to a murder investigation."

DeVane paused, but did not face her.

"I told him I would keep this out of the paper and away from the police, if I got the right answers." Rita waited.

"Quit badgering me. I'll tell you what I know." DeVane turned around.

"Deal."

DeVane came back to the table, but neither of them sat.

"Where were you the night of Ellis' murder?"

"What day was that?"

"Twentieth of September, a Saturday."

"With Hillman at Burning Tree," DeVane answered.

"Witnesses?"

DeVane thought for a moment. "Yes, a couple of other senators and admin assistants."

"Do you know someone by the name of Miriam Blalock?" Rita asked.

"Who?"

"Never mind. Last question—what was the subject of Bobby Ellis' last story?" Rita focused hard.

DeVane licked his lips. "I don't know. I guess I thought it was about Charles Strutt. He seemed to be hanging around his office a lot."

Chapter 22

Rita slid the small UPS box out of her trunk. Bobby's brother had phoned her two days before to say that the West Virginia police finally sent him the package with the rest of Bobby's things. In his distress, Edmund Ellis never asked about any other clothing or effects Bobby had with him; he had simply accepted the plastic evidence bag with the smaller items as all he was due.

Rita had told him to send them immediately. Now she lugged the box into Bobby's apartment, still unrented and furnished with his few belongings. She turned the key and entered the meager rooms Bobby Ellis had arranged as the staging area for his return to former glory.

A chill shivered along her backbone. She was violating that vulnerable and hopeful place again. She could not give in to that emotional response though or she could never do her work. Rita marched past the psychic stop sign into Bobby's bedroom.

Here she placed the box beside Bobby's bed. Carefully across the comforter, so that each item was clearly separated, she laid the following: grey flannel slacks, a pair of Gold Toe socks, an undershirt and briefs, a belt, a shaving kit, two long-sleeved polo shirts, a sweater, a leather bomber jacket, and a pair of scuffed Docksiders.

The leather jacket and sweater Rita placed across the two pillows then descending the bed she placed the slacks and belt with the polo shirts alongside, underwear and socks and shaving kit, Bobby's shoes. She then pulled a manila envelope out of the box. Inside were the things the police had previously given Edmund: the fatal tie, the valet set of car keys, the wallet, and the full set of keys she had found when inspecting Bobby's apartment the first time. She spread these along the bottom of the bed. The death scene photos were still tucked inside the envelope.

"Talk to me, Bobby," Rita said from the end of the bed. She visualized him dressed in the slacks and polo shirt and concentrated on that image of the man.

He stood woodenly before her like a cigar store Indian. His lips were stone, his eyes blank, a bruised ring around his neck. A lump rose in her throat and she closed her mind to the image her mind had so vividly constructed.

"It's not going to work like that," she whispered. She stared at the clothing. The thought arose of a missing article so that she slid the photographs out of the envelope and tried to decipher any missing piece. Bobby Ellis died in a pair of slacks and a T-shirt.

"One undershirt," Rita said. "One pair of slacks, underwear, socks." She checked the corresponding items on the bed. These were unworn. She decided the missing items he was wearing had gone with Bobby's body from Friendly Mortuary to the Maryland undertaker with whom Edmund had arranged Bobby's funeral.

"The keys." Rita picked up the full set and the valet set. "Did you leave home without your apartment keys? No, I've already decided that somebody took these off your body or out of your room. That person had to take them in order to get in here and search."

Rita segregated the two sets of keys to an open space on the bed. "But is there anything else here to know?"

She stared at the bomber jacket. She had already checked the pockets, but she went through again. She caressed every seam, fondled the lining, but found no hiding places or stashed goods. She re-checked the pockets of Bobby's slacks and glanced over the polo shirts to the belt.

"So why didn't you hang yourself with your belt?" Rita picked it up and pulled the smooth leather through her hand as though it were a snake. Again and again she ran it across her palm.

"Guys in jails hang themselves with their belts. It's strong enough to hold you. You would know that." Rita gripped the buckle in one hand, doubling back so that when she snapped the leather, it cracked like a rifle shot. She set the belt beside the car keys.

She passed over the underwear and went to the shaving kit. She drew out a disposable razor, a travel size shaving cream, deodorant, dental floss, toothpaste and a toothbrush with a glob of paste dried in the bristles.

"You were in the middle of brushing your teeth," Rita said. "Somebody snuck up behind you?" Rita shook her head. "No sign of struggle in the bathroom and besides you would have seen them in the mirror."

Rita took the toothbrush into Bobby's bathroom and stood in front of the mirror. She closed her eyes. "It's time for bed and I'm brushing my teeth. Somebody's in the room, but I go ahead anyway. No." Rita paused. "Yes, that's it. Somebody knocks on the door. An urgent knock. I don't take time to rinse, but go to see who's there."

Rita hurried back to the bed. She placed the toothbrush with the keys and the belt.

"Now what?" Rita paced across the room. "The killer confronts me. I laugh and tell him no way. The killer pleads. I say, forget it. The killer gets pissed and grabs my arm to talk sense into me. I fight back. He's too big and I know this, but instead of trying to calm him down, I get more belligerent."

Rita paced faster across the room at the end of the bed. "I make him madder. It's a real fight, but the guy is way too much for me to handle. I'm scared but it's too late now. He has me by the throat and I can't scream and I'm losing consciousness."

Rita halted. "It's over." Her knees wobbled. "Now the killer panics. He has to cover himself. He needs a quick getaway. He thinks of the suicide. Why? Because he knows me, knows I have the drug history, the recent rehab. Yes."

Rita turned to the bed. "The killer picks up the first thing he knows could be a noose." Rita grabbed the belt. "Why wasn't it this?" She reached for the tie with the other hand and glanced from one to the other as if weighing their value. "Where was this tie that it was so handy?"

Rita stood at the end of the bed surveying the clothing she had arranged there. The tie and belt were the only possibilities for a ligature in Bobby Ellis's things. Of course, the killer might also have been able to work one of the cheap thin bath towels into a noose, but the tie and belt were the best bets. But why the tie?

"Bobby, I know you weren't wearing a tie to brush your teeth." She checked the label. It was an expensive silk, an Armani, not one a man would choose to go with Ellis' L.L. Bean casual.

Rita surveyed the bed again. The bomber jacket, grey slacks, two polo shirts.

"Why in the hell were you packing a tie?" Rita asked the scattered items as she stared at the two casual shirts.

She caught her breath. "I'll tell you why you weren't packing a tie. Because you don't wear one with these shirts." She held the ligature high for scrutiny.

"Whose fucking tie is this?"

♏

Charles Strutt emerged from the limo as Rita approached the entrance to the Cock and Bull, a power lunch den already thronged with the hungry and the hunters. Though Rita reached the door first, Strutt cut her off and marched through. She shook her head and followed after.

Strutt stood at the maitre'd station. He was in his early fifties, tall and Kennedy-esque, looking as though he had been coiffed and shaved by some movie make-up artist. As Rita studied him, she considered how remarkably he resembled the publicity photo on the back of his new book *Trade-off: How America Gets Cheated in International Markets*. It had been a great success with Rush Limbaugh fans.

While she thought about how much fun it would be to watch him pose a little longer, she stepped up. "Senator Strutt, I'm Rita Mars."

Strutt looked down at her, his eyes traveling from her face to her shoes and then making a return trip. "I was expecting someone much taller."

"Yes, well, my writing does make me seem larger than life."

"I beg your pardon?"

"Never mind."

The maitre'd seated them in a corner. Upon taking his chair, the senator pulled a sheaf of papers out of his breast pocket and set them on the table. He then slipped on a pair of reading glasses.

"You don't mind, do you? I have a roll call vote at two thirty and I have to go over my notes on the bill." Without waiting for a reply, he gestured for the waiter and ordered two Caesar salads and two Pelerines.

"Do you have my questions answered also?" She folded her arms across her chest.

This stopped Strutt in mid-perusal of his legislation notes. "My God, did Randy forget to give them to me?"

"Senator, I didn't give you any advance copy of my questions. I was hoping to have a few minutes of your time and candor on the Bobby Ellis case."

"Ellis." Strutt teased the name. "One of my constituents?"

"No." Rita sighed. "He was a reporter who was murdered recently and I'm working on the case. It was suggested that he might have been doing an investigative piece on you."

"On me?" Strutt snorted and peered over his glasses. "Nothing to investigate. Nothing to find. Reporters are always swarming around my office, but I don't remember anyone in particular."

The waiter delivered the salads and Strutt dug in. "Would you read that sentence?" He slid a page over her bread plate and poised his index finger at the third of a long list of bullet points. "Are they saying my constituents are split or do they mean Congress is split on that?"

Rita stared at the man who watched her in earnest anticipation of an answer. Finally she glanced down. "Congress."

"Hmm. I didn't realize that was the case." He absently forked a mouthful of romaine.

"Senator, I need to ask you some questions about this murder."

"Go right ahead." Strutt checked his watch. "Just need to be back on the floor by two thirty."

"Do you know who Bobby Ellis is?"

Strutt never lifted his head from his reading. "Heard the name, but I don't think I would know him if I fell over him."

"Did you know of anyone working on any investigative pieces on you?"

Strutt pulled a Mount Blanc from his jacket and scribbled a note on the paper he was reading. "Not directly. As I said reporters are always buzzing around, especially now that this healthcare thing is the hot item. I get calls about television interviews and newspaper articles, radio call-ins. You know how it is."

"No, God damn it, I don't know how it is." Rita pounded the table with her fist so that the flatware jingled and the water slopped in the goblets.

"What is the problem? I came here willingly by your invitation and now that you find I can't help you, you get irate." Strutt peered over the reading glasses at Rita.

"I want your attention for five minutes."

"But you have it. You know I'm a busy man. I'm not here to manufacture material for your newspaper."

"I want to know why there was a rumor that you were the center of an investigative reporting piece," Rita insisted in such a loud voice that people at the next table looked over.

Strutt pursed his lips in anger. "Don't start threatening me. I don't have to put up with this."

"I'm not threatening. I want to know what you know, that's it."

Strutt studied her for a minute. "Would you mind proofing this statement? I'm reading it before the committee meeting today, and I didn't have time to go over it with Randy before I left."

Rita's jaw dropped. She closed her eyes to let her anger dissipate in the darkness. "Give me the goddam statement. But I want an answer." She snatched it out of Strutt's hand.

"If you want to know what reporters, what news organizations, and what stories I've been involved in, all you have to do is contact Randy Wyman, my chief of staff. I don't keep track of those details. I don't have time." Strutt shook his head.

"Give me that pen," Rita said. She lined through a few words and wrote new ones above. "Passive voice sucks." She handed the paper back.

Strutt glanced over the changes, his lips moving as he read. "I think you're right," he smiled. "It is much better this way."

"You're welcome," Rita said.

"Look at the time, I've got to get back. I'm not even going to be able to finish my salad." Strutt stood up. "Call Randy. I'll tell him to expect you. He'll have information."

Rita called after the departing senator. "Wait, do you know a Miriam Blalock?"

Without turning around, Strutt called back. "Ask Randy, he'll know if I do."

Chapter 23

The fog draped an impenetrable billow across the city. The bright lights of Independence Avenue were blurs of sodium orange and the Reflecting Pool was lost. Rita could barely read the street signs before she was on them.

The day had been warm, but the Canadian front, which had steamrolled the landscape, forced walkers off the streets around the Capitol. Cars, headlights suddenly glowing like approaching eyes, floated slowly through the intersections. Only the buses seemed unintimidated as they lumbered along, chuffing huffs of greasy black smoke and screeching their brakes.

"Jesus." Rita's Jeep caught the edge of a curb as she misjudged the distance. She'd been driving for forty-five minutes and still no parking space in sight. At last, she took a chance and nosed the car into a No Parking zone near the Viet Nam Vet's Memorial. Surely no cop would be giving her a ticket tonight.

She pulled the collar of her pea jacket close to her cheeks. The cold stung her eyes to tears as she jabbed the keys into the pocket with her father's lighter. Beyond she recognized the ghostly shrine, which was her destination.

The illuminated Lincoln brooded on his marble dais. He seemed a thoughtful god considering the fate of nations. Rita jogged the tiers of marble steps toward his benevolent presence. At the temple entrance her footsteps echoed through the Doric colonnade.

Tourists were scarce on a night like this, and with the fog choking out all but an illusion of the city beyond, Rita felt alone. For an instant she wished she'd worn the heavy shoulder holster with the 9mm. As quickly, she scoffed at herself. For a moment she thought she smelled cigarette smoke then she jumped when she heard footsteps behind her.

"Evening." It was a park policeman in a brown uniform and oil black slicker.

"Hi," Rita said.

"Can I help you with something?" The ranger paused in his rounds.

"I'm waiting for someone."

"Not a good idea on a night like this."

"I'm fine, but thanks," Rita said.

"I can wait with you for a few minutes."

So chivalry isn't dead, Rita thought. "Thanks, but he'll be along any minute."

The ranger walked off to continue his tour into the night.

Why in the hell did this guy want to meet here, Rita asked herself. She checked her watch. And why the hell was he fifteen minutes late? She eased toward the towering legs of Lincoln and leaned her back against the platform over which he presided. It was easier to deal with somebody who attacked from the front. Rita started whistling "It's Off to Work We Go" from Snow White.

"Nice tune."

The voice made Rita jump again. "Why did you sneak up on me?"

"Sorry." Randy Wyman laughed. "Just wanted to see if I could." He stood with his hands on his hips, his tan cashmere coat a perfect fit, his shoes polished and his pants cuffed.

"Don't do things like that. You scared the hell out of me."

"You aren't carrying a gun?" Wyman asked.

"I never carry and tell," Rita answered.

Wyman walked up close, too close. Rita took a step back.

"How unusual," Wyman said. "I thought all detectives had guns."

"I didn't say I didn't have one."

"I see. And you know how to use it?"

"Yes," Rita answered abruptly. "But it's too cold for idle chatter out here. Why couldn't we meet in your office?"

Wyman inched back into her personal space. She could smell his sweet cologne. "Too much going on there with all the media hype on healthcare. Reporters see you hanging around, they're liable to get the wrong impression."

"And what would that wrong impression be?"

"Oh, you know, some back room stuff. Do you have to take any martial arts to be a detective?"

"Why, are you considering it?"

"Just curious. That's all."

"Your boss said I could ask you a few questions and that you'd give me some straight answers." Rita looked up into his eyes, which were hard and dark like shining black marbles.

"Go ahead," Wyman said. Before she could respond, he asked, "So do you?"

"Do I what?" Rita snapped.

"Know martial arts."

"What is this? Are you interviewing me for *American Gladiators?*"

"The senator uses security types every once in a while for sensitive projects. You never know, you might want a job here sometime."

"I had a job here. I left it for meaningful work," Rita answered.

"Just trying to be helpful." Wyman rocked back onto his heels.

Rita watched her breath curl into smoke as she talked. "Your boss said you could tell me about how many times Bobby Ellis came see you."

"He didn't," Wyman said.

Rita figured that Strutt had already warned his chief aide about what he'd told her earlier that afternoon. "Never saw him?"

"He wasn't a regular, no consistent contact. Would you like to go somewhere for coffee?"

"No thanks. I'd like to ask these questions and move on."
She continued. "So, you had no idea he was writing a story on the senator and his office?"

"None. In fact, I would have been surprised. Ellis was strictly small time. Check out the stories in that series he did. Tired pieces. No ambition. He had had it."

"That's your opinion?" Rita asked.

Wyman shrugged. "Everybody knew it."

Rita could feel the heat in her cheeks. "When did you see him last?"

"Can't remember."

"You're using the Republican defense?"

"Very funny. Look, Ellis hung around the offices and the pressroom, but not around Strutt's office. Don't take my word for it. Check it out with the secretary. Ask LeGrande's people across the hall." Wyman stared pointedly into Rita's face.

"Strutt said you could tell me if he knew a woman named Miriam Blalock." Rita stared back.

Wyman laughed. "Congressmen know only as much as their staffers. It's a good thing for the republic that we're so smart. And no, he doesn't know anyone named Miriam Blalock."

"Do these guys ever do anything for themselves?" Rita asked.

Wyman opened his mouth to respond.

"Never mind I don't want to know what it is." Rita cut him off.

Wyman again marched across Rita's invisible line into very personal space. "I'd like to help," he offered. "Tell you what. Give me your address and telephone number, I'll nose around and get back to you with what I find." He held out his hand.

Without giving ground, Rita handed him a card from her coat pocket.

"Cold hands, warm heart," Wyman said as he attempted to grasp her fingers. Rita pulled away.

Wyman turned the card over. "Business address. This is a very public place—Washington. If I do find something, I'd like to pass it on in private. Strutt doesn't need bad press. How about your cell number?" He handed her a gold pen from the inside pocket of his topcoat.

Rita paused to consider then figured what could it hurt.

"Anything else?" he asked as he tucked the pen and card inside his coat.

"Not for now."

Wyman turned for the marble steps, halted, and turned back to Rita. "By the way, you might want to check out Ellis' last target. Hillman wasn't the only one in that office with something to hide. His assistant, Mr. DeVane carries quite a secret from the past. A leak of that little gem could have killed Hillman—and DeVane."

"How do you know that?" Rita asked.

"I know everything," Wyman answered. "That's my job."

♏

She hated this place. Rita waited at the south entrance to Patuxent Institution. It was a fortress of the damned, like purgatory where you served an indefinite time until you were clean enough for heaven—or in this case, the real world. Karin taught GED classes here once a week.

A guard with a blank face took Rita's name and checked his list. He nodded without a smile or any other betrayal of acknowledgement. Assuming she knew where she was going, he settled back into his guard post and let her ramble down the hall to the next locked passage. The entrance gate clanged shut. Rita never looked behind. The idea of no exit made her want to run.

After three more locked doors and check lists, Rita was on the corridor where offices lined the wall. She peered inside Karin's door, but the small room was empty. Rita made herself at home behind the battered grey metal desk.

It was a small, typically institutional room with cream-colored block walls and nondescript vinyl flooring. The walls were bare except for an empty cork bulletin board and prison safety warnings printed on orange copy paper. Gunmetal grey filing cabinets crowded the open space.

Rita leaned back in the desk chair. It was the one state provided item which offered some semblance of human comfort. It was new and comfortably upholstered and had a high lumbar contoured back. From her assumption of authority, Rita studied the things that changed this room from "an office" to "Karin's office."

On the desk were two cheap black picture frames. One held a photo of Karin's sister, her husband and two nieces. The other was an old photo of Karin and her sister with children playing at the water's edge on the beach.

Rita smiled at this picture.

"Thinking of teaching a class here?" Karin had been standing at the door unnoticed.

Rita jumped out of the chair. "Relaxing."

Karin carried a metal clipboard. She held it tucked to her chest, both arms crossed it, much the way a schoolgirl might carry her books. But it was no incidental action. The metal clipboard was armor against haywire inmates who attacked teachers with cleverly devised weapons.

"Anything new?" Karin went to her chair, dropped the clipboard, and sat.

Rita perched on the edge of the desk. "Not much. A minor run-in with the worst of Washington."

Karin leaned forward.

"I met with Randy Wyman, Charles Strutt's chief of staff, to get some information the good senator promised. He made it some big secret deal where we rendezvoused at the Lincoln Memorial at midnight. I felt like I was in some thirties spy film."

"And?"

"And—those Hill staffers make me want to throw up. Everything's a fucking power play." Rita shivered.

"But did you get anything?"

"Stuffed sinuses, a parking ticket, and an interesting sidelight on Hillman's best boy, DeVane."

Karin put her finger to her lips for an instant. "What was that?"

"Wyman said DeVane had a very ugly skeleton in his closet and that DeVane wouldn't have wanted that secret to see the light of newsprint. I'd have to agree that if I were DeVane, I wouldn't want my failed embezzlement career on page one."

"You checked it out?"

Rita nodded. "I did some electronic file rifling from the newspapers in Hillman's home state of Pennsylvania. Sure enough on the first pass, DeVane's name retrieved two stories from the *Wilkes-Barre Sun*. The young and altruistic director of American Family Relief got caught with his fingers in the till. Over a hundred thousand of well-intentioned donation dollars found themselves transported to DeVane's bank account rather than to the single poor families they were intended for."

"DeVane sure wouldn't want a reporter to splash that information around. It could cost his boss as well as himself. Do you think Hillman knew about it?" Karin said.

"Maybe, maybe not. DeVane did probation rather than time. He made restitution with the help of his family—and admitted he had a gambling habit, which he gave as the reason for his foray into crime. Part of his probation hinged on rehabilitation treatment." Rita answered.

"But even if he had remained a straight arrow, a story like that could destroy his career. I think it would also damage

Hillman so close on the heels of that mystery money article."
Karin glanced at her watch.

"A motive maker if I ever heard one." Rita slid off the desk.
"I'm going to chat again with Mr. DeVane. But for now, I would like to invite you to dinner."

"Sounds like a wonderful thing to me." Karin tossed her clipboard into her desk drawer and slid her briefcase from underneath it.

"And your day? Any strange noises from your charming ex?" Rita led the way to the door.

"Not a peep."

"The silence is making me crazy."

"I've always heard that good things come to those who wait."

They came to the first locked gate. A camera overhead allowed an unseen sentry to magically slide back the bars.

"Not my strong suit," said Rita.

"You're going to make something happen?"

They paused briefly at the second gate and again the barrier fell away.

"That I am." Rita gestured for Karin to go first.

Karin hesitated and then marched ahead. "That makes me nervous, but I wish you good luck."

Rita grasped her hand. "Thanks, that and a rabbit out of my hat should pull me through."

Chapter 24

Bullfeathers Grill was jammed with lunchers on their respective roads to glory. All the tables were filled, mostly with parties of two, men who looked as if they had all dressed from the same closet. Babble level hovered at the high end of the decibel scale as waiters wove through the masses. The maitre'd's eyes glazed with indifference when Rita entered.

"We won't have anything for an hour," he yawned.

"Doesn't matter. I'm meeting somebody who's already here." Rita craned her neck to spot the quarry.

"Feel free." The fact that she was meeting an established honored guest generated a flicker of interest in the maitre'd. He swept his arm toward the diners as a blessing for Rita to proceed.

She saw her target rise from a table near the back and slip around a corner where she knew the rest rooms were.

"Got a piece of tape?" Rita asked quickly.

The request flustered him enough that he did not inquire for reasons, but searched beneath the lectern and pulled out a desk roll to offer.

In the meantime, Rita ripped a piece of notepaper out of her portfolio and scribbled on it.

"Thanks." She stuck half the tape strip onto the paper and wedged her way toward the rear of the restaurant. At the men's room door, she plastered her notepaper—Out of Order—and swung wide the door.

It was a cramped space in beige tile. Two urinals and two black stalls faced the door. The muzzy air smelled of cigar smoke and industrial deodorizer.

"Excuse—hey, wrong room." A grey-haired dignitary tucked himself hurriedly into his high-powered flannels as Rita brushed by him at the urinals.

She peered under the stalls. One pair of Bally's rested side by side.

"I said wrong room." Mr. Grey Hair was making her presence his cause.

"Plumbing inspector." Rita flipped her PI badge. She held the door for Mr. Grey Hair to exit. He glared but left without further comment.

Behind her she heard the shuffle of shoes and the jingle of pocket change.

"You can stay put DeVane." She rapped the stall door with her knuckle.

Pants legs drooped around the Bally loafers as though the wearer was readying to pull up and make a run.

"Who the hell's out there?"

"Somebody who's pissed that you lied to them." Rita answered.

DeVane said nothing.

"No, it's not a constituent," she said, "and I don't have a gun so you can sit back down."

DeVane hesitated then did as she said. "You said you didn't know Bobby Ellis except for the number he did on your boss."

The stall was silent.

"You said you had little dealing with him. You guessed he was doing a story on Strutt. You forgot a story he had on you. You forgot because it was such an old story, right?" Rita rapped the stall door again.

DeVane answered, "I don't know what you're talking about."

"Bullshit. The translation for that doublespeak is 'how much do you know.' Am I right?"

DeVane said nothing.

"I said, am I right?" Rita pounded the door with her fist.

"You're right." DeVane's voice was low.

"So tell me about that fucking story in your own words— and remember I already know how it goes. I'm just looking for more lies."

"Ellis had the story. He came to see with a photocopy from the *Scranton Sun*. I was scared. I saw my whole life flashing in front of me."

"So you hunted him down and killed him."

"No, goddam it. I thought you knew the story, smartass."

"Go on," Rita said.

"I begged him not to print it. Ellis was a decent guy. He knew what it was like to come back from big time addiction.

He heard me out. In fact, he said that the sniffing out he'd done before confronting me confirmed I was square and hadn't taken any wrong turns into relapse. He cut me a break." DeVane said.

"And after that?"

"After that I was grateful. I felt I owed him. A couple of days later I called him about a gut instinct I had on something."

"You sicced him on some other unsuspecting slob," Rita said.

The feet stirred under the stall door and the changed jingled. "It was a good lead."

"Ok."

DeVane paused. "I told him I thought Strutt was taking money to drive the healthcare thing through."

"Charles Strutt is taking money to push healthcare."

"I think so," DeVane sniffed. "You know, Hillman's on that committee too so I'm on top of what goes on. Anyway Hillman's opposed to a lot of stuff in that legislation. Strutt started out in the same place, but all of a sudden within the last three months, he's done a 180. It's like some alien took over his brain—or some deep pockets bought his influence. He's been spinning weird interpretations on all the stuff he formerly disagreed with, making it sound like Mom and apple pie."

"Talking out of every side of his mouth to cover any possible constituent concerns?" Rita asked.

"No. It's different than weasel words. It's a campaign. You know, you say something long and hard enough, you start to believe and then so do the rest of the people you say it to."

"The PR approach to good government."

"Exposure is everything." The shoes pushed their legs to a standing position. A zipper hissed and a belt buckle clanked. Pete DeVane emerged.

"Welcome to the real world," Rita said.

"This was pretty embarrassing," DeVane said. "Why the hell can't you ask for an appointment?" He walked to the sink to wash his hands.

"And you'd just clear your calendar so I could make you uncomfortable?"

"Ok, so you're right. I wouldn't." DeVane tore off a paper towel. "But the men's room?"

"I like a captive audience," Rita laughed. "So Ellis took off after Charles Strutt. He didn't go without proof."

"I didn't have much to go on, just a hunch," DeVane said. "I sent him some contribution lists that had a lot of unusual organizations—things I'd never seen on PAC lists. I sent some memos that Strutt had written to committee members. It wasn't that solid, but it gave him a place to start hunting. Ellis set up a mail drop for me under the name Anne Rice and I was to send him stuff as I got it."

"Anne Rice?"

DeVane laughed. "The vampire author. Ellis had a thing about politicians as vampires."

"Sounds like Bobby." A lump rose in Rita's throat but she choked it down.

"He was a decent guy. I'm sorry about what happened to him." DeVane reached to touch her arm, but she moved away.

"He didn't deserve what he got." Rita swallowed hard one more time. "So where is the mail drop?"

DeVane gave her the Silver Spring address which she'd already visited, the place where the mysterious Miriam Blalock got her mail. He told Rita that he'd never been there and had no idea if it was still in Ellis' name. But he did give her the box number. He also told her he'd stopped gathering information after Ellis' death.

"Start again. Anything," Rita said. "Send it to me. You have my mailing address in Baltimore. I'm going to finish Bobby's story."

"It didn't get him anywhere—and he's dead," DeVane warned.

"Only the good die young."

"I'll nose around some more," DeVane promised. He gestured toward the door and Rita led the way.

"One more thing." She turned to face him. "That story on you is old. It didn't just fall out of the sky. Somebody wanted to slam you—or Hillman—by hurting you. Any ideas as to a perpetrator?"

"This is a tough game," DeVane said. "Opponents will do what they can to neutralize you. Partisan politics is one step above gladiators at the coliseum."

"Then I want you to think who had something to gain by blowing your credibility or your boss's," Rita said. "Get back to me on that."

"Could be a long list."

"Make it a short one—one where the prize is big enough for blood sacrifice."

DeVane nodded.

The men's room door burst open and the maitre'd flung himself inside, his face red and eyes wild. "What the hell is going on in here?"

Rita flipped the PI badge again, so quickly the maitre'd continued to stare at the space where it had been.

"Plumbing inspection. Water pressure's down and there's no hydraulic percolation in your toilets. Get your maintenance people to check it out. I'll let it pass for now, but I'll be back next week for verification."

She held the door as DeVane walked out. She followed, leaving the maitre'd speechless inside.

♏

It was a calm sea and Rita, her parents, and brother floated placidly in a skiff over glassine waters. Suddenly the sky purpled and the boat rocked to ever growing swells until the tiny craft rocketed like a billiard ball on a well-banked shot. Her mother cried. Her father laughed. Her brother hugged the boarding rail while she endured buffeting with distant stare and cold eyes.

"Help!" her mother shouted.

"No one can hear you," said her father.

At last the skiff toppled. She alone could keep her head above water. Her father sank immediately. Her mother and brother flailed with arms stretched toward her. She had to save them, but just as she was about to touch their fingertips, waves crashed between. Over and again Rita pounded the water with frantic strokes but she seemed to be frozen in place.

In a flash she knew her mother and brother were gone.

Rita bolted upright in bed. Her T-shirt clung with sweat to her breasts and her mouth was hot and cottony. The Great White Hunter stopped his paw licking to stare curiously.

"What are you looking at?" she said.

The Great White Hunter resumed his bath and Rita lay down on her wet pillow. She rolled her head to check the clock. It was 3:45 a.m. and she knew that sleep was gone forever. She jumped in the shower, then dressed in jeans, running shoes and layered sweaters against the October chill. The Great White Hunter had already snuggled a nest into her abandoned comforter.

"Clean the house while I'm gone." Rita scratched his head and saw him open a wary eye.

On the way out of the driveway, she braked when she noticed the shiny reflecting eye of a deer just inside the pasture. Rita tapped her horn and the animal cleared the fence.

At the 7-Eleven, she stopped for coffee and a package of cupcakes. Two bleary-eyed teens stared into the soda cooler while a scruffy bearded clerk, hardly older, kept watch. A truck driver came in for cigarettes followed by an off-duty nurse looking for the same.

"It is always this busy this time of night?" Rita asked.

The clerk shrugged and said nothing, not even the amount she owed. Rita had to check the register screen to find out.

"Too much MTV," Rita said as she opened the cupcakes.

She cruised the Jones Falls Expressway, a traffic horror story at rush hour, but quiet and toured only by police and drug dealers at this time of day. The city was a silent light show downtown where office towers glowed in other worldly orange and blue fluorescence.

On one corner across from her office were two men in sweatshirts, hoods up, who exchanged cash and plastic baggies. On the other corner, nestled on a cozy grate was a figure in a filthy overcoat, Chuck Taylors and a knit watch cap.

Rita slid the Jeep into a space directly in front of her building. Out of nowhere staggered a drunk reeking of dirt and Mad Dog 50-50.

"Gotta dollar to spare?" The drunk pitched forward and clutched at her arm.

In reflex, Rita shoved him. The drunk flew helplessly backward onto the brick facade behind, his head butting and ricocheting off the wall. For an instant, Rita and the drunk eyed one another. Then the drunk bent his head and slunk away.

"Hey, I'm sorry." Rita thrust her hand into her pocket. "You scared me. I didn't mean to push you."

The drunk scampered around the corner like the Norwegian rats who ran the alleys at night.

Rita walked to the alleyway, but did not enter. "I said I'm sorry. Here's a dollar. Come on back."

A trash can lid dropped to the street and rolled to a clattering fall. Rita could see nothing in the darkness. She turned around and went to her building.

"I didn't mean it," she mumbled to herself. "He scared me."

♏

Something was wrong. Rita knew it before she hit the lights. It was a disturbance in the air, a strange scent, a feeling.

Once the light went on, she saw it all. The waiting room furniture was tossed and every drawer in Bev's desk was pulled out. Rita rushed into her office where the case files were housed in a credenza. These drawers as well as all her desk drawers were fully extended.

The TV was still in the corner. Her PC still sat on her desk. The petty cash box still had over a hundred dollars and the business checkbook rested in plain sight in her middle desk drawer. Not a robbery.

Cautiously Rita riffed through the case files, but none appeared missing. She realized the only real disturbance was in the case files. The other desk drawers were open to cover the target of the intrusion, but which files were they after? Impossible to tell.

Rita plopped herself into her chair and swiveled into deep thought. This was certainly not about the side case she'd just taken on, a woman searching for her birth mother. Bobby Ellis? The files on that case were at her house. Rita got up and flipped the manila sheaves in the E section. Nothing else seemed controversial enough to inspire mayhem.

She went to her chair. Round and round she swiveled. It could be that she'd scared the thieves off when she'd come up the steps. Maybe.

Two patrolmen showed up. One was a rookie, the other a couch potato old timer who yawned when she met him at the door. The young guy was thin and Italian looking. He kept a tight-lipped professional face while the chubby cop just seemed bored.

"What was taken?" The fat guy asked and nodded toward the rookie who was flipping over a notebook.

"Nothing I can see," Rita said.

The young guy scribbled. The old guy sauntered around Rita's desk.

"Damage?" he asked.

"None," Rita answered.

The older policeman picked up the silver frame on Rita's desk. Enclosed was an old photo of Rita and Diane on a Cayman beach. The old cop's eyebrows danced a curious step.

"So you're filing a report on house wrecking?"

"This isn't a house and last I checked, this office fits a B and E description."

The young cop looked up from squinting at his notebook.

"Lover's quarrel?" The old cop asked.

Rita glared. "What the hell are you trying to say?"

"Just a thought." The old cop stole a glance at the beach picture again.

"Look, I'd like to enter a report on this breaking and entering." Rita walked to the young policeman and tapped an angry finger on his notebook. The officer said nothing, but did watch the finger poke his page.

"So what story you want in this little fairy tale?" The old cop went to the door. "No sign of forced entry."

"Are you going to write this report or not?" Rita jammed her hands on her hips.

Chapter 25

Rita careened off the exit ramp onto the Jones Falls Expressway. It was a little after six and a hard bar of red streaked the black horizon as a promise of the approaching sun. A few more headlights bobbed on the other side of the highway where early commuters began their lemming-like trek into the city.

"Get the hell out of the way," Rita screamed at a lumbering newspaper delivery truck. She veered to the left and zoomed past.

On her flight Rita kept a sharp lookout for police as she alternated irritating glances at her car clock. "Jesus." Rita swerved for a motorist who idled along.

The Jeep nosed into the dip at the end of her driveway and bounced, gravel spitting backward, as Rita raced toward her house. She flung open the car door and without bothering to close it, dashed into her house.

Panting, she halted just inside. She closed the outside door, which opened onto her sunroom, leaned her back against the jamb, and held her breath to listen. The baseboard heat gurgled, but nothing else made a sound.

The wooden steps in the living room creaked. Every muscle tensed as Rita floated across the floor to the French doors, which opened onto the living room. The whoosh of brushed carpet. Rita flattened herself to the wall in case someone should come through those French doors. The Great White Hunter sauntered across the threshold. He stopped to stare at this unexpected visit from his owner.

"Why the hell aren't you a big ole mean dog?" Rita hissed. He yawned, stretched and padded over to the food bowl.

Rita took in a deep breath and crept through her living room, staying close to the wall. The dim light of morning gave her some cover, but a sense of otherworldliness as well. The steps in this old farmhouse were over a hundred years old. No way could she sneak up to her study without sending a signal.

She held the railing and ascended as softly as she could close to the wall. At the top step, she halted to listen again, but she heard nothing except her own shallow breathing.

A quick glance confirmed that her home office and files were intact. She checked the bedroom, behind the shower curtain in the bath, the closets and under the bed in the guest rooms. The house was empty.

Rita walked into her bedroom and sat on the edge of her bed. Her body trembled with the aftermath of rage. She swallowed hard and took a deep breath.

"Son of a bitch." She picked up the phone on her night table and dialed Mary Margaret.

"Did you get anything on Miriam Blalock yet?"

"Rita?"

"Yes. Did you?"

"You sound funny, like you've been running or something," Mary Margaret said.

Rita related the story about her office and her recent interviews on the Bobby Ellis case.

"You're getting warm," Mary Margaret said.

"I know. I've made somebody real nervous." Rita watched the Great White Hunter jump on her bed and land like a feather.

"You gotta be careful."

"I'm always careful." She stroked the luxurious fur of the cat who nudged her hand.

"I didn't find anything on that Blalock woman. Maybe it's an alias."

"Maybe."

"I have friends in the State Police. I want to give you a name in case you need it."

Rita took the name and thanked Mary Margaret. "Well, I'm going back to clean up my office."

"Keep in touch, Slick."

"Always." Rita hung up the phone.

♏

The office was locked and still a mess as Rita tooled along I-95 toward Silver Spring. Rush hour traffic on this route was like a bumper car ride with drivers jockeying for position and thrusting within inches of major collisions.

The manager who had been on duty last time was gone. The new guy was older, a retiree who glared out at the world with suspicious darting eyes. He wore suede brogues and red suspenders over a wrinkled white shirt. He didn't know who Miriam Blalock was either.

Rita fished Bobby Ellis' keys out of her slacks pocket and went to the box Pete DeVane said he used to send information. She inserted a small key but the tumblers didn't turn. She checked the box number and then tried a different but similar key.

Inside the mailbox were a number of papers that Rita pulled out. She went to her car to examine them. She had five committee meeting transcripts with highlighted sections. She had newspaper articles and a copy of a visitor's log page from Senator Strutt's office. She also had the Federal disclosure notice from Washington's powerful public relations firm, Titleton Associates, which listed a major European pharmaceutical industry association and several foreign drug manufacturers as clients. Finally she had an extensive list of contributors to Charles Strutt's political treasure chest.

She drove back to her disheveled office where she spent the next two hours putting things into order. With files and desks back to normal, Rita got on the phone.

"Pete DeVane," she said. In the background she could hear Brett Hillman shouting.

"Uh, he's tied up right now. Can I have him call you back?" The secretary asked.

"You idiot, are you trying to sabotage my career?" Hillman screamed.

Rita did not hear the reply. "I'll hold."

"It could be a while," the secretary warned.

"You have to find out everybody's position on that bill. You can't guess. You can't assume. Do you hear me?" Hillman yelled.

Again the reply was too low.

"I'll hold," Rita assured her.

"Now get out of here and get to each one of those committee members and ask how the hell they're going to vote. Do you hear me?" Hillman was still yelling.

There was a pause and then someone picked up her line.

"Peter DeVane." he announced.

"A staffer's life must be an interesting one," Rita said.

DeVane paused. "Yeah, a cross between that of God and a galley slave."

"Well, I want you to feel as comfortable with me. Where were you last night and early this morning?" Rita asked.

"What do you mean?"

"I mean what I said."

"I was here in this office until after one a.m.," DeVane said. "I was working on the voting profile for the healthcare bill. You've already heard what a resounding success my analysis was."

"I did indeed. But what I really want is proof you were where you said you were."

"I've got the building log that the guard keeps."

"Good, then I want to see it. And I appreciate the help." Rita hung up.

♏

The meal in Rita's kitchen that night was strangely silent except for the scrape of silverware on plates. Rita told a joke about a vacuum cleaner salesman. She had to explain it to Karin. Then she asked Karin if she'd heard anything from her husband.

"Nothing," she said. "I think he's moved on."

Rita stopped eating and looked up.

Karin cupped her chin in hand as she spoke. "I was thinking that work on my house should be done within the next week. I'm going to move back in there as soon as I can."

"You don't like my housekeeping?"

"Don't be absurd." Karin said. "I feel as though I'm in your way here."

"Ah, yes, the line of women I haven't been able to bring home and seduce." Rita pushed a ravioli with her fork.

"That's not what I meant and you know it."

"You're not a bother. You're not in my way," Rita said.

"I know and you are very kind for saying that. But I really think Douglas is over it all. He's not easily scared off, so if he were still interested in coming after me, I think we would have seen something."

"He's still Dr. Demento in my book," Rita said.

"And he is in mine," Karin responded, "so my theory is that he's found some new potential victim he is in the process of wooing and wowing. He doesn't have the time or inclination to punish me anymore."

Rita put down her fork and leaned across Karin's table. "You really believe that?"

Karin looked into Rita's eyes. "I think that you can only obsess on one thing at a time. It is the nature of the condition."

"That's a profound but evasive response." Rita said.

Karin picked up her plate and turned from Rita to take it to the sink. "Yes, I really do think he's found someone else who has his full attention and focus. And speaking of evasive, I'd like to know what you're not telling me about the Bobby Ellis case."

Rita jerked her head up. "What do you mean?" She grabbed her own plate and followed Karin.

"I mean you've walked and talked like a robot since you came in. You've hardly said a word and those you did speak were not funny and easy like your normal self." Karin turned to face Rita. "You're all tucked in so as not to give something away."

Rita's eyes scanned Karin's face.

Karin resumed dirty dish duty at the sink. "Your choice."

"Somebody broke into my office."

Karin spun around. "Why didn't you tell me?"

"You'd be afraid for me." Rita handed her the glasses from the table and the empty salad plates.

"I would like to know what's going on," Karin answered. "Especially since you're wearing a gun all of a sudden."

"You could tell that?" Rita patted the holster snugged under her left arm.

"I'm not blind and you were stiff as a board when I hugged you hello. Why should you be afraid and I'm not allowed?"

"I'm not afraid." Rita picked up the bread plate from the table and emptied the crumbs into the garbage can.

"You always carry a gun for trust?"

Rita laughed. "Sure. It inspires me to trust people won't do me in."

"Well, you must not trust me very much." Karin took Rita's arm and made her look into her face.

"It's not that." Rita sighed. "I didn't want you to worry. And, yes, I'm a little edgy that whoever broke into my office is the person who killed Bobby."

She lowered her eyes from Karin's. Then she revealed that the police had been more combative than helpful, that she had rushed home to make sure no one had struck there after she'd left, and that she was certain this was the first of succeeding incidents in an effort to destroy her case.

Karin made Rita sit down while she made coffee. "How are you going to protect yourself?"

Rita explained about the call to Mary Margaret and the offer of assistance from the local State Trooper. She also told her that increased vigilance was her only hope. "Even if I declared I was off the case tomorrow," Rita said, "whoever is on my trail, feels I know too much. That's why this thing's gotten physical. There is no turning back."

Karin nodded in agreement. "Do you think you'll need a body guard?"

"Can't do my work that way." The gun felt heavier on Rita's shoulder as she adjusted the leather strap.

"What about when it's just you in the house?" Karin asked.

"I'll be all right. Believe me."

The two women stared at one another.

"I refuse to run or hide," Rita said.

For a long time, Karin sat without speaking. At last she said, "So where are you on this thing now anyway?"

Rita told her about visiting the mail drop and retrieving the items DeVane had sent Bobby. She went into the living room and returned with those papers from her briefcase.

"Everything is about that damned healthcare bill." Rita waved the papers at Karin when she sat down at the table again.

"Any specifics yet?"

"DeVane thinks Charlie Strutt's mixed up in some kind of scheme to bulldoze this bill through. These transcripts he gave me show how he did a complete about face within one month of total denouncement."

"Do you think he's alone in this?" Karin asked.

"I don't know. But I know the most powerful lobby firm in D.C. represents some major foreign players on this, and I have a list of contributors to Strutt's political machine. I'm going to have to go through each one of them for financials to find out." Rita shoved the two-page contributions list toward Karin.

"Looks like a day's work."

"I'll be a bleary-eyed accountant when I'm done."

"Just make sure you're alive when you're done." Karin looked at Rita.

"I'm going to do my best," Rita replied.

Chapter 26

There must be a reason it's always grey when I come to D.C. Rita thought to herself. She swung off DuPont Circle onto Massachusetts Avenue, the city's Embassy Row. Flags, like jousting tournament banners, furled rippling color into the drab streets. Swarms of black Mercedes crouched along the curb and an occasional security guard in pressed suit and dark glasses stood on watch at a doorway.

She checked the address she'd scribbled on the back of her business card. The twin elephants at the Indian Embassy kept their stone heads down as she passed. The Iranian grandeur of a more flamboyant era had all been auctioned, replaced now by the stark facade of zealotry. It was such a contrast to the brilliant glass of the architecture across the street in the fortress of the wild Brazilians.

Rita glanced again at her street number and nosed her Jeep along the curb where the red, white, and green flag lay still in the November cold. The marble steps to the Mexican embassy were empty, but even before she was out the door, a cadre of dark suited men were beside the car.

"Senora," the leader said in an official and heavily accented voice, "you cannot park here. This is reserved for the ambassador's car." The man's face was square and flat, his frame small, but muscled. The two men backing him up apparently went to the same body building classes.

Rita got out anyway. She looked up and down the street. "He's on his way?"

"Senora, the ambassador is on delegation in Canada."

"Then he won't be needing his parking space." Rita turned away and locked the door.

"I must ask you to move your car." The two men behind the leader closed ranks.

"I have an appointment." Rita decided she'd played enough; maybe one she could have handled, but these three were likely to give her serious bruises.

The spokesman stiffened as if this were a possibility, he was unequipped to deal with. He looked at his backups.

"Who are you to see, Senora?" The man's tone was only slightly less thawed.

"Senor Gutierrez, head of your trade mission here." Rita stared into the brown eyes of the security man. They remained unmoved, like a chunk of dark quartz.

The man nodded to one of the men behind who scurried up the steps and inside.

"Nice day, don't you think?" Rita said.

The two guards stood in a robot pose as if their function had been turned off until the next circuit was set up.

"How about those Redskins?" Rita folded her arms across her chest. "Some game Sunday, wasn't it?"

No response.

"Think they'll take the World Cup? How about the American Cup? "

The door of the embassy swung open then and the messenger returned with only a nod of his head as communication.

"Please follow me." The lead security guard turned. His backup disappeared quickly inside as he led Rita along a red carpeted hallway, past pre-Columbian art works and intricate woven wall hangings.

They came to an office where a secretary sat at a huge mahogany desk. She was an American, blonde and tall. When she stood to talk in whispers to the guard, she towered above him by a good three inches. When the security man finished and left, she eyed Rita.

"Senor Gutierrez will be with you shortly." The blonde resumed her seat and stared into her PC monitor.

"Thanks." Rita looked around the office.

More Mexican wall hangings, Conquistadoran breast plates and helmets tastefully displayed on dark wood paneling. Behind and to the left of the secretary's desk were double oak doors, richly carved and polished, brass handles gleaming. The thickly carpeted room was silent except for the padding of the secretary's fingers on her keyboard.

A young man entered the room, another American. He reminded Rita of the Hill staffers, same starched shirt and braces, same expensive shoes and cuffed suit trousers. The man handed a sheaf of papers to the secretary, smiled at Rita and left.

"You know," Rita said in her best let's get friendly voice, "I always think of embassies as hiring only people from the country they represent."

The woman looked up warily as if she were considering this as some subterfuge. She apparently decided Rita was harmless and answered. "Oh, no, there are a lot of Americans who work here."

"It must be really interesting for students to have a chance to work in this environment."

"They're really not students. We hire a lot of ex-government people, you know, who have experience with how things work."

Rita nodded. "The fellow who was just in here reminded me a lot of the young guys you see on the hill."

The secretary smiled. "He used to be a staffer on the Senate Foreign Relations Committee, but we offered him a better salary. They don't pay that well over there."

"Well, then you can get some pretty knowledgeable people," Rita said.

"We do," the secretary said.

"And some pretty influential people," Rita added.

Something about that sentence made the secretary halt. "Um," she said and bent her head toward her PC to resume working and to signal the end of her chat.

The double doors opened and two men emerged. Both were Americans, both carried briefcases. They walked in lock step and exited without saying anything to the secretary.

Rita looked up expectantly, but the secretary kept on typing.

"My appointment was at eleven," Rita said.

The secretary continued to face her PC screen. "Senor Gutierrez still has someone with him."

Rita sighed and checked her watch. She got up to saunter around the room. Having inspected quickly all immediate surroundings, she started into the hall. As soon as she cleared the doorway, the two silent, but well-dressed thugs who had assisted the official greeter stepped out to bar her way.

"We don't allow guests to wander around by themselves," the secretary said.

"How about a guided tour?" Rita grinned at the two guards who said nothing, but held their ground.

"You'll need to wait here for Senor Gutierrez." The secretary kept on working.

Rita turned and went back inside. The pop-up goons disappeared on either side of the doorway.

"You'll need to wait here for Senor Gutierrez." Rita mimicked the secretary under her breath. "I could see the Pope with less intrigue. I could see the President."

She addressed the oblivious secretary. "I can see God with less bullshit than this."

The woman looked up, eyed Rita, then went back to her PC.

It was quarter to twelve when the double doors opened and a tall man, aristocratically thin in a grey suit that perfectly complemented his silvering hair, entered the room. Rita had a straight shot inside that inner office. This was Gutierrez and there had been no one else in that room with him.

"Senora Mars." Gutierrez made straight for her and offered a polished hand. Gold cuff links pinned tight starched cuffs at the end of his jacket sleeve. Rita thought she saw light sparkle from his gleaming white teeth.

"Senor Gutierrez." She shook his hand and marveled at the softness. In cold weather, her own hands roughened and chapped with even the most diligent care.

"I must apologize for the delay." Gutierrez's accent was more subtle than the goons who guarded the castle. "And now I find myself pressed for time. Perhaps we could reschedule so that I may give my full attention. I'm afraid I am on my way now to a luncheon meeting at your White House."

This guy was as smooth as Bela Lugosi sucking up to his next victim. "But I have only a few questions."

Gutierrez's arm floated around but did not touch her back. With his other arm, he indicated they should walk. As they exited, the two pop-up protectors fell in behind. Rita gave them a quick glance, but they stared ahead as if they were alone and unaware of the couple in front of them.

"I would gladly answer them on my way," Gutierrez said, "but my car will not be able to return you."

"I'll take you up on your offer."

Suddenly one of the silent menaces behind, shot around to open the front door of the embassy. Again Rita gave him a stare, but he ignored her. A pearl grey stretch Mercedes idled discreet exhaust behind her Jeep. The other guard was already at the back passenger door.

The interior of the limousine smelled of expensive leather, cologne and cigar smoke. Between the passenger accommodations and the driver was a tinted glass partition controlled by buttons on either door of the back seat. A wet bar, a television, a fax machine, and two phones made up the accessories for any and all anticipated diplomatic needs. Rita wondered if there was a button back here that raised machine guns on the front and rear in James Bond style.

Gutierrez spoke in rapid Spanish to the guard holding the door. The guard closed the door and went to the driver's window. Rita could make this out barely through the darkened glass that separated the front from the back. All the other windows were deeply tinted as well, though seeing out was far easier than seeing inside.

"Relax, Senora Mars. Please." Gutierrez reached for the wet bar.

"No thanks."

Gutierrez shrugged and leaned back into his seat.

"Senor Gutierrez, have you ever heard of a reporter by the name of Robert Ellis?" Rita asked.

Gutierrez pursed his lips, then shrugged. "I do not know the names of each individual reporter in this city. Should I know him?"

"He was, I believe, working on a story about the new healthcare bill."

"But then so is every reporter in your country." Gutierrez smiled. "I see so many."

"He was working on it from a different angle, not so much was it right or wrong for this country to enter into this agreement, as it was a story about how influence is brought to bear without regard to that right or wrong." Rita watched the man's eyes.

Gutierrez blinked and seemed to study something at the street corner where the limousine had stopped for a red light. "Like your Woodward and Bernstein, this reporter?"

Rita continued to watch. "Yes, he was like those men."

"And where are they now—Woodward and Bernstein?" Gutierrez asked.

"They're retired from the newspaper"

Gutierrez smiled. "That is not exactly how I meant that. I meant did they achieve some celebrity? Did they not write books and gain place? Do they not today have what you call clout?"

"So?"

"We are passing your Supreme Court." Gutierrez pointed at the massive facade through his tinted window.

Rita ducked her head to catch a glimpse.

"It is a beautiful neoclassic building honoring the law of your land. Above you see the robed figures who represent the purveyors of justice." Gutierrez tapped on the window. "Do you know that the architect sculpted in figures of himself and his friends among that lofty company?"

"Senor, we're getting off the subject." Rita's eyes narrowed.

"Only a little." Gutierrez laughed then pointed again as the limo swept around a corner. "Now I will get to the point."

Rita craned her neck for this new lesson in capital architecture. The car glided by a mammoth fountain depicting the agony of Neptune at the death of his godlike children.

"It is so ideal and muscular, that fountain, and so eloquent in meaning."

Rita waited.

"It is myth, that ideal of beauty and justice, is it not? Your capitol is where men enter marble halls with ringing words of justice and honorable action, but where each day is a common marketplace of trading base commodities for favor and power. This is true and you, among a few, really understand that." Gutierrez turned to Rita.

The limousine idled to a halt and a guard who had been riding shotgun for the chauffeur sprang for the trade consul's door to hold it.

Rita slid out behind him. "Are you going to answer my question or not?"

"I do not know your Robert Ellis. I do know that my country has pursued an honest course according to the guidelines your own officials have assigned for us to work under, and that includes contracting lobbyists to speak for us."

Gutierrez walked up the sidewalk to the delegation awaiting him at the glass entrance at the White House.

Rita started after him, but the powerful arm of the Mexican bodyguard stretched like a rail crossing barrier. "I'm going to finish Ellis' story, Gutierrez. I'm going to know where the skeletons are buried. And I'm going to find out if you had anything to do with Bobby's death."

Chapter 27

Rita hated the silence. She glanced up from her desk to the empty outer office. Bev was at the dressmaker's trying on evening gowns. When she was there, Rita sometimes got annoyed with her chatter. When she was away, Rita missed her.

Always the lone wolf on her own diverse trail, Rita ran hot and cold for companionship. She wanted people, but when they got too close, that itch for solitude scratched at her psyche and she put in hard distance. Blessed are the unthinking for they shall never wonder at the perversity of their actions.

Rita sighed and picked at the potato chip crumbs on the foil, which of late had sealed in the heat of her corned beef on rye. She'd been going over Senator Charles Strutt's contributor lists. Nothing jumped out.

The phone rang.

"RM Investigative Services," Rita said.

The male voice asked to speak to the head of the agency.

"This is Rita Mars."

"Ms. Mars, this is special agent Les Folger with the Baltimore Bureau of the FBI, and I'd like to talk to you about your recent visit to the Mexican Trade Mission at their offices in the Mexican Embassy."

"What about it?"

"We have a complaint from Mr. Jorge Gutierrez about your behavior there yesterday." Folger cleared his throat.

"Oh, really? And what was the Senor's major problem?"

"Mr. Gutierrez says in his official complaint that you were belligerent and abusive and that you refused to leave when asked politely by the embassy staff security."

"Polite in Mexico is when three goons try to intimidate you by not speaking, but ganging up three to one?" Rita balled up the sandwich foil and threw it at the trashcan. It bounced off the rim.

"In the statement, Mr. Gutierrez states that security had to escort you from the premises. In my official capacity as liaison for the Washington bureau, it's my duty to inform you of the complaint made against you and to instruct you not to return to the embassy. You are not to telephone them or in any way reinitiate contact with them. Is that understood?" Folger sounded like he read from a policy and procedures manual.

"I don't get to respond?"

Folger answered. "This is a foreign relations matter referred through channels at the State Department. Embassy personnel are not to be harassed. I must advise you that if you don't comply with these instructions, you won't get off with a verbal warning next time."

"And what's the next step, Herr FBI? Loaded tacos at a hundred paces?" Rita reached for the foil ball and slam-dunked the trashcan.

"Ms. Mars, I don't know what your background is or your experience in these kinds of things, but you won't be able to just blow this off. You can mouth off to me; I'm only the messenger. But if you cross the line, you're going to be in bigger trouble than you might have bargained for."

"I'm not bargaining for trouble. If I wanted it, I'd just go in and take it."

"Your funeral."

"What a quaint expression," Rita said. "I guess that was the line Bobby Ellis ran into."

"Who?"

"Thanks for the warning, Folger. I'll try to stay out of any Taco Bells." Rita hung up. Instantly she dialed Mary Margaret.

"What's the matter, Rita?" She heard Mary Margaret take a sip of coffee.

"How do you know something's wrong?"

"Slick, I've known you a long time. You get that authoritative 'I can take care of myself' tone when you need help."

Rita let the comment prickle her scalp. She closed her eyes, took a deep breath and concentrated on changing her tone. "It's no big deal."

"Jesus, Rita, are the Feds after you?"

"Hey, do you know something I don't?" Irritation rubbed her voice like sandpaper.

"Had to be somebody big and nasty. 'No big deal' is the dead giveaway. The smaller you try to make stuff, the bigger it must be. I know you."

"So, will you help me or not? This mind reader act is getting on my nerves." Then Rita added with a quiet sliver of contrition. "It IS the Feds."

"Who?"

"FBI?"

"Why?"

"Supposedly for harassing a Mexican trade mission rep."

"What the hell were you doing?" Rita heard Mary Margaret thump her coffee cup onto her desk.

"I wasn't harassing that asshole. I had an appointment. He agreed to see me."

"He didn't give you the answer you wanted so you proceeded to pound him into the ground."

"I did not."

"This is me you're talking to."

Rita frowned. At her third-floor window, a pigeon had been marching back and forth on the ledge as if he were keeping guard. She rolled her desk chair over and rapped on the glass to make him fly away. "He lied."

"Tell me exactly what you did." Mary Margaret said.

"I asked him some questions about Bobby Ellis. That's all. He pretended he didn't have time to see me and asked did I want to ride in his limo with him to a meeting at the White House. He was oh-so-Latino charming. But when I asked him the questions, he gave some goddam lecture about the myth of American government and politics. He stonewalled and—and I said a few things. That's it."

"Like what exactly did you say?"

"I said I'd bury him if I found out he had anything to do with Bobby's death."

"Jesus, Rita."

"And I mean it."

"No doubt."

"Ok, I acted out, but this guy just wants me off his trail. As far as I'm concerned this is your basic rotten in Denmark move. I'm not backing down, "Rita said.

"I'll call around," Mary Margaret sighed. "What was the name of the agent? Maybe I can find out what's going on. I still have a lot of contacts."

"Thanks, Smooth."

"And while I'm calling, do a few Hail Marys."

"She won't be listening. I'm not Catholic."

"Then make a pitch to St. Jude. He'll listen to anybody."

"Oh, you're just so damned smart, aren't you?" Rita hung up the phone.

♏

The staff cafeteria at the Paxtuxent smelled of vinyl flooring and old grease in spite of the stainless steel decor that exuded a hard brightness that had nothing to do with light. Rita had eaten here once or twice when she was working on the Lyle Solomon story.

Solomon was a murderer, a rapist, and an unrepentant. He was also a horribly abused child and quite possibly a multiple personality. He had never sought leniency, and Mary Margaret even speculated that the behavior he exhibited at the end of his spree, indicated he was looking for suicide by cop. But he was taken alive. Waiving all appeals, he was dead by lethal injection within two years.

In this building, Rita always had the sense that someone was going to close in on her from behind. She made Karin choose a table near the wall where Rita could sit facing the entire room.

"The FBI called you?" Karin rested her fork in her salad bowl.

Rita talked with her mouth full of French fries. "Umm, no big deal."

"Why are they getting involved?"

"Could be a couple of things. Could be they want to be left alone—like Garbo—and that's a real possibility. They might see me as some kind of wing nut off on a tangent." Rita looked at Karin and smiled. "Though how they could have gotten that impression is truly beyond me."

Karin smiled back and shook her head. "You went in like the caped crusader?"

"Moi?"

"Vous."

"I was assertive and adamant at the end of our meeting when Gutierrez wouldn't answer questions." Rita tilted her head back and laughed.

"I see."

"But there are some other possibilities about dragging in the Feds."

"Like there's something to your accusations and they want you off the trail right now?" Karin pointed her salad fork at Rita.

"Bingo."

"Or they're nervous about bad publicity and they want to institute spin control on any possible links to the most remote of scandals."

"You're such a clever girl – and not as mean as Mary Margaret." Rita stuffed more French fries into her mouth. "But whatever, I'm going to stick around like a bad dream."

"You will be careful?" Karin's smile dissolved.

"You're the one who has to carry armor." Rita tapped Karin's metal clipboard, which lay on the table. "And speaking of that—Dr. Demento?"

"No news is good news," Karin said.

Rita nodded.

m

Georgetown hustled with its usual snarl of fashionable traffic—lots of low-slung Mercedes convertibles with bored Washington wives at the wheel. Students, who would be the next wave of law merchants and king makers, strolled the cobbled sidewalks with flush knapsacks and equally flush wallets. Rita slowed at the traffic light and made her turn.

Titleton Associate's office was a huge brick building just past M on Wisconsin. Clones in dark suits with briefcases strode through the glass doors like doctors on their way to the bank. She did catch a glimpse of one woman, young, but no less prepossessed than her male counterparts.

The receptionist, an all-American type with blonde hair and blue eyes, sized up Rita. "May I help you?"

"I have an appointment with Dalton Foster." Rita glanced up at the twenty-five-foot windows that rose like cathedral panes into the reaches of the three-story open atrium.

Clients with appointments seemed to have a soothing effect on the receptionist. She smiled demurely through her red lipstick and touched a button on an electronic telephone that might have come from the bridge of the Starship Enterprise.

"Third door on the left on the second floor."

Rita waded through the surf of expensive carpet. On the stairs she passed a cadre of Koreans trooping in file to exit. She passed a conference room, long and wide, centered with a massive walnut table and chairs ample enough for men in armor. The chandelier was worthy of Cinderella's ballroom.

Another blonde haired, blue eyed woman greeted Rita in Dalton Foster's outer office. "Please go in."

"The Stepford Wives get jobs as secretaries," Rita whispered to herself.

"Ms. Mars, it's a pleasure to have you visit. I'm very familiar with your writing. I've been a fan." Dalton must have just come back from a conjugal visit with his money in the Cayman's. He had a deep tan, accented brilliantly by his ultra-white, starched collar and the gold wristband of his watch.

"Even when I accused your firm of the Ted Turner approach to the war in El Salvador?" Rita took a seat without waiting for an invitation.

"You mean when you said it was our job to colorize the Sandinistas for American consumption?"

"You did read my article."

"It's my job to know where the potholes are—and how to minimize them." Dalton sat back in a leather chair that couched his body like King Kong's palm.

"Well, now that we know which side each of us is on, I'd like to ask you a few questions about your new cinematic production."

"Which is?" Foster asked. Behind him, a wall-sized modern artwork gave him an aura of emerging from some cosmic force field.

"Healthcare legislation."

Foster nodded. "So we have a contract with the Mexican Trade Consul to represent their interests in this country." He frowned. "But I would hardly compare this lobbying effort with the El Salvadoran program—which, by the way, was also strictly on the up and up according to guidelines handed down by State Department."

"I have reason to believe that a friend of mine, Bobby Ellis, was working on a story about this bill." Rita studied the inlay detail work of Foster's desk. The piece reminded her of an ornate bunker.

"Ellis sounds familiar." Foster squinted and the sun weathered lines around his eyes crinkled. "Wasn't he the guy who killed himself?"

"I don't think it was suicide." Rita watched Foster's face for telltale signals of lying.

"And you think I did it?" Foster leaned forward in his chair so that the leather creaked in surprise.

"I think Ellis found something about the new healthcare program that cost him his life."

Foster smoothed over his shock then stood in defense of his honor. "Impossible. And you're certainly barking up the wrong tree here. You as well as anybody should understand we don't have to kill people to get our way."

"Money doesn't work on everybody." Rita stood as well.

"I used to think that." Foster came around the desk to escort her out.

"It wouldn't work on me."

Foster studied her for a moment. "Maybe not, but it would work on someone else to dilute your impact."

Rita stared straight into his face. "My point exactly about how Bobby Ellis got to be dead."

Chapter 28

Rita stood at her kitchen window. The room was dark except for the red eye of the coffee maker. At 5 a.m. on November mornings with the sun still snug behind the horizon, the backyard glowed in the unearthly blue of a mercury lamp on the barn.

Strewn across the kitchen table were papers where Rita left them for the night before. Second cup of coffee in hand, she turned for a glance at her futile readings then looked again through the window. A fox trotted across the driveway, his brush sweeping the asphalt.

She hated the silence. Too many unquiet pictures of the past surfaced in tranquility—her father raging, her mother crying. Maybe that's why her life was so unsettled. Activity was the remedy for remembrance.

"Hey, come here." Rita reached to stroke The Great White Hunter who rubbed his good morning greeting against her sweatpants.

She picked him up and sat in a chair at the table. As soon as she let go, the cat jumped to the floor.

"In ten years, you'd think you'd get used to sitting in my lap and being petted—like other cats," Rita said.

The Great White Hunter purred.

"But you're not like other cats, are you?"

The cat nestled his head into Rita's hand.

"That's why we get along so well," she said. "Neither one of us is like what we're supposed to be."

The Great White Hunter sauntered away to his food bowl.

Rita grunted, got up and turned on the kitchen light, which exposed her hours of failure from the night before. She gathered the strewn papers into two piles and set one pile at her left, one at her right. She had one page remaining on which was a list in her handwriting. She studied it for a long time.

"How long have you been up?" Karin shuffled into the kitchen. She wore an extra-large sweatshirt as pajamas. On her feet were thick rag socks.

"I'm sorry. Did I wake you up?" Rita asked.

"Not really. I just had a sense something was going on down here. Got some extra coffee?" Karin reached into the cabinet for a cup.

"Plenty." Rita poured coffee into the offered cup. "But you don't get up this early. Go on back to bed; I'll call you when a reasonable hour appears."

"I'm too awake. Any luck?" Karin pointed at the papers on the table.

"No." Rita pulled a package of frosted cinnamon buns from the breadbox.

"I'm sorry I interrupted last night."

"Didn't matter. I'd been staring at this stuff for hours before you got here. I probably needed the break and getting away today will give me a fresh perspective when I get back to this." Rita handed Karin a plate with a hunk of the pastry.

"I'll just strap these to my thighs."

"No calories if you eat them early enough in the morning."

"Oh, really?" Karin took a big bite and said with her mouth full, "In that case I'll set my alarm and start eating lunch and dinner before I go to work."

"Good idea." Rita chewed her pastry, but her eyes wandered to her handwritten list.

"What are you looking for anyway?"

"Well, I've got Charles Strutt's list of contributors in this pile." Rita tapped the papers on her right. "And I've got Titleton's foreign client list here." She tapped the papers on her left.

"I remember that much from last night, but you were pretty fuzzy on the rest." Karin said.

"I'm looking for something to jump out, something that looks like illegal payoffs, something that Bobby Ellis might have stumbled on when he was working his story."

"I'm still not getting it. Sorry, I'm really dense on this."

Rita smiled. "You're not alone. This stuff is very complex to read: easy to manipulate and hide in. Anyway, here goes."

She took a swig of coffee. "It's big business for American PR firms to hire former government honchos and solicit foreign interests to pay huge fees for entry to federal agencies and our lovely legislative bodies that these honchos came from."

"Well, I do get that much." Karin said.

"Ok, so Titleton has the contract for the Government of Mexico and for the Mexican Free Trade Association because they have some guys working for them who retired from our Commerce and State Departments. Their job for this specific contract is to smooth the way for Mexican business here. But I just can't connect the dots on Mexico and U.S. healthcare."

Karin nodded and took another bite of her pastry.

"Over here we have Charles Strutt, the head of the Senate Commerce Committee who has taken, according to Pete DeVane, a serious about-face on his anti-healthcare stance. So, what I'm looking for is evidence in his list of contributors that Strutt's getting some kind of back door money from Mexico. And if I knew what they were trying to buy in this legislation, it'd be a whole lot easier."

Karin picked up Rita's handwritten list. "And these are?"

"These are my guesses as to how either of the Mexican groups could have disguised their names in order to circumvent the law against direct foreign contribution."

"Not a big list," Karin said. "This doesn't look like enough groups, given contribution limits, to make a serious buy off."

"I know." Rita ran her fingers through her hair and rested her forehead on the table. After a moment she sat up.

"Mind if I make a suggestion?" Karin studied Rita's list. "You've concentrated on groups that have something to do with trade. Maybe they called them something else to disguise their involvement."

"Yes." Rita brightened. "That's it. Why didn't I think of that? I even wrote a story about how foreign business helps organize community consumer groups and study groups, any kind of body they can leverage to make them appear like just another U.S. company." She gave Karin a high five.

"The best thing is that I got a list of last years' contributors to Strutt's war chest and I can go through to see who the brand-new donors are. I can slim down the list, then run down info on all the new kids on the block." Rita made a face. "Yuck, hours of research."

"But it'll be worth it," Karin said.

"Yes, I think it will."

"And while you're scrubbing that list," Karin yawned. "I think I'll take in another dose of caffeine."

"Good therapy." Rita was already lining out the repeat contributors. "I have an interesting total of fifteen first time organizations."

"Would you think fifteen is enough for a big amount of money? I mean, aren't foreign interests limited in what they can give?"

"Sure and they have to report those contributions to the Federal Election Committee. However, if they get American companies or individuals to form these PACS, they can funnel an unlimited amount of soft money. Independent PACS don't have the same kinds of restrictions." Rita eyed the buns quickly, but turned away.

"Clever," Karin said.

"Very. Some of those new contributors have very interesting names—Texas Consumers' Association; Americans for Central American Study; Plastics Council of North America."

"They sound so authentic," Karin said.

"Most cons do." Rita answered.

♏

Later Karin met Rita at her office around seven; they had a date for dinner. The wind whistled off the granite ledges at Rita's windows, forcing bedded pigeons to bury their heads deeper beneath their wings. When Karin entered the office was dark except for the glow of the PC screen on Rita's desk.

Karin switched on the light. "You'll ruin your eyes."

"Too late. I already had a nasty habit that did that." Rita let her reading glasses slip down her nose. She peered up at Karin to grin.

"Finding anything?" Karin came around the desk to look over Rita's shoulder.

"Everything." Rita rubbed her eyes. "The onion is peeling, slowly but surely."

"You found a connection in those new contributors?"

"I found *the* connection," Rita said. "That great patriotic organization called Americans for an Open Market Economy."

Karin pulled up a chair. "So, dazzle me with details."

"I hired a paralegal in DC to do most of the grunt work, and she sent these file transfers over today on the first batch of contributing PACs she finished investigating. This is how it appears to be going. On the surface, it seems like a bunch of independent U.S. consumer and trade groups are getting together in righteous fervor to support this healthcare bill. What the paralegal is finding out, what I told her to look for, is a parent organization. If there was even a mention of some other affiliation, she was to run it down."

"All roads lead to Americans for an Open Market Economy?" Karin asked.

"Exactly, and she's not finished with half the list I sent." Rita rubbed her eyes again.

"You're exhausted."

"Only a little."

"Like somebody's a little bit dead." Karin sniffed.

"I can't sleep." Rita launched herself from the chair and paced in front of the desk. "I'm going to bring this case to conclusion. I'm going to find Bobby's killer."

"And it just might be these Open Market people?"

"I've got to find out who they are, where they came from." Rita returned to her chair. "I know that you wouldn't, but promise you won't say what I told you just now—about this group?"

"I would never," Karin promised.

"I can't let them know I understand the scheme. It's too early in the game. They could scatter. I have to herd them into the canyon." Rita switched off her PC.

"This is a very dangerous course you're on." Karin led the way as Rita pointed to the office door.

"Maybe." They stood in the hallway. Rita turned off the light and locked her office door.

Karin grabbed her arm when she started down the hall. "Not maybe. Bobby Ellis is as dead as they come. He must have found this same entrance to the tomb."

"What a great analogy." Rita smiled and started walking again.

"Listen to me." Karin snatched at her coat sleeve. "This isn't some high stakes poker game or the usual Washington mud wrestling. This is real stuff. You've got to protect yourself."

"Ok, ok. I'm going to." Rita turned away again.

"Tell me how."

"In the car—on the way to dinner," Rita said.

"Now."

"Geez, you're touchy."

Karin waited without speaking.

Rita sighed. "First, you won't say anything. Second, my inquiries will be exceptionally less confrontational and open than Bobby's. Third, I've got a packet of information with what I know so far in my safe deposit box. I'm keeping nothing with me so even if I get ransacked again, the assholes won't find a piece of anything. Do I get the *Good Housekeeping* seal yet?"

"What you just said has nothing to do with what I asked. How are you protecting *yourself*, you, Rita Mars?" Karin touched Rita's coat sleeve again, but with a feel of comfort and protection rather than urgency.

Rita swallowed hard. She undid the buttons of her overcoat and pulled back the lapels of the jacket she wore over her turtleneck. The seasoned leather straps of her shoulder holster harnessed the left side of her body. The Glock 19, plastic miracle of firepower, was a dark hulk under her arm.

Karin bowed her head. "I don't know which is worse. Them with a gun or you with a gun."

Rita quickly let her coat fall back into place. She buttoned it. "Thanks for that great vote of confidence. I happen to be an excellent marksman."

"That's not always enough," Karin said, "but it'll do for now." She linked her arm through Rita's as they left the building.

"Yeah," Rita said, "that makes me a little nervous too."

♏

Cafe Hon nestled among the tired, but eager storefronts in Hamden. It was a working class neighborhood that union members and skinheads and big-haired blondes called home. The streets were narrow, crowded on opposite curbs by pick-ups and muscle cars. But while the neighborhood leaned far to the right, Cafe Hon enticed even raving liberals to its tables for honest pot roast and hand cut fries and pies to die for.

"And speaking of our most recent conversations," Rita said. "Still nothing from Demento?"

She and Karin sat waiting for coffee and lemon meringue pie.

"Nothing from Douglas." Karin smiled as the waitress, cracking her gum, set the coffee and dessert before them.

"What do you think that means?"

"One of two things. Giving up or surprise attack."

"I don't like the second option." Rita stuck her fork into her meringue.

"Time is the only answer. There's no quick and dirty way to the bottom line here," Karin said.

"A common dilemma of our times." Then Rita added. "I do want to share one other juicy item about the Bobby case though. The tip I got about Mr. Peter DeVane's sullied past— I decided to explore a tangent off that angle. I made a list of all the people Bobby was in contact with over the last month, then I ran a search of old news on about twenty folks."

"You found some things?"

"Looks like a few people could have skeletons they don't want to see daylight. And guess what? One of those might be our friendly and helpful Randy Wyman, though his smacks less of intentional evil than overzealous brutishness."

"What was it?" Karin asked.

"An accident while he was in college. Seems he was on the wrestling team. He paralyzed one of his opponents. But the article was awash in tearful apology and regret." Rita stabbed a bite of pie.

"He paralyzed an opponent?"

Rita shrugged. "Wrestling—it can happen."

"What other transgressions did you find?" Karin asked.

"Nothing very interesting. A handful of drunk driving arrests, a disorderly conduct, no secrets to kill for."

The pie gone and the coffee dregs in their cups, Rita counted out bills for the check and she and Karin stepped onto 35th Street. The 7-Eleven across the way was a gathering point for black leather jacketed boys in engineer boots. Some strode growling Harleys, exhaust swirling in the November wind.

"What's next?" Karin studied the gang outside the convenience store as she waited for Rita to unlock the Jeep passenger door.

"I'm going to call on DeVane and Wyman to ask about Americans for an Open Market Economy."

"You said you were going to investigate them secretly," Karin said.

"I am." Rita nodded. "But you have to stick your head up sometime in a turkey hunt."

Chapter 29

The galleries of the Senate overflowed with future constituents bused in from surrounding school districts. Middle and high school students, populated the close set wooden seats, and were, for the most part, respectful of the theatre unfolding below. As a by-product of C-Span, Senators came to the microphone, one by one, to wave their patriotism and declaim homilies for the annual Thanksgiving proclamation.

"Do you think these kids really believe this is what government's like?" Rita whispered to Kate Harrigan.

She sat beside her in the less crowded press section. The audience in this part of the ceiling was far less respectful and attentive. They did, however, have the decency to sleep without snoring.

Kate, Rita's journalist contact, yawned. "Those boys on the floor sure hope so. They want these children to go home and tell Mommy and Daddy they saw their very own Senator saving the world for truth, justice and the American Way."

Rita shook her head. "Can you imagine watching this on TV all day?"

The two women laughed until a teacher herding her seventh grade class took it upon herself to reprimand them with a "quiet or else" glare.

"So how are you coming on the Bobby Ellis thing?" Kate asked.

"Good. I'm doing good," Rita lied. She stared down at the speaker's podium where Charles Strutt advanced for his five minutes of video glory.

"So?" Kate turned to give full attention.

"So what? No, I don't know who did it. But I'm going great guns on the story he was working on. And Bobby was right about one thing, shit is going to hit the fan when it all comes out."

"Was it Hillman?" Kate asked. "Is he mixed up in this? I heard he had some ugly little harassment secrets he didn't want to rise up out of the grave."

"Hillman? Harassment?"

"Guess that wasn't it," Kate said, then added, "or are you just trying to throw me off track?"

"No, no, I didn't know about any of that. But Kate, I can't tell you yet what the story is. I don't have it all, and I can't afford to have it leaking." Rita leaned back in her seat while she watched Strutt talk.

He had a strong voice and a well-coached Walter Cronkite delivery. If he'd done *War of the Worlds*, there'd have been twice the number of suicides.

"Come on, you know me." Kate leaned closer.

"Yeah, I know you're the best news reporter in this bureaucratic berg." Rita stared straight into her eyes.

"Ok, I understand. No hard feelings."

"But I promise to share it with you first if you do me a favor." Rita glanced around to check if anyone was listening.

Kate nodded and leaned close again.

"I want you to let it out that I'm on to something big in Bobby's last story."

Kate kept her eye contact steady. "You're the bait in the trap."

Rita blinked. "I'm the bait in the trap."

♏︎

When the show was over and the students were filing through the halls toward their pose for an 8x10 glossy with the Senator of their choice, Kate and Rita split up. Kate headed back to the press quarters while Rita marched to an office on the second floor.

"Not you again. You're a bad dream." Pete DeVane brushed past her in the reception area of Brett Hillman's office.

She followed. "Dreaming men are haunted men.'"

DeVane halted and turned. "Where did that come from?"

"A poem by Benet."

DeVane turned and resumed his forced march. Rita was at his heels.

"I'm busy," he said.

"Me too," said Rita

"Well, good for you."

They were in a labyrinth of cubicles now, and DeVane disappeared into one. Rita rounded the corner as he tapped a computer key. A screen full of text popped into view. He sat down and ignored Rita who planted herself in front of his desk.

"I want Hillman's contributor lists for this year and last."

"I want the Redskins to win the Superbowl."

"I've got the better chance."

DeVane shot her a look. Before the discussion continued, another Hillman aide came in.

"The vote's coming up on that grant for the University of Florida," the man said without acknowledging he'd interrupted a meeting.

DeVane sighed. "Tell Hillman this is the deal. Vote yes. Preston from Florida will vote for keeping that Navy base open for him and he'll help deliver a few extra from his committee if he comes back with a promise on the farm subsidy for citrus growers."

The other aide nodded and left.

"You guys make me sick."

"So leave." DeVane scrolled through the material on his PC.

"If people only knew now things worked in this 'I'll scratch your back' game—and how much it costs them." Rita rolled her eyes.

DeVane stopped to face her. "People don't give a damn. The only thing they understand is that their Senator got money for their state. That makes them happy and they vote to prove it. Some of them are too dumb to know how it happens. Some don't care. There're only a few nit-picking Puritans, like you, who want to grind the process to a halt."

Rita started to speak, stopped and began again. "Just give me the contributions lists."

"Write me a letter the way all good constituents do." DeVane returned to his PC screen.

"If I go through channels, it won't be pretty."

DeVane's fingers froze on the keyboard. He waited then tapped a few more keys. In a few seconds, pages started emitting from the laser printer in the corner of the cubicle.

"Now will you go away?" he said.

"Only maybe. It depends on what pops out of that machine."

DeVane continued to work on his computer as Rita stood watch at the printer. It finished as DeVane stood and came around the desk. Rita gathered the lists and followed after him.

At the office doorway she almost collided with Randy Wyman as he entered Hillman's office and stopped to speak to DeVane.

"Did you get those reports on healthcare I sent?" he asked.

"Uh, yeah, but I haven't had time to look at them yet." DeVane jerked his thumb at Rita.

"How are you doing on the Ellis case?" Wyman smiled.

"I'm making great progress on the story he never got finished," Rita said. "It's an interesting piece."

"Oh? I thought no one knew what he was working on." Wyman said.

"Hey, we were supposed to be in that committee meeting five minutes ago," DeVane said. "Let's go." He was out in the hall.

"Tell me about it as we walk," Wyman said to Rita.

"A good reporter doesn't tell her story until press time," she said.

"You sound like you're well along. I was going to ask if there was anything I could do to help."

"I'll keep that offer in mind." Rita smiled.

"It must be a hell of a story." Wyman slowed.

DeVane was far ahead of them. Rita stopped walking and Wyman with her.

"It's going to be a killer," she said.

♏

Something wasn't right. Rita rolled her head toward the digital clock. Three a.m. Had that sound been in a dream or was it here and now?

Karin was at a PR event with a client in New York. Bev was with her; they planned a day of shopping after the last seminar. They would be back by train tomorrow night.

The Great White Hunter, recently coiled into his usual deep sleep curl at the end of the bed was awake. His head cocked toward the bedroom door. One ear twitched.

Rita sat up and strained to listen. Was that her breathing or someone else's? She stopped. Nothing. Just as she resumed, she heard it again. A thump, shallow, but distinct. The Great White Hunter rose and stretched toward the sound.

Her old farmhouse creaked, settled, sighed, and shifted. Rita had lived here long enough to identify and sleep through most of the house's familiar cadence. This sound was not one of them, and Rita's curse and gift was the ability to hear everything within striking distance, even from the deepest sleep. That gift was the vestige of her unpredictably violent childhood.

The Great White Hunter poised on the edge of the bed, looked back at Rita then softly dropped to the carpet. Rita, in sweatpants and T-shirt, eased herself from the bed and slipped into a pair of sneakers. From the peg rag on the wall, she drew the Glock from her shoulder holster, patting the butt to make sure the clip was in.

Sweat beaded on her upper lip. She checked the window by the driveway but saw no car. Then she tiptoed into the bathroom and peered through the blinds, no vehicle there either. Maybe it was a squirrel on the roof or a raccoon in the basement.

Rita stole to her bedroom door and listened at the stairs. The bottom step creaked. She squeezed her eyes shut and thought about what to do.

Shoe leather shushed on another wooden step. The Great White Hunter stood at the top and stared down. Rita tried to scoot him away with her foot, but she couldn't touch him without jeopardizing her position.

The intruder was drawing closer. Rita could hear leather sliding on the handrail. He was taking it slow, one step at a time with a pause to listen at each.

Rita's mouth tasted of old pennies and she got a whiff of cigarette smoke that quickly evaporated. She held her breath, the barrel of the semi-automatic resting like a kiss against her lips. She touched the trigger and with her free left hand reached for the light switch that would shower the stairway with light.

The intruder took another step up. He was more than half way up now. The Great White Hunter stood transfixed, staring. With his perfect cat vision of the night, he had the eye witness view.

Rita flipped the switch. Instantly hundred-watt candlepower drenched the stairwell. She paused a moment for the intruder's reaction. The Great White Hunter blinked, but continued to look down the steps. There was immediate silence, followed by the scramble of retreat.

Rita aimed her weapon and then leaped to face the stairs. She saw a Nike disappearing into her living room. She hurtled down the steps in pursuit. The wooden back door was thrown open and the aluminum storm door still hung outward into the night.

Through those doors in the blue mercury glow from the barn light she saw the dark figure of a man, running across her driveway. At the rear of her six acres was a huge horse farm, not visible from the main road, but which was accessible by a private paved drive that ran along her pasture fences. She guessed the man must have parked along that drive. It was rarely traveled, completely dark and a perfect spot from which to approach her house undetected.

She pounded across her driveway. Ahead she heard the thudding feet of her quarry. Once off the driveway and beyond the barn, the mercury lamp was no help. There was a section of open ground between her two unused pastures. The man raced through this area.

"Stop or I'll shoot." Rita could see nothing as she stopped, braced herself and aimed toward the sound of running.

Crack. She saw a white fire burst and threw herself to the ground. She knew that she must be backlit by the mercury glow. If she dropped, he would be as blind as she. Crack. He shot again.

"Jesus." Her face pressed to the dirt.

Rita dug her elbows in to steady her hand and snapped the trigger for a few frenzied rounds. She heard a car door thud and the ignition catch.

She jumped up and sprinted the last yards to the private road. The oily smell of exhaust permeated the cold November air. Tires screamed and peeled rubber as the car fishtailed on the road.

"Goddam you." Rita pumped the trigger and sparked the darkness with her own firepower.

She heard bullets slam to metal. She heard the smash of breaking windows, but in the light of the street lamp at the end of the private drive, she watched a dark BMW fishtail out onto the main road and roar off.

"Fuck you." Rita fired into the air.

She did not chase the car, but stood shivering in the night. Her teeth chattered as she bowed her head and dropped her arm with the gun clutched in hand. For a long time, she stood there in that half slump. Her knees were too wobbly to carry her back to her house. Her mouth was open and slack. She gulped deep draughts of air.

Inside her house she stared at the kitchen wall phone. Should she call the police? Waste of time. She made coffee instead. It was almost four.

The Great White Hunter sauntered in and rubbed against her leg. She reached down to scratch his head.

"Who was it, kiddo?" she asked. "Who was that fucker?"

The Great White Hunter purred, but kept his secret.

Rita paced the kitchen as she waited for the coffee to brew. She had to exorcise this experience, share the burden of its intensity or it was going to thrash her. Who to call?

She picked up the phone.

"This had better not be a trivia question about a thirties detective movie you're watching." Mary Margaret's voice was thick with sleep.

"No, this is a trivia question about who the hell tried to shoot me in my own house."

"Rita, Jesus, are you all right?" Mary Margaret's voice grew suddenly clear and strong.

"I'm having a bad night. I just need to talk to you for a minute. I'm sorry I woke you up." Rita ran her fingers through her hair. This was a dumb idea.

"I'm getting dressed." The receiver dropped to the floor, but was quickly retrieved. "Call the police."

"I just did, dammit. And I'm not calling any others," said Rita. She took in a long slow breath.

"Are you sure the shooter is gone? Lock yourself in until I get there. I'll call—"

"I'm fine. Somebody broke in. I chased him. We both shot off a few rounds, but—"

"My God, are you hurt? Did you shoot him?"

"No, look, I'm really sorry I called. I just, I just—I needed to say what happened. Ok?"

"I'll be right there." Mary Margaret hung up.

Rita listened to the drone of the disconnected line for a minute then hung up. She poured a cup of coffee and sat in her kitchen with all the lights off.

Before she could take the first sip, tears, like desert rain, coursed down her cheeks.

Chapter 30

Death calls demanded sobriety. Rita laughed when her father told her that. Not so that he'd know, of course, but in the hidden way children of alcoholics keep feelings to themselves. But she didn't laugh when he went on to explain that you owed the survivors your pain and guilt of being alive. The unspoken grief of mothers and fathers, of husbands and wives, of children demanded no less.

Rita punched the numbers on her telephone. She'd been in the office for two hours on this Saturday morning and had come in here specifically to phone Edmund Ellis with a status report. She'd filed, dusted, paced, and stared out the window to stall.

"Dr. Ellis?"

"Yes." The voice belonged to a man much older than the trim mid-fifties man who had contracted her services.

"This is Rita Mars. I'm calling with an update on your case."

"You found him." Ellis' voice was flat.

For an instant, Rita was confused. It sounded as though Edmund was expecting her to find his long-lost brother. But almost as quickly she made the leap to his real question.

"No, I'm sorry. I don't have the murderer yet," she said.

Ellis on the other end was silent.

"I've been in a depression," he said after a while.

Rita squeezed the handle of her coffee cup. What was she supposed to say to that?

"I'm sorry." Rita paused a beat and went on. "I do have some information though, and I'd like you to know where we stand as of now."

"I have dreams," Edmund said.

"Dreams?"

"At night and even during the day. Flashbacks, I guess."

"Have you gotten any counseling? Families of murder victims need time and help in coping with this." Rita watched the oils swirl on the surface of her cold coffee. She was in this conversation now and there was no way but ahead.

"I keep seeing the funeral director—he was just a kid really—pulling back the sheet. I watch his arm, like a ballet dancer, in slow motion."

"Dr. Ellis, maybe I can call you back later if this is too painful. Or I can send you a written report," Rita offered.

"Then I see his face. It's white and firm, like a mask. Then I see the purple-black ring of bruises on his throat." Ellis kept on.

Rita held her breath.

"I see it over and over."

"I'm sorry."

"I want it to go away."

Rita did not respond.

"I don't think about catching the killer anymore. All I can think about is how I want this picture to go away."

"Have you talked to anyone else about this?" Rita asked.

"The only thing I want right now is for the last memory of my brother to go away. And I feel guilty," he said.

Rita heard a catch in his voice as if he cried quietly. "Is there anything I can do to help you?"

"Maybe if you find the murderer, the pictures will stop."

"I was calling to tell you where I am with that," Rita said.

"I must sound deranged," Edmund said. "I'm sorry. Let me know what you've found."

Rita could see that magical light in the tunnel. She sat up straight in her chair and went down the list of notes she'd made for Edmund's briefing.

She believed that Bobby's death had to do with his investigation into backroom dealings on the upcoming healthcare agreement. She had a list of suspects. No, she couldn't share them at this time with Edmund; she couldn't jeopardize her case with any kind of leaks. Her strategy was to make it widely known that she was going to complete Bobby's last article in the series and that she was well into the work he'd started. The killers might then come after her and in so doing, reveal themselves.

"Aren't you afraid?" Edmund Ellis asked.

"I don't think about it," Rita answered.

ℳ

"Hey, baby," Bev said when she realized it was Rita on the line. "Solve any whodunits today?"

She was at home now and getting ready for a long run on the fire trails in Gunpowder Park. Snow hung like a threat in the grey air and the wind clicked the branches of the bare trees, but she needed to run right now.

"I'm not cut out for this job," Rita said. "Not tough enough."

"Who said?"

"Me. I'm a fraud, Bev." Rita tied her shoe with the phone snug under her chin.

"You think you the only one who gets the dark moment? You think you're the Lone Ranger in the shadow of doubt?"

"No, dammit." Rita snapped a knot in her laces. "But there's doubt and then there's the epiphany of self-revelation."

"Damn, girl. You talk like an English major."

"Well, I was one—and don't try to make fun of me." Rita unraveled the knot and re-laced her shoe.

"I ain't makin' fun, Rita Mars. I'm tellin' you, like the person I am who loves you, you got the right stuff, honey. But that don't mean there ain't gonna be days like this."

Rita sighed.

"Did you talk to Dr. Ellis?" Bev switched to her professional tone.

Rita stared out the window. The pasture was brown, the sky dead grey. "Yes, I talked to Edmund Ellis. I gave a sterling report to the good doctor that conveyed to him that I'm clueless."

"But you're not clueless," Bev said.

"No, but I have a great imagination about why Bobby's dead, and I've got a suspect list big enough to cast a Charleton Heston Bible movie. Hey, I've got two U.S. senators, the entire industrial lobby, and the State of Mexico," Rita shouted.

When she was finished, Bev said nothing.

"I shouldn't have called. I'm too pissed," Rita said.

"What happened when you phoned Edmund Ellis?" Bev asked.

"Nothing," Rita said. "I can't tell you right now."

"Don't hang up yet."

"I'm going to run. I have to," Rita said.

"Call me when you get back. You hear me, girl?"

"I hear you, Bev. I'll call."

It was cold on the fire trails. The wind shook the pine n-eedles and tugged on aging branches that creaked with every gust. Gusts stung Rita's eyes until they teared. Still she ran for more than an hour and when she came home, she checked in with Bev, took a hot shower, fell into bed and slept a mercifully dreamless sleep.

♏

"Are you feeling any better?" Bev greeted Rita at the front door to her condo. Karin was attending an awards dinner and Rita was to pick her up later.

Rita lowered her eyes as she entered. "Ok, so I'm a big baby feeling sorry for myself." She stood like a scolded child and waited with her coat on for Bev to acknowledge her apology.

"It's ok." Bev took the coat. "But beating yourself up ain't gonna get rid of that frustration. Did the run help?"

"Yes." Rita followed Bev into her kitchen. "I know that somewhere in my head about not beating myself up. It just isn't strong enough to stop me sometimes. "

Bev handed Rita a wooden spoon and assigned her the stirring of the spaghetti sauce while she prepared a salad. "And what happened today? Obviously it had something to do with Edmund Ellis."

Rita told her about his depression and flashbacks. "Edmund Ellis is eaten up with grief and guilt and I'm calling to tell him I have exactly nothing."

"This isn't about Edmund Ellis." Bev held Rita's eyes with a fixed bayonet gaze.

Rita's breath ran shallow. She struggled to flight, but Bev had her pinned. She heard herself say, "The man is haunted. His talk about the recurring nightmare of Bobby unveiled at the funeral home is unnerving."

"Reminds you of something."

"No. I feel sorry for the guy, that's all. That image coming back over and over."

Bev said nothing.

Rita went on. "It made his pain so real, so palpable that it came down that phone wire into me. Like in *The Exorcist* when the demon tries to take over the priest. The demon gets to him even though he doesn't get control."

"Did you ever get this feeling before?" Bev met Rita's eyes more gently this time and gave her room for escape.

Rita looked away at the stove where the digital clock numerals gleamed in green. "Maybe it is about me. I mean all those years I spent on the newspaper. I loved the game, the hide and seek. I was a good seeker. There were a few times things didn't pan out—I was pissed, but hell, I rode off in another direction after truth, justice and the American way."

"And now?" Bev asked.

Rita let out a long slow sigh. "Now I have to make this work. I have to find the answer to this riddle or I can't do anything else."

Bev's face clouded "Why?"

"Because I can't. Edmund Ellis needs to know the answer."

"Some riddles don't have an answer. You can't fix Edmund's pain. Finding the killer is no guarantee he'll stop being haunted. He has to deal with his pain—you got to deal with yours," Bev said.

"I'm not the one in pain," Rita countered.

Bev placed the salads on the table. "Don't give me that line, girl."

After dinner they retreated to the living room, Bev on the sofa, Rita sprawled in a chair. They watched some old Law and Orders on Netflix while Rita chattered with a running commentary.

"Instant suspect," she mumbled. "Nice and clean."

"Play that dumb act and spend all day everyday stacking the deck against one guy."

"Oh, a clue only Sherlock Holmes would have picked up."

"Quiet," Bev said after a while.

"Pisses me off the way they make it look so damned easy," Rita said.

"I'm turnin' this damn thing off," Bev said.

"I'll be quiet." Rita slumped deeper into the chair.

But it didn't last long and finally Bev tapped the power button on the remote control.

"Hey," Rita said. "Aren't we going to watch the end?"

"This is the end for me, baby." Bev got up and went into the kitchen.

"I'm sorry." Rita followed. "I should have stayed home and groused by myself. I didn't mean to ruin the evening."

Bev poured water into the coffeemaker. "Want some?"

Rita nodded. She sat chin in hand, elbow propped on the table in a pose of dejection. Then she checked her watch. She had to leave in twenty minutes to pick up Karin.

"I'm sure it's very frustrating." Bev measured coffee into the filter.

"I have a strong sense that the murder has something to do with a newspaper story on foreign trade—but I can't make the connection. From there, I leap to a whole country, the U.S. Senate and God knows who else as suspects. I have assholes rearranging the furniture in my office and breaking into my house. And I can't even find a broad named Miriam Blalock." Rita slapped the tabletop with flattened palms.

"Now there's a name from the past." Bev flicked the switch on the coffeemaker and joined Rita at the kitchen table.

"What?"

"It's the name of the vampire Catherine Deneuve played in The Hunger," Bev said.

Rita sat up straight and stared across at her. "Did you say vampire?"

"Yes, Lord, she and that boy, David Bowie, were these—"

"Oh, my God." Rita touched her temple.

"What?"

"I'll call you tomorrow," Rita said, "and take a rain check on the coffee."

♏

She'd been awake all night, waiting for the darkness to peel back. Even after she'd picked up Karin and ensconced her safely in the guest room, she could not calm down enough for sleep. She'd paced and jingled a set of keys and drank coffee. And now a thin pink streak signaled the start of the race. She wasn't going to wait to say goodbye to Karin.

The Great White Hunter watched in detached silence as she threw open the closet door and jammed into her overcoat. He yawned as she jogged to the Jeep and warmed the engine. He curled back into sleep as she flew down the drive.

I-83 was already stirring as early commuters from just over the Pennsylvania line scuttled southward to city jobs. The Baltimore beltway was a straight shot to I-95 where she punched the accelerator and launched toward Silver Spring.

Unhindered by state trooper interference, Rita was at the private post box location a little after six. The doors weren't open yet. The sign on the glass front said hours were six to ten on weekdays. Rita pounded on the door.

The old man whom she'd met last time took his time in getting to the lock. Through the windows Rita could see his set jaw and red face.

"Just hold your horses," he sputtered as Rita blew by him when he turned the key and inched open the door.

"Damned pushy women."

Rita was at the mailbox she'd stared at so futilely before. She held the unknown key on Bobby Ellis' key lob and poised it at the lock. With eyes on the prize, she watched the little silver of sliver enter—and turn.

For a moment she stared at the papers stuffed inside. "Thank you. Thank you," she said and pulled out the box contents with one hand.

It was freezing, but Rita opened the trunk of the Jeep. There on the empty bay she started sorting.

"Hillman dirt." She tossed a contribution check copy.

"DeVane's skeleton." She placed this beside the check.

"Hillman dirt." Another photocopied check.

"Kickback story." She started a third pile.

She had four stacks of information when she was done, each relating to one of the stories in Bobby Ellis' news series.

"He had a source," Rita mused. "Somebody long before DeVane started sending him things."

She glanced around her at the cars now entering and leaving the mailing service lot. Quickly she gathered the papers in her trunk and stashed them in the spare tire well.

"Nothing on healthcare at all," Rita said as she slammed the trunk and locked herself into the car. "How very curious. Could the source have turned into a subject?"

She backed out of her parking space. "And who the hell is Miriam Blalock?"

Chapter 31

Snow sifted on the Capitol. The scene reminded Rita of one of those water-filled toys where you shook the plastic dome and fake flakes swirled a blizzard around a one-inch Frosty the Snowman.

One difference, this scene was busier—and noisier. It wasn't cold enough to deter the protest group du jour. This Wednesday afternoon session was devoted to agriculture. Bundled in parkas and mittens, the marchers hoisted signs decrying the irradiation of tomatoes and such for the beautification of the local grocery's produce displays.

"Looks aren't everything" one sign said.

"You are what you eat" said another.

Rita skirted the band of hearty dissidents and jogged the marble steps. She wondered how those guys could keep it up. She'd walked only two blocks and already she couldn't feel her toes.

"Got your story yet?" Kate Harrigan whispered as Rita sat down with her in the pressroom.

Rita glanced over her shoulder. Three people bent over laptops tapping out copy. One woman sat in the corner with a cup of coffee and a briefing paper.

"No," Rita whispered back.

"Damn." Kate appeared to lose interest.

"I need your input."

This created new interest in Kate's face. She whispered again. "What?"

"Just some opinions," Rita said.

"You certainly know how to push a reporter's buttons." Kate frowned. "This isn't about Bobby Ellis?"

"Not really. I was thinking about doing a profile piece for the *Atlantic* on the key players in the healthcare fight." Rita smiled and nodded.

"So, what's the deal with the Ellis case?" Kate settled her big boned frame into the squeaky desk chair.

"I'm still working on it." Rita looked Kate squarely in the eyes.

"And?"

"And nothing. I have some leads that I'm following," Rita looked around the room again in the way that old jockeys watch a post parade.

"Rita, you sound like some goddam police PR nerd." Kate shook her head. "What opinions do you want?"

"The key guys on the hill in the pro healthcare camp. Windsor, Layman, Hillman and Strutt; what's their story on why they're backing this?"

Kate sighed, tilted her head for a moment and started speaking. "Windsor is straight out of Dante's seventh circle. An opportunist with a capital 'O'. He has his Hill rats taking polls every five minutes to figure out which way the wind blows. With Illinois' heavy industry rusting away to nothing, his constituents are looking for cheap medicine."

"Makes sense," Rita said.

"Layman, our human rights hero from the great state of Oregon believes we can cure what ails America with a coverage for all program." Kate rubbed her thumb and forefinger together.

"Hillman?"

"Go figure. Somebody must have promised him a pork prize for Pennsylvania if he votes for this thing. All he cares about is staying in office. He'd sell the Statue of Liberty to the Chinese if they promised to give him money for re-election."

"A true statesman." Rita laughed.

"As are they all."

"And how about Strutt?"

"A man without a brain."

"Strutt?" Rita said.

"Hell, he looks good on TV and sounds good when he talks. Only trouble is he's really a hand puppet. When you come from the kind of money he does, you can hire people to make you look like anything. He happens to look like a Senator." Kate's face crinkled into a sly grin.

"What's so funny?" Rita asked.

"We had a guy just like this a little while back. They made him look like a President."

They both laughed again.

"Nobody in it for logical, moral or economic rationale?" Rita said with a sigh.

"Honey, you worked this Hill. Is there something you forgot?" Kate checked her watch.

"Ok, I'll get out of your hair." Rita stood. "Thanks for the sketches. They will help."

"Anytime." Kate stood up with her and shook hands. "Take care of yourself. Let me know when you find something out about Bobby."

Rita nodded. That stubborn lump rose in her throat again.

"Hey," Kate called after her as she was leaving, "and let me know when that *Atlantic* piece comes out."

Rita stuck her hands in her parka. Kate's profiles gave her nothing concrete and the conversation served only to remind her how far she was from answers. Miriam Blalock was starting to get on her nerves.

She marched up the Capitol atrium spiral stairs instead of taking the elevator. A troop of Girl Scouts passed her on their way down. It was warm in this old mausoleum and she was starting to sweat in her pea jacket.

She stopped at Hillman's office. As usual, the waiting supplicants outnumbered the seating. The receptionist cast a reluctant eye, but said nothing as Rita proceeded to DeVane's cubicle.

"Whipping up constituent pabulum?" Rita said to DeVane's white-shirted back. He hunched over the keyboard; Christmas wreaths adorned his expensive white braces.

"Go away." He didn't turn around.

"I want a minute."

"You've already had it." DeVane kept typing.

"Look, I want to find out who killed a friend of mine. You knew him. He was a decent man," Rita said.

DeVane stopped typing. After a moment, he turned around with a look of resignation. "What do you want?"

"Beware geeks bearing gifts," Rita said. "I've been snooping contribution lists and looks like somebody's wheeling in a Trojan horse."

"Can you speak in less picturesque language?" DeVane shook his head. Dark circles under his eyes gave him a depraved look.

"I'm finding that a lot of the groups pumping money to support healthcare are actually subsidiaries of an umbrella organization with a very Spanish accent." Rita rested her fists on DeVane's desk and leaned into his face. "*Comprende?*"

"Avoiding the limitations on foreign donation." In spite of the dark circles, his eyes sparked to life.

"You're a very quick boy," Rita said.

"And you think Hillman?"

"I made no accusations. Just keep what I said in mind." Rita started to leave, then bent back down.

"Are you Miriam Blalock?" She was almost nose-to-nose with him. She smelled his toothpaste.

"What are you talking about?'

"See you around," she said and left.

The next office was Strutt's. This time the receptionist got on the phone to security.

"How's the case coming?" Randy Wyman asked when she appeared at his cubicle. He obviously got more sleep than his harried counterpart DeVane.

"Like an avalanche down Everest," Rita said.

"Sounds dangerous." Wyman leaned back in his chair.

"Going to be for some people, especially some people who are working on the healthcare bill." Rita watched his eyes. They never blinked; they stared straight at her.

"In what way?"

Rita repeated what she'd told DeVane.

"Can't be. The committee's worked damned hard on this. It's a good piece of legislation. It works. It helps a lot of people. It makes medical care affordable." Wyman tapped the desk with his finger. "We've come too far to let some jerks torpedo this with stupidity."

Rita shrugged. "Just an advisement."

"I'm going to look into it immediately. You have my word," Wyman promised. He stood up and offered his hand.

Rita took it. "Miriam Blalock."

Wyman blinked. "I beg your pardon?"

"Let me know what you find," she said.

ᕬ

Rita liked this part of town where her office was. It was seedy enough to be out of public scrutiny—a must for clients insisting on discretion—but close enough to be on regularly patrolled streets. Of course, the mayor would have everyone believe that all streets were so well guarded. In this age of municipal economies though, it was the high bracket tax base and tourist areas that got real attention.

The problem here was parking. She had a space in a lot a block over, a block lined with shabby storefronts, cheap eateries, and dingy bars. During the day, heavy traffic kept danger at a distance, but at night opportunistic thieves and drunken brawlers ruled.

Rita preferred parking along the curb just outside her building, but tonight a dented pickup and an ancient Buick took up the two legal available spots. For an instant she considered parking illegally, but the fine was a cool one fifty. She also considered forgetting her mission to browse old newspaper files electronically for any past dirt on her Senatorial suspects.

She took a test spin around the block hoping that maybe one of the vehicles would have moved. No such luck. She wasn't about to be paranoid about a half block of dark pavement either.

In the lot she waved to the elderly black man who barricaded himself into his warm lighted booth at night. He was asleep with an Orioles cap over his eyes and didn't return her greeting. Rita surveyed the lot as she got out. It was a great spot for an ambush.

The wind was quiet tonight, but the cold was bitter. She pulled her pea coat collar around her cheeks while her breath streamed in clouds between the upturned lapels. Before starting for her office, she took another quick look around and patted the 9mm under her arm. She left her hand inside the coat with her hand on the butt.

A police paddy wagon rumbled along Calvert Street in no particular hurry. As she looked south, she saw the dancing lights of Baltimore's Block, home of the topless dancer, the Swedish Bookstore, and every assortment of addictions and diseases imaginable.

To the north it was darker; street lamps dotted the deserted sidewalks. Much farther up, were the staid houses and perennial gardens of Guilford, but in this immediate area were warehouse docks and closed cafes. Two blocks up a cat slunk across the street.

Rita crossed Calvert and headed for the corner where her building was situated across from the courthouse. It was darker on this side of the street. One of the lamps was out. A stinking steamy wisp rose like swamp fog from a sewer grate.

"Hey."

The sound made Rita jump. It was at her feet.

"Gotta quarter?" The words were almost indistinguishable.

She could barely make out the lump curled at the corner of the grate.

"Just need a quarter."

Rita took a deep breath, reached into her overcoat pocket and tossed down a dollar.

"Thankee." A claw-like hand squirmed over the sidewalk and retrieved the paper. Like an animal, it scurried back into its den.

Rita patted the butt of the Glock once more. The plastic handle was warm and reassuring.

At her building's foyer door, Rita fumbled with the key. She had to take her hand off the gun in order to get the right key into position off her key ring. The lock turned and she entered. The only light was the green exit sign. The overhead was out.

She stepped on something crunchy. As soon as her loafers tread on it, she knew it for crushed glass. The overhead wasn't burned out. Someone had smashed it.

Immediately she pivoted and reached for the glass door's metal handle, but a strong gloved hand chopped her wrist.

"Fuck." She jumped back, but could see only a big male figure in jeans and a ski jacket.

The man grabbed at her and she ducked. Her wrist ached with the force of the blow, but she jabbed her hand inside her coat for the Glock. As she did, the attacker punched her in the chest. She reeled as the blow knocked the wind out of her and she stumbled against the wall.

Rita sucked in oxygen. She had to stay conscious or she was dead. She spun away and made for the stairs. Having been in the building for over a year, she had a good sense of the place even in the dark, and she figured she had a better chance for safety if she could make it to her office. The attacker would surely have more trouble finding his way. It was the only hope as his body was between her and the outside door.

For a moment she was ahead of him, but he recovered quickly and was on her heels. She couldn't pull the 9 mm and run at the same time. Her coat was still buttoned. To halt now was to throw herself into his hands.

She raced to the top of the stairs and, in the pitch darkness, threw herself on her back on the slick marble floor and launched herself backward. The attacker lost her immediately. As he ran up the steps, he couldn't hear the wool coat sliding on the floor. He paused at the top.

In that moment Rita snatched the Glock from its holster, thrust it toward the stairwell and blasted off half a dozen rounds. Fire burst from the muzzle, but not enough light to illuminate her attacker.

Even as she fired, Rita inched along the wall and got herself into a standing position. When the roaring blast of the Glock quieted, she could hear herself panting. Saliva dripped from the corner of her mouth.

She didn't know if she'd hit him or not, but she could hear rubber soled shoes pounding down the steps. She lurched toward the railing in time to see the man throw open the outside door and fly out.

"Jesus Christ," she said to herself. "Jesus Christ."

She leaned her back against the wall and let herself slide to the floor.

Chapter 32

Stalking moon. The cold white face peered from behind scudding billowed clouds. The eerie illumination made Rita recall black and white movies about werewolves.

The Jeep purred as Rita surveyed her house from the back driveway. Every light was out. Karin went to bed early but usually read herself to sleep. Even the guest room was dark. The fluorescent dial of Rita's watch told her it was half past one.

She let the Jeep idle at the back door instead of pulling into the carport. She looked at her house and then on to the scattered farms who were her neighbors. It was a clean, solid sanctuary.

How many times as a child she'd ridden through such areas as these and yearned for the bright warmth that seemed to lie just behind the curtained panes. She pictured quiet respectful families around happy dinner tables. She imagined peaceful refuge in the lamplight.

Rita leaned back on the headrest. For a moment she closed her eyes, and in that darkness, transported herself to rooms of anger and shouting. She'd run away from there, but the ghosts followed wherever she went. Her hand reached for that battered chrome lighter in her pocket.

She opened her eyes. She didn't want to be alone and the fear had to be spoken. It was her only hope for release from its hold. Rita made no effort to quiet the closing and locking of her back door.

"Who is it?" Karin's voice was hesitant from the top of the dark stairway.

"Me."

"Are you all right?" Karin hurried down the steps.

"I'm ok." Rita stepped in from the biting November cold. In the warmth of the house, she felt her body tension diminish. Tears welled in her eyes.

"What happened?" Karin seized Rita by the shoulders. Light shown down only from the mercury light on the barn. The rest of the house remained dark.

"An unexpected guest at the office." As she stood there, Rita fidgeted. "Look, I'm sorry that I woke you up at this ungodly hour."

"I'm making coffee." Karin marched toward the kitchen.

Rita followed. "You have to get up early."

"You have to tell me what happened." Karin flicked the lights in the kitchen. "Fill the coffeemaker—and start talking."

Rita did as she was told. "I told you about the regular Mormon Tabernacle Choir of suspects I have."

Karin nodded as she pulled a glass container from the freezer.

"Well, I subscribe to the theory that people don't suddenly do something out of character, like rob a bank or kill their mother."

"Yes, precedents of some sort usually crop up." Karin measured coffee from the freezer container into the coffeemaker.

"So anyway, I was going to surf through computer files keying on the names of the healthcare committee senators and staff to see if I could dig up any previous dirt—other than Pete DeVane's little gambling faux pas. I got to my office and the building foyer was pitch black. I thought the light was burned out, but when I stepped on broken glass, I knew somebody had broken it. I started to backtrack in a big hurry, but some big dude whacked my hand off the door handle." Rita felt her mouth go dry again as she told the story.

"Oh my God." Karin put her hand to her mouth. "How did you get away?"

Rita relayed the problem of the topcoat buttoned over her shoulder holster and how she'd made her dash up the stairs, and the subsequent raking of the stairwell with 9 mm shells.

"You called the police?" The coffee was finished, but Karin made no move to pour.

Rita turned her back and reached into the cabinet for cups. "They could tell me nothing." She walked to the coffeemaker.

Karin grabbed her arm. "You can't just set yourself up as a target like this."

"Look, this may be the only way to draw this guy out."

"This may be the way you end up like Bobby Ellis and what good is that?" Karin's voice was stern.

Rita stared at her. "I don't think I've ever seen you angry."

"I don't want to see you dead because of some heroic Rambo notions you're entertaining."

"I do NOT have any Rambo ideas," Rita banged the counter and the coffee cups rattled.

"Then what are you doing?" Karin's voice lowered to a strong steady level.

Rita paused. "I'll call somebody." She faced the coffeemaker and focused on pouring.

"I know how much this case means to you. But throwing yourself in the path of the train isn't going to make it stop." Karin took a cup from Rita.

"Nobody could really protect me anyway," Rita mumbled as she joined Karin at the kitchen table.

"Mary Margaret offered to help, didn't she?" Karin asked.

"I'll talk to her tomorrow." Rita gulped her coffee and burned the roof of her mouth.

♏

In the morning, the office was silent, offering no hint of the previous night's violence. Cautiously, Rita peered through the door before she entered. No signs of search as there had been from the last such intrusion.

She figured that her assailant had had enough after her shooting and did not return last night. She went inside and turned up the thermostat. This November morning was brutal, icy with a steady raw rain. Bev had a gown fitting and was coming in late.

Rita hated grey days like this when she had to be in the office. With the granite building and the pale blue paint, the interior seemed dingy like the inside of a cell. She flicked on the fluorescent lights to brighten up the place.

In front of the computer, Rita shook the rain off her parka and tossed it across her visitor's chair. Then she snapped on her computer and flipped the lid on her large coffee—extra cream and sugar—while the machine booted. She'd brought in a supply of doughnuts for her quest through the electronic jungle.

The first name Rita keyed into her newspaper files was Miriam Blalock. Might as well, she thought, just to double check, though she was certain the name was an alias for Bobby's Capitol Hill source. No matches.

Rita sighed and typed in Charles Strutt's name. Bingo, she assembled hundreds of matches. He was a senator, what did she expect? One by one she scanned the news files that mentioned his name.

Ok, so she now had a profile of the man's complete career. He'd started making headlines at twelve when he became an Eagle Scout—he'd obviously had an eye for good press even as a kid. He'd received a scholarship from his state delegate when it was time for college—Kate must have been right about his scholastic tendencies. The scholarship was a political perk and had no connection to intellectual ability.

On and on Rita scrolled through the electronic files. The three doughnuts were gone. The last of the coffee was a cold, sugary ooze. At the last file which included Strutt's current status and a quote on the healthcare legislation, Rita ended the search with a keystroke and sat back to rub her eyes.

She had many more names on her list. She crossed off Strutt, the dumb but devoted elected official who'd had not so much as a parking ticket that made the news. From the things she'd read, she decided he wasn't a candidate for murderer.

It took several hours, but Rita went through the newspaper files on each of the senator suspects on the healthcare committee. Not one item she uncovered would have made her think twice about digging deeper into their pasts. She had a headache and her eyes watered.

"Smooth, it's me." Rita tapped her pen on the desktop as she talked.

"How's the Ellis case going?"

Rita hesitated. "Slow."

"Any leads at all? Find that Miriam Blalock broad?"

"Uh, yeah. It's an alias, somebody on the Hill who was Bobby's source." Rita drew X's on her notepad and walled them into a box.

"Somebody who may have wanted him out of the way after a while?" Mary Margaret asked.

"That's my guess. I'm thinking that either Bobby found something about the source or that Bobby's murder was a warning for the talker to keep his mouth shut." Rita drew bars down the boxes.

"You had any trouble since the break-in at your house?"

Rita paused. "No, nothing." She stabbed the pen into the center of the notepad.

"Better keep a sharp eye out though. If he killed one person, another's no big deal. Whoever it is has a big stake in keeping things quiet."

"Yeah."

"Want me to call one of my trooper buddies?"

"No, Smooth. I'm fine. I'll let you know if the situation heats up though." Rita gritted her teeth on the lie.

"Are you telling me the truth?"

"Swear to God," Rita said. "On my Catholic honor."

"Oh, yeah, that's good," Mary Margaret snorted. "You're not Catholic and you called Jean Paul II, the Pontoon."

Rita smiled. "Hey, if the shoe fits . . ."

"Don't play with this, Rita. I can't take another funeral right now."

"You know me, Smooth."

"All too well, my girl."

"I've got it all planned," said Rita. "We're gonna rock together on the front porch of the old folks' home."

"Just remember that," Mary Margaret said.

"How could I ever forget?"

Chapter 33

Two women with blue hair wearing orchid corsages crowded one the loveseats in Brett Hillman's waiting room. Beside them was a man in a hand sewn grey silk suit with a briefcase of soft and expensive leather. He tried to keep a respectable distance from a couple and their teenage son, the family attired in their best nylon polo shirts and vinyl loafers.

Pete DeVane came out of his office and offered Rita a thin binder.

"How come your attitude's so different these days?" Rita asked as she took it from him.

"I get carried away here." He ran his fingers through his hair. "You spend every minute chasing obscure details and you end up with a very narrow view. You forget the larger world and the meaninglessness of what you're doing outside a tiny sphere in a corner of the universe."

Rita noticed for the first time that Devine's blond hair was thinning at the fringe of his forehead. "A particularly New Age perspective if I ever heard one."

"Then I take it you're a New Ager yourself. Kate says that's why you left the *Star* after all those years."

Rita studied the man before her. "Maybe neither one of us are. Maybe we got tired of the *illegitimi carborundum.*"

"Yeah, I'm getting there." DeVane's voice was weary. "Anyway, here's your scrapbook—or rogue's gallery—depending on your perspective."

Rita took the binder and opened it. Inside were plastic photographic inserts with black and whites and news copy pictures. Charles Strutt and Brett Hillman filled the first sheet. Following were the other major senatorial players on the healthcare committee and after that were photos of their chief legislative aides. DeVane and Randy Wyman, both in candid shots from formal fundraisers, were the last two.

"Thanks for taking the time," Rita said. "I know it's a premium around here."

"I hope it'll help." DeVane held out his hand. "And that you catch the bastard."

Rita nodded as she accepted the peace offering. "Me too." She held his hand for a lingering moment.

♏

Rita cruised around the lighted fountain in the center of DuPont Circle. Male couples, walking close, hurried away from the biting cold. One man in a dark warm-up suit and running shoes walked a yorkie. With everybody home and curled inside against the November night, Rita couldn't find a parking place.

She passed Bobby Ellis' old apartment once and then came around again. Somebody else was living there now. The lights were on, curtains drawn. From her car, the place looked warm and homey and not like the empty shell so recently chilled by death.

Brake lights went on. Rita nosed the Jeep along the cars lined at the curb. Back and forth, the old BMW finally extracted itself from the tight space and roared off toward downtown.

Rita slipped the Jeep in effortlessly. I may not be able to track down a murderer, she thought to herself, but I can sure parallel park. Too bad it's not a vocation.

She pulled the collar of her pea jacket close around her cheeks and drew DeVane's binder off the passenger seat as she got out. It was late, too late to be in this part of town alone whether you were a man or a woman. The Glock was in her right coat pocket. She carried the binder under her one arm and kept her opposite hand in communication with the weapon.

Young Joe Friendly hadn't been too clear on the time of Bobby's Ellis' death. But with his estimate she added time necessary to get from Harper's Ferry to this neighborhood. She was grasping at straws at this point, but she knew no other paths to chase down. She was going to hunt these streets in search of anyone who may have been about at this hour on that night. She was going to show them her photographs. And if she was very lucky, she was going to yell Bingo.

She hailed the man with the yorkie as he approached her. "Excuse me."

"I don't have any spare change." The little dog paused to sniff at her slacks cuffs, but his master snapped the leash and maintained his brisk pace.

"I'm not begging for money." Rita trotted after him.

The man didn't turn around. "And I'm not interested in women either."

She stifled her anger impulse. Instead she caught up and strode beside him. "I just want a minute of your time. It could save somebody's life." My own, she thought to herself.

The man with a bored and bothered sneer halted. The yorkie pranced around his feet.

"I want you to look at some pictures. See if you might have noticed any of these people around here within the last month or so." Rita motioned toward a gas lamp standing in a yard.

The man followed, dragging his fluffy charge. Rita opened the binder. The man stared down at the first page and said nothing.

"Look familiar?" Rita was losing patience with the guy, but figured slugging him wasn't going to get her anywhere.

"No."

Rita flipped slowly through the book. The man registered nothing. Meantime the yorkie pawed his warm-up pants, begging to be held. When she came to the end, the man shook his head, snapped the leash so that the little dog jerked to all fours, and they both stalked off.

"Have a nice evening—asshole," Rita mumbled.

For an hour afterward she made an ever-widening circle out from the center, which was Bobby Ellis' apartment. Her goal was a two-block radius where she might encounter regulars at this time of night in this neighborhood.

She stopped at one point to check her map under a streetlight. She heard the scrape of tennis shoes on sidewalk and turned around. Three young men in sweatpants and hooded sweatshirts stopped when she did, just one block back. Rita touched the Glock's handle with her leather-gloved hand.

For another block they followed her, slowing when she did, speeding up as she did. At the same time, they managed to close the distance between them and her. Even in the chill she could feel sweat bead at her temples.

Finally they made their move. Rita heard the slap of rubber on pavement as they raced behind her. Instantly she turned, hoisted the Glock over her head and fired. The boys froze in unison, turned heel and sped off in the opposite direction.

"Welcome to the nation's capitol." Rita shook her head.

Her feet had lost feeling and her fingers were numb. She was hungry and tired and hadn't seen another damned person to speak to in the entire time she'd been hunting out here. She had one more corner to turn and she was out of here.

Around the corner was a neighborhood grocery/drugstore/ liquor store. Inside were the young Korean proprietor and his wife behind the counter. They nodded silently as Rita walked in.

"Hi," Rita went to them. They smiled at first. "I was wondering if you'd mind helping me with something."

She put the binder down and opened it to the first page. The grocer and his wife looked at each other as their smiles died. Both took a step back. "No trouble with police," the man said.

"I'm not the police," Rita answered.

The wife gave her husband a fearful glance. He said, "No trouble with neighbors."

"This isn't about the neighbors." Rita explained Bobby's death and that she was checking to see if any of the people pictured in the book might have been around here that night.

The wife and husband consulted each other with a silent study of faces. At last the man said, "We will look."

"Thank you." Rita turned the pages slowly, giving them time to take in and consider.

"This one," the wife piped up suddenly. She touched the face with her finger. "This one here."

Her husband nodded eagerly. "I remember because very unusual—man come in so late at night to buy dish glove."

Rita looked down at the photograph they had selected. "You're sure?"

"Sure," the wife said. "Very strange man wash dishes late at night."

Rita nodded and closed the binder. "Thank you. You've been more of a help than you'll know."

Chapter 34

She thought about soldiers. She had interviewed survivors of Vietnam in her time, but she'd never been there. Their eyes were windows to infinity. She'd seen that look in every face. Only now did she begin to understand, and she smoothed the engraving on her father's lighter.

It was dark in the Belfast Valley. Barn lights were beacons in the night; street lamps were few and far between out here. And marquee across distant house fronts were red and green and blue sparkles of early Christmas decorations. Karin still had three more hours of sleep before her alarm went off.

Rita sat on the edge of her bed to look out the window. She could see the interstate from her hill and even at this late hour, traffic flowed. In one hand was the Glock, unusually heavy at this moment. In her other hand was the extra magazine.

The Great White Hunter purred and rubbed against her leg. She reached down to scratch his eager upturned head and brush the fine blond hairs off her black warm up pants.

"Got to go, kiddo," she whispered to the cat. Uninterested he jumped to her bed and nestled among the pillows where she'd never slept that night.

She wore a black silk warm up suit over silk thermals. It was too cold to attend a rendezvous in a skimpy outfit and too dangerous not to dress as light for flight. Running would be impossible in her loafers and pea coat. She strapped her shoulder holster on over her jacket. No use pretending.

Rita skipped down the steps and into the kitchen. The house was dark except for the photosensitive nightlights that went on when the sun went down. If anybody was lurking around outside, she didn't want them to have a clear view of her.

In the kitchen she reached for her cell phone. Instantly the touchtone pad lit as she hit one of her speed dial buttons. She left a message for Bev at the office; Bev would be Karin's contact for the day. Rita hit the speed dial again.

"Now what?" The voice on the other end was gruff with sleep and annoyance at being wakened.

"Smooth, I need to tell you something."

"What the hell time is it?"

Rita heard her fumble with a clock. "Look, I need to get on the road. But I want you to know . . ."

"You found him, didn't you?" Suddenly the voice was clear and awake.

"Found him?"

"Bobby Ellis' killer."

"I think so."

"And you're going somewhere to meet him?"

"That's about it," Rita patted her left jacket pocket for the extra 9mm clip.

"Dammit, girl, have you lost your mind? Where are you going? Tell me. I'll go with you."

"What I wanted to tell you was that if something happens to me tonight, you need to know it wasn't an accident or a mugging or anything it might be cooked up to be. Ok?"

"Dammit, Rita," Mary Margaret yelled into the phone. "Are you crazy? Let me call somebody. I can have them follow you. This guy would never know you weren't alone."

"Can't trust that, Smooth," Rita said. "Now look, I don't have time to explain the whole thing. I wrote it up though and I put it in my safe deposit box. Anything happens, you get the bastard." Rita took a deep breath.

"Don't do this, Rita. You're not a cop, let alone an undercover cop. This is too dangerous." Mary Margaret grew calmer, more coaxing now.

"The train has left the station." Rita checked her watch.

"I'm putting a bench warrant on your ass," Mary Margaret said as Rita hung up the phone.

If something happened tonight, she'd never get to say goodbye to Karin. She hadn't said anything before bed because she didn't want to lie. She didn't wake her now because she might be someone who could talk her out of it.

At the back door, Rita drew out the Glock and inspected the clip. She patted the extra in her pocket. She pulled a black watch cap out of her closet and onto her head. She was on her way to Washington.

In the years she'd written investigative pieces, she'd had showdown after showdown. It was all shadow boxing. This one sued the newspaper; another one called her names on a TV show. Talk was big and there had been some pushing and shoving. She thought about Mary Margaret's words. Maybe she wasn't prepared for this.

Too late to turn back she'd said to Smooth—and it was.

♏

At night Washington was the Emerald City. Gold sodium glow from the streetlights promised richness and beauty. In truth, it was a labyrinth of dangerous avenues through the heart of a once mighty kingdom. Pirates owned the streets and citizens fled with the sun to suburban safety beyond the asphalt moat called the beltway.

Traffic was light. Rita knew her route precisely. Like Gawain meeting the Green Knight, she rode unerringly to the temple of the majestic Lincoln. He reigned in white marble bathed in godlike light.

He had said he'd meet her at the base of the statue. Rita took up a position out of the spotlights behind a column. Her watch said she had fifteen minutes until 4 a.m., his chosen hour. The fifteen minutes came and went, but her appointment did not appear.

Rita kept her place.

She did not have to look at her watch to know that time flowed on. In the early morning hours of this nerve center of the country, it was quiet. Car lights had not passed for a long time. She saw no policemen or passersby. She and the enshrined president sat without speaking in his temple.

She heard leather on marble and ducked deeper into the shadow of the column she hid behind. A man emerged on the far side of Lincoln's mammoth dais. He wore a black scarf with a black topcoat and black leather gloves.

She didn't remember Randy Wyman as that tall or solid as he appeared now. He surveyed the interior of the memorial. With both hands in his pockets, he stepped forward and looked around again. When he was ready to retreat, Rita spoke.

"I didn't stand you up."

Wyman's head jerked toward the sound of her voice. He stepped back. "I thought you had." He laughed. "I have the information I told you about."

"I have some information for you too."

With his left hand, Wyman reached into the breast pocket of his topcoat and extended a manila envelope. He shielded his eyes against the glare of the monument's spotlights. His right hand stayed in his pocket.

"Where are you?" he called out in the general direction of her hiding place.

"Here I am." Rita stepped from behind the column. She had the advantage of herself in shadow, Wyman in full light.

"What are you doing?"

"Keeping my distance." Her hand flexed and she thought about reaching for the Glock, but did not.

The two stood like gunfighters at dueling pace from one another.

"You were Bobby's source," Rita said.

Wyman said nothing.

"Until he found something out about you that he couldn't walk away from. That's when you killed him." Rita watched the right coat pocket with Wyman's hand inside.

"DeVane has certainly fed you a line. You don't believe that bullshit, do you?"

"DeVane didn't have to tell me a thing," Rita called to him. "I learned it all by myself. I learned a lot of things. I know that you paralyzed Dennis Phelps when he threatened to keep you from the NCAA wrestling championship."

"That's a lie. That was an accident," Wyman yelled.

"I know that Bobby kept a mail drop under the name Miriam Blalock and you were the source for dirt on people who stood in the way of what you wanted."

"Bobby Ellis was a washed-up news junkie who couldn't write his own name. If it hadn't been for me, that series would have been a pile of worthless print." Wyman's face reddened and the veins in his neck strained tight as he shouted at her.

"He found out you masterminded this little Mexican jumping bean scheme with contribution funds. He found out you became an agent for the Mexican Trade Consul. He knew that Charles Strutt danced to whatever tune you played. You had him line up with healthcare, a piece of legislation that, on his own, he would never have supported. You got paid and Mexican contract pharma outsourcers got the lion's share of manufacturing for the healthcare bill's med fulfillment."

"He knew nothing." Wyman's black-gloved hand coiled from his coat pocket like a cobra.

Rita saw the glint of shining chrome. In turn, she grabbed for the handle of the Glock and ran behind her column.

"The idiot was too stupid to put two and two together." Wyman ducked behind the Lincoln dais into his own shadow shield.

"Not true, he was a real mathematician." Rita kept an eye toward the spot where Wyman disappeared, but was wary of a sudden attack from the darkness if he ran around the statue to come up behind her.

A burst of fire from the rear of the dais and a splatter of 9mm shells chipped the marble column she used as cover.

"He was stupid." Wyman's voice floated in the darkness and Rita had no idea where he was.

She backed to the next column on the dark west portico. She could hear herself panting and sweat trickled down from the watch cap. She flattened herself and hoped that the black warm up suit was camouflage enough. The smell of cordite spiked the cold still air.

Another burst of gunfire and Abraham Lincoln's brilliant aura exploded. Wyman had blown out one of the floodlights.

The massive marble hall sank into the dusk of reflection from faraway streetlights.

"Shit." Rita hadn't seen where the shots came from. She held her breath to listen for footsteps. "Were you the asshole who broke into my office?" Rita called out. She peered around the trunk of her column.

Wyman did not reply.

"Were you the asshole you who broke into my house?" Rita ducked around the column for a quick look and back again.

Wyman kept his silence and Rita could feel a rivulet of sweat trickle down her cheek.

Maybe he left. Maybe he'd run away. This was a perfect opportunity to escape after all. He'd thrown the place into darkness and kept her guessing and under cover long enough to make a clean getaway.

Rita stepped away from the column and padded in front of the darkened Lincoln, pressing her body against the cold marble throne. Before she reached the other side, a chattering blast of bullets raked toward her from behind.

Rita dropped to the pavement and scuttled away on her knees and elbows. She had no idea where Wyman was. In the dark, she touched something and picked it up. Wyman had taken off his shoes so that she couldn't hear him when he ran.

Rita was at the front of the monument. Down the marble steps were the park and the Viet Nam wall, the reflecting pool, safety. She thought Wyman had run off, but maybe it was she who should escape.

Blam. Blam. Blam. Explosions rattled one after another. He was on this side of the dais again, near the back. He must have seen her silhouette in the feeble glow from the street. Rita retreated to the front of Lincoln again.

If she ran down the long flight of marble steps, she'd be a perfect target. She had no idea now if he would sneak up around the statue from the side where he'd fired or double back to attack from the opposite side.

Unbelievable. She was trapped in an open portico, a national shrine and park, a public place. Damn, Mary Margaret was right. She knew sources and grammar. What the hell did she know about a firefight?

"If you think, you'll get away with this, you're crazy," Rita yelled into the depths.

"I will or I won't. But at this point killing you loses me nothing." Wyman's voice came from the side where he'd fired— or was it the back?

Rita crouched to her combat crawl position again and maneuvered toward the opposite end of Lincoln's perch. After every move, she stopped to listen. If she crawled around the bottom of the dais, maybe she could get the drop on Wyman who'd be looking for a standing figure.

When she reached the edge, she paused and ducked her head around for a quick look. She saw nothing but blackness. It was this or nothing. Rita began her crawl down the dark side of the statue.

"What a clever idea." Wyman tromped her neck with his stocking foot.

Rita's face smashed to the freezing marble. She saw stars from the pain in her nose as it whacked the stone. The Glock, although still in hand, was trapped beneath her throat.

"Just like your stupid friend. You newspaper people make me sick. You're so smug, so damned righteous."

Rita edged the plastic weapon just a little on the slippery floor as Wyman talked. She knew that if she gave it a sudden jerk to freedom, he'd blow her head off. She could feel him bending over her; his gun was aimed straight at her skull.

"Oh, and you're not?" She moved her gun a bit more.

"It's a game. The people with the power, with the balls to take it and make things happen, win all the marbles."

The Glock was almost out. Only the tip of the barrel jutted into her chin. She had to keep him talking.

"Ok, smart guy, so what are you going to do with me? Think you can still take all the marbles after you've killed me?" The Glock was free. Rita's finger rested on the trigger.

"Well, I might as well tell you since . . ."

The blast of her own gun rang in her ear. She saw fire from above and Wyman's gun exploded. A spray of chips and marble dust from his errant shot rained in her face.

She squeezed her eyes shut and waited to die. She heard sucking breath and a groan. Instantly she was on her feet. Behind her was a convergence of park and city police.

Randy Wyman lay on his back, his mouth gaping, lips moving without words. She could see the blood seeping from the hole in his starched white shirt. It flowed like black ink across a blank page.

As a platoon of policemen charged up the steps, she stepped aside and began to throw up.

♏

Rita sat in her living room in the early morning hours after she'd made her statement and the DC police released her. Mary Margaret was there when they brought her in. She was probably at work by now.

Rita didn't remember driving home. It was a blur. The only memory that was clear and recurrent was that last pitiful image of the dying Randy Wyman.

"I didn't mean to kill him." Rita had said that five times now.

Karin sat beside her on the sofa, arm around her. Two undrunk cups of coffee on the table before them. Karin stroked her back.

"I know," she said in a low reassuring voice. "I know."

"I just wanted to catch him—like in the newspaper when you write up the expose and the rest of the world takes the right action."

Karin let her talk.

"Then it came down to him or me." Rita looked up into Karin's face. "You want to hear something crazy? You know what it took to make me pull that trigger? I thought about Bobby and I got the rage. I didn't think about saving my own life. Jesus."

"You're safe," Karin said. "That's all that matters for right now. And maybe you'll need to talk about it. I know a psychologist who works with FBI agents on things like this."

"I don't know."

"You'll like her."

"I'll think about it." Rita reached for her coffee and finding it cold, stood up. "We need to warm these up."

"Don't stuff this, Rita." Karin followed her into the kitchen.

"The good news is it appears that Dr. Demento is gone. You can go back to your life—and your own house—soon." Rita poured fresh coffee into the mugs she'd just emptied.

Karin sighed and took the cup Rita offered. "Can I set up the appointment for you?"

"I'm fine. Really." Rita touched her coffee to Karin's in a salute.

She smiled, but her eyes wandered away as the image of Randy Wyman's body flashed in her mind's unforgiving eye.

Chapter 35

Rita's Jeep leaned hard into the curve of the exit ramp. Karin had dressed and gone to her office to see clients; she had appointments until eight that night. This was to be Karin's last night in Rita's house; tomorrow she would pack and go back home.

It was a hard, cold evening. A silvery half-moon rested among a sprinkle of bright stars. She could see the dark shapes of deer as they foraged for leftovers in the stubble of harvested corn and bean fields. Light showed through bay windows, and frost sparkled on the frozen grass.

As she pulled into the joint driveway that she shared with the Mondieus, she glanced over at their house. Loretta, in long coat and earmuffs, stood in her front yard where a floodlight focused on the foil-adorned door. Rita pulled onto the parking pad behind her house and then walked over to Loretta's.

"Good evening, my dear," Loretta said. "Loretta Mondieu." She held out her hand.

"Rita Mars." Rita shook Loretta's hand. "I live next door."

"Well, it's a lovely time for Christmas now isn't it?" Loretta asked.

"Yes, it is."

"You really must come and see my decorations, my dear. How long have you lived there, did you say?" She took Rita's arm gently and guided her toward the front of the house

"Six years, Loretta."

"We really should try to see more of one another." Loretta eased Rita into the brilliant scope of the floodlight. "Isn't this a beautiful door?"

But Rita was distracted by something other than the door. Loretta's stone goose, Scarsdale, was ready for an entirely different season. The statue wore a colorful full skirt, a low-cut peasant blouse, and a charming straw hat clustered with shining plastic fruits. Tiny bananas dangled seductively over Scarsdale's eye.

"Loretta, did you dress Scarsdale yourself?"

Loretta turned from admiring her front door. "Why yes, I did dear, but I had some help from this charming woman who lives next door."

"Loretta, I live next door." Rita squatted next to the small statue.

"No, dear, a lovely chocolate woman lives next door. Exquisite taste really. She made the suggestion and helped me prepare the outfit."

Rita stood up and shook her head.

"It is so festive, don't you think?" Loretta asked.

"Oh, Bev is festive all right."

"You should stop in and introduce yourself next door," Loretta said. "I'm sure that nice lady wouldn't mind."

"I'm sure," Rita said. "Now you had better get back in the house where it's warm." It was Rita's turn to guide Loretta.

"And give my best to Uncle Hodge," Loretta said.

"I'll do that, Loretta." Rita watched as the older woman cautiously climbed the three steps on her back porch and disappeared inside the house.

The interior of Rita's house was toasty with heat from the two wood stoves. She smelled the scents of chocolate and piecrust baking and heard Mozart emanating from the second floor.

"Home from the wars, honey?" Beverly skipped down the stairs and rounded the corner into the living room. She wore a white velour warm-up suit trimmed in gold. Her immaculate white leather sneakers were a perfect complement, as were her shining gold button earrings.

"You dressed the duck like Carmen Miranda?" Rita pulled off her pea jacket and scarf.

"Scarsdale is a goose, honey." Bev went to the wood stove to toss in another log.

"What were you thinking?" Rita followed Bev into the kitchen.

"Cherry pie—your favorite." Bev opened the oven door for a peek. "And chocolate chips, last batch out." She offered a heaping plate in Rita's direction.

"But Carmen Miranda?" Rita caved. She took two cookies and sank into a chair at the kitchen table while Bev poured her a fresh cup of coffee, replete with a hint of cinnamon.

"Loretta loved it and it was the perfect lawn ornament for this white bread territory you live in." Bev sat in the chair next to her.

"White bread?"

"Name two properties owned by somebody other than an Episcopalian," Bev asked.

Rita thought for a moment.

"I rest my case," Bev said.

"No cookies for you?" Rita asked.

"Honey, I'm watching this figure like a hawk. Um hm. This girl is going to be *The Hippo's* Miss January this year."

Rita gestured for more cookies

"You doin' all right? You know, after the shooting?" Bev asked with a deep furrow across her perfect brows.

"I'm ok," Rita said, her mouth full of cookie. "Thank you for asking. For being here for me."

Bev was silent for a moment. "Always, baby." She offered Rita the cookie plate again, but Rita shook her head. "I've eaten enough sugar today to put me in diabetic shock."

"This is not the time to be cool, Rita," Bev said. "Talk to somebody if you need to."

Rita stared into Bev's dark eyes, then lowered her own. "I will, Bev." She sank back into her chair.

"Don't push everything down to hide it."

Rita reached for a cookie, stopped herself, sat back again.

"You're tough. It's what's carried you through the devastation—every time." Bev stood and picked up the cookie plate. "Thassit, baby. Make it happen."

"Bev, I'm glad you're here." Rita stood and hugged the muscular six-two-frame around the waist. "I need to hear things sometimes."

"Ain't that the truth," Bev said, sliding foil over the cookies. "If it weren't for me, you wouldn't be havin' any style at all. You'd be wearin' them ugly flannel shirts and big ol' clunky sandals with argyle socks, and no good lookin' woman would be takin' a second look at you."

"Well, I still don't have the eyebrow plucking down pat yet," Rita laughed.

"Hey, every good thing has its time, baby."

Car lights arced across the parking pad behind the house.

Bev looked at Rita and tensed for action. Rita glanced out the window. "Karin VanDreem. We're going to stay here tonight and then she's going back home tomorrow."

Bev's eyebrows raised.

"Don't even think it," Rita said.

A knock on the back door, then Karin entered with a bag of groceries. "I thought I would pick up some dinner just in case." She smiled at Bev who returned the acknowledgement.

"I was just getting ready to go down to the gym," Bev said. "And since you'll be here tonight, I'll go on home."

"Please don't leave on my account." Karin looked to Rita.

"Not a problem, we don't want to keep Bev trapped way out here in the country. She's a city girl." Rita took the bag from Karin and set it on the table.

"I'll get my stuff," Bev said. "Rita, I want to show you a plumbing problem you've got in the upstairs bathroom. "Scuse us, we'll be right back."

"I'll unpack the groceries," Karin said.

"A plumbing problem?" Rita asked as they headed up the steps.

"God, you are dense." Bev pulled Rita into the bathroom and closed the door.

"What?" Rita whispered.

"You still need to be careful. There are less people out here than the neighborhood where that crazy doctor almost killed the both of you. And who knows if anybody was working with that Wyman guy."

"I'll be fine. I feel safer here."

"You know, complacency can get you into trouble."

"Ok, I can see that, but I'm on guard."

"Good. You know how to reach me. And—your weapon—ready?" Bev opened Rita's jacket. "Where the hell is it, girl?"

"It's in my room."

"Have it ready," Bev said.

"I will," Rita promised.

"Think you could pull the trigger—after Wyman?"

"Of course, I can pull the trigger. For God's sake . . ."

"I'm asking can you pull the trigger?" Bev said.

Rita looked into Bev's eyes.

"If you do what you're doing now, you're a dead girl."

Rita squared her shoulders. "I can do it, Bev."

"I can't lose you, girlfriend."

"I haven't gotten lost yet," Rita replied.

"I'm calling you before bedtime."

"I'm fine."

"You make me nervous," Bev said.

"I make everybody nervous," said Rita. "That's my job."

"Take care of yourself."

"I will, Bev."

They hugged, Rita opened the bathroom door, and in a few minutes, Bev's black SUV disappeared down the driveway.

♏

During dinner, Rita said little. Karin chattered about the day's client meetings.

"Bev left some great dessert," Rita said as they cleared the dishes. "Go relax in the living room. I'll make coffee."

In the living room was a big ceramic wood stove. Having been fed by Bev, a healthy fire blazed through its smoky window. The Great White Hunter lay on the carpet near the brick hearth.

"I brought a little of the pie and the cookies. We can sample both." Rita sat a wooden tray on the cocktail table by the sofa where Karin sat.

"This is wonderful." Karin helped her arrange the coffee cups and dessert plates on the table.

"It makes me feel that things are returning to normal." Rita said.

"It makes me feel the world is safe again," said Karin.

"Oldies?" Rita walked over to the sound system and switched on the radio. "I can't take too much contemporary stuff anymore."

Karin laughed.

Rita turned and rejoined Karin on the sofa. The Dell Vikings were finishing up *Come Go With Me*.

"Bev bakes a mean cherry pie." Rita offered a plate.

"This is the most relaxed I've been in a long time," Karin said. "This is a wonderful house."

"Thanks." Rita broke off a piece of pie with her fork.

"You and your partner lived here?"

"Eleven years." Rita sipped her coffee.

"I'm bringing up painful memories," Karin said.

"I'm just tired of talking about it."

"Sorry."

"It's ok," Rita said. "Really. So—how about that pie?"

"Delicious. Bev is a remarkable person," Karin said.

"I'll drink to that." Rita saluted with her coffee cup. "A special forces queen on the battlefield and in the kitchen."

"Should we talk about what happens next?"

"I don't know who's more compulsive, you or me." Rita smiled. "But no, we're not going to talk about Dr. Demento or

Bobby Ellis or world hunger. Tonight we're going to sit in front of this fire, drink coffee, eat sweets, and rest our pretty little heads."

"Listen to Marvin Gaye," Karin added. His smooth voice warmed the room with "What's Goin' On."

The Great White Hunter opened one eye, yawned and curled in a different direction. For a long while the two women leaned back into the sofa without speaking. Gradually the fire in the stove belly waned to flickers of blue and orange.

Rita sighed. "The major drawback to wood stoves." She roused herself from the comfortable cushions and went to the hearth. She threw in two more logs and stoked the crumbling embers to ignite the new wood.

"Hey, it's snowing." She closed the stove door and went to the window that opened on the vista from the top of the hill to the road and the panorama of the valley to the south.

Karin glanced out the window behind the sofa. "I don't see anything."

"Come over here, look down the drive," Rita said. At the bottom of the hill was a streetlight, few and far between out in this part of the county.

Karin came to the front window.

"If we turn out the light . . ." Rita switched off the ceiling light.

"Ohh. It's so pretty. Makes being in here feel even more cozy."

Rita and Karin stood by the window and watched the tiny flakes dust the pasture and the trees.

"We used to dance sometimes," Rita said.

"Excuse me?" Karin looked puzzled.

"Sometimes when it was late at night, when Diane and I were alone, when the music was on. We'd turn off the lights and dance right here in the living room."

Karin started to speak, but said nothing.

"Memories pop up like that sometimes," Rita said.

From the radio came the voice of Johnny Rivers. *Slow Dancing.*

"I've never danced with a woman," Karin said.

"Oh, come on, even straight women have danced together," said Rita.

Karin reached for Rita's hand. Rita led. She could feel the heat in her face as Karin followed. Rita sensed that familiar lump in her throat, the rise of memory and loss. Karin's hair smelled like ripe apples. Rita swallowed hard. She would not let emotion win.

Rita moved her partner around the room. Deftly she danced past the cocktail table, the edge of the hearth, the sleeping cat—and Karin moved with her.

When the song ended, they were standing in front of the wood stove. Their faces illuminated by the rosy light of the fire.

"Are you crying?" Karin said as she leaned back a little from Rita.

"I never cry." Rita's face was inches from Karin's. She searched in her eyes.

Karin did not look away.

Rita leaned forward. For an instant, she hesitated and then touched her lips at the corner of Karin's mouth.

Cigarette smoke, she swore she smelled cigarette smoke, and she was afraid.

Chapter 36

One minute Rita was staring into Karin's eyes. The next the house went black.

Karin jumped. "What is it?"

"We're at the end of the transmission lines out here. Electric goes off all the time." Rita squeezed her arm for reassurance. "Do you smell cigarettes?"

"No, why?"

The dancing light from the wood stove grill cast devilish shadows around the room. Rita started for the phone.

"Wait," Karin whispered after her and grabbed at her sleeve.

"I'm just going to report this to the electric company."

"We're the only ones." Karin pulled Rita back. "Look."

The lone streetlight at the end of the drive still shone. Rita went to the side window. Loretta's nightlight glimmered in her bedroom window. The mercury light on the barn was gone.

A rattle at the back of the house.

"Stay with me," Rita whispered in Karin's ear. She led her by the hand as they made their way to the stairs.

The front door knob ticked a turn as Karin and Rita passed.

"Shit."

"He's here." Panic quavered in Karin's voice.

"My cell phone is upstairs—with my car keys and my gun." Rita hoped she sounded more composed than she felt. Her heart was pounding against her chest and her mouth went dry.

Karin dug her nails into Rita's hand. "My phone's in the car."

Rita whispered again. "Stay close to me. If anything happens, run outside and get to Loretta's house."

"What about you?"

"Just do what I say. Got it?"

Karin nodded.

They began their stealth ascent on the stairs. At the top, Rita felt sweat beading around her hairline and on her lip. Her hands were shaky, but she gripped Karin's to keep herself steady.

Upstairs there was no fire to cast even a dim light. The two women halted on the top step. Rita put a finger over Karin's lips. She nodded to let Rita know that she understood not to cry out.

The Glock 19 was in its holster slung from a coat rack peg on the front of the closet door. The car keys and cell phone lay on the dresser top. Rita reached for her gun.

Her eyes were getting accustomed to the dark, and she knew the house well. It wasn't bumping into furniture that worried her.

From downstairs came the creak of the back door hinges. Rita froze. Karin jumped behind her. Rita put her finger over her lips again. She could feel the tears on Karin's face.

Rita gave her a quick hug and then reached for her weapon. She felt for the magazine; the clip was in. She flicked the safety off and took a deep breath. Then she listened. Her every nerve fiber tensed, ready to catch a creak, a cough, a scrape. Nothing.

The gun in her hand calmed her. Her hands steadied. She and Karin inched toward the dresser. Rita groped the top. She found the keys, but the cell phone was missing.

"Shit," she mouthed to herself. Where had she left it?

She touched Karin's arms with both hands as if to set her in place. She then walked carefully to the bedroom door, shut and locked it.

"It'll buy us a few minutes," she whispered to Karin when she returned. "We're going out the window."

"He might be out there." Karin pulled back.

"And he might be in here and he might be setting the house on fire. Who knows," Rita whispered, "but we have a better shot at escape out there. In here we're cooked."

Rita motioned for Karin to stand on one side of the window, away from the glass. She stood on the other and turned the sash lock without a sound. Each woman put a hand on the window to push slowly and quietly up. Rita rested the gun on the sill and slid the screen open as well.

Outside a dense cold settled on the night. A fine mist of snow still fell from the sky. The flat porch roof extended just outside.

"I'm afraid of heights," Karin said.

"Good, that would be two of us," said Rita. "Just don't look down."

"How are we going to get off the roof?"

"Just get on it first, please," Rita whispered back.

With the first step Karin's foot slipped and she grabbed in panic at the windowsill.

"Don't try to stand. Stay on your hands and knees," Rita advised.

While Karin cautiously made her way onto the roof, Rita tiptoed to the bedroom door to listen. Nothing.

Doubts crept in. Where the hell was the intruder? What if it was just some freak wiring problem? No, she said to herself. Better to take the chance and look like a fool.

She smiled to herself at the news story: Woman falls to death after crawling onto snow-covered roof. Police suspect idiocy. Film at eleven.

"I'm freezing," Karin said when Rita came to the window to follow her on the roof.

Rita reached in and grabbed a sweatshirt lying across a handy chair. Karin pulled it on.

"And now that we're here, how are we going to get down?" Karin asked.

"We're taking the air stairs." Rita crawled to the edge of the roof and peered through the darkness. The snow gave some semblance of light to the landscape, but out here in the heart of the country, night was very deep.

"What are the air—oh, no. No," Karin hissed at Rita. "I am not jumping off this roof. It must be a twenty-foot drop."

"Twelve. It's a twelve-foot drop." Rita said.

"Oh, great."

"You're not going to jump. I'm going to lower you down. I'm the one who's going to jump."

"I'm afraid," Karin said.

"Get as close to the edge as you can. I'll hold your arms. You'll be ok."

"I can't," Karin said.

"You will," Rita commanded.

Karin inched to the roof edge. Rita surveyed the snowy crust on the lawn far below. No footprints. If she could only get Karin down without a sound.

"Now listen," Rita whispered in Karin's ear. "After I lower you as far as I can, you'll drop to the ground. Run immediately to Loretta's house. Do not stop. Got it?"

"I need to wait for you."

"No, no matter what happens, you'll do what I say."

"I don't want to leave you," Karin said.

"We don't have time to play this game."

Karin nodded.

Slowly, Rita helped Karin make her way over the edge of the porch roof. Rita's arms ached with the effort. She peered over the side; Karin was looking up into her face, awaiting the signal. Rita nodded as Karin braced herself. She dropped with a soft thud on the frozen grass below.

Karin looked back. Rita made a shooing motion with one hand and Karin dashed across the lawn and driveway. She disappeared in the shadow of the oaks that separated Loretta's property from hers.

Rita's toes were numb now and her fingers stung from the chill. A noise behind her—had someone opened the bedroom door? Rita stuffed the Glock into the back of her waistband and gripped the edge of the roof. The guttering was going to slice her hands to ribbons.

The bedroom door scraped open. Its ancient hinges strained against the dresser.

"Damn."

She could take a leap or she could attempt to maneuver the porch posts. A drop from this height could leave her unable to run.

She stooped to grasp the edge of the roof.

"You're not planning to fly away, are you, Ms. Mars?"

Still on her knees, Rita turned to face Douglas Sevier who stood at the window, a Sig Sauer in his black-gloved hand. A demonic mist swirled from his mouth as he spoke.

Rita snapped her arm behind her back and snatched the Glock from her jeans.

"Any minute the police are going to be here." Rita, still on her knees, aimed the gun barrel up at Sevier's chest.

"The telepathy police?" Sevier smiled as he stepped through the window and out onto the roof. He took a step toward her.

Rita shrunk back and thrust the Glock forward. "I'm warning you." For a moment, she thought of just throwing herself off the roof, but he'd have her for sure if she snapped her leg. If only she was confident enough to try and stand.

Sevier edged forward and leaned down into Rita's face. "You can't do it."

Before she could react, Sevier punched her gun hand with the Sig's barrel. He whacked her squarely on the knuckles. Pain shot up her arm as her Glock slid along the snow coated shingles and came to rest in the gutter.

"When I finish with you, I'm going to saunter next door and dispose of potential witnesses." Sevier leaned so close to Rita's face that she could smell the peppermint.

She heard speaking but not the words. Her mind spun like a tire in mud. There was no chance of kicking at Sevier and knocking him off the roof. The Glock was gone. To lunge at him was certain disaster.

She was going to die.

Rita looked up. All she could see was the glint in Sevier's eye and his white teeth. He pushed the gun against her throat. She swallowed hard as the cold metal pressed on her jugular.

She sensed a presence then. There was movement and the cutting *swoosh* of mass and velocity splitting the night air. Rita heard a soft thud with the crunch of bone.

Like a great crow, Sevier flew over the edge of the roof to the frozen lawn below. A muscular figure in black towered over her.

"Goddam, girl. I told you. I told you, you couldn't pull that trigger." Bev dropped to her knees in front of Rita. "And now, here you scare me like you're going to be killed. Jesus." Bev hugged her tight and they rocked back and forth on the snowy shingles.

Rita closed her eyes and let the tears fall, let herself collapse into Bev's arms, let herself come back to the land of the living.

"You were right," she whispered to Bev. "I froze. My head took over and I started thinking about having killed someone."

"It's ok, baby. It's ok." Bev still held her.

Rita stopped after a moment. Bev let her go and helped her to her feet. Both peered over the roof at the broken figure below.

"We need to call the ambulance," Rita said.

"Just the police," said Bev. "He was dead before he left the roof."

Rita hugged her one more time and then they crawled back inside her house.

♏

Hours later, on the dark side of morning, Rita and Bev and Karin sat with Loretta and Leonard Mondieu in their kitchen. Silently they sipped hot chocolate together. The house smelled of evergreens and sugar cookies. There was no death here, no threat or danger. It could have been the night before Christmas and all through the house.

The blue gumball police lights had long since left, along with the ambulance. The statements were in the books; the inquiry to be scheduled. Rita had contacted her attorney who had done such an admirable job of lifting her from general lock-up on her last police adventure.

"Isn't it a lovely night, dear?" Loretta asked Rita. "I made these cookies myself."

"They're delicious," Rita answered. She turned to Bev. "So how the hell did you know to come?"

"I called on the bat phone, dear. More hot chocolate?" Loretta asked Karin.

"The bat phone?" Rita stared at Bev.

Loretta whipped a flip phone from the pocket of her fleece robe.

"I gave it to her," Bev said. "It's programmed to dial one number, mine. I told her if she . . ."

"If I saw the devil again, I was to push the button on the bat phone. And I did." Loretta swelled with pride.

"You saw him?"

"Dear, I see everything that happens at your house."

"Everything?"

Loretta smiled and nodded.

♏

In the morning Rita helped Karin pack and followed her to her house in Guilford to help at the other end. When the boxes and suitcases were empty, they sat at Karin's kitchen table with coffee and cookies.

"I remember this scene," Rita said. "This is where I came in."

Karin nodded and smiled.

"I'm sorry the way this ended," Rita said.

"I think it was inevitable." Karin touched her hand. "The path Douglas chose—it was a matter of time."

"I can still be sorry," Rita said.

"Yes, you can and I thank you for that. And why did you ask me about cigarettes just before the lights went out."

"I smelled the smoke, strong. I've noticed for a long while I seem to catch that whenever something bad is about to happen. Reminds me of my father."

They sat in silence for a long while.

"So . . ." They spoke at the same time and laughed.

"You first," Rita said.

"I'm going to sell the house, move to a smaller place. I'll work on putting my life back together," Karin said. "And you?"

"More leaping tall buildings, saving the world, that kind of thing." Rita glanced at her watch. "I'm meeting Smooth downtown in an hour. She's helping me with a runaway case."

Rita stood up.

Karin came around the table and held out her arms. "I'm glad I got to spend time with you."

They held each other close. Rita was the first to release. Karin followed her to the door.

Rita turned as she twisted the handle. "Just one thing."

"And that is?" Karin asked.

"Don't die wondering," Rita said and stepped outside into the sun.

Acknowledgements

I wanted to write and never imagined beyond my word choice and my storytelling all the complexities and decisions and plain grunt work that a published life demanded. For the support of those pivotal people who believed and yet will never see a finished book - I am forever grateful to my grandmother, May Dixon for my love of learning; to Mary Gay Calcott, the woman who taught me how to write, and to my forever friend, Mary Alice Brittingham. This work honors them.

And for enduring the "read this, please and give me honest feedback," for hours of my unavailability and obsession, I so grateful that you hung in there with me. I owe my partner, Dotty Friedrick, for her encouragement and unfailing support in spite of my changeable moods. I am grateful for the support of Carol Steinitz, who gave good counsel at my lowest moments and always spoke with the calm voice of reason.

I would especially like to thank, Caitlin Berve, a writer whose writing, editing and work ethic I admire and respect. She is responsible for the quality of the editorial work performed on my manuscript. She kept me on track with the task list, reminding me of things I had no idea I needed to do. Left to my own devices, I could not have gotten through the sheer mechanics of publishing.

VALERIE WEBSTER has been a triathlete, a writing instructor, a crime reporter, a member of Sisters in Crime and the mentoring program of Mystery Writers of America. She is the author of DRIVEN: A RITA MARS THRILLER, wherein she incorporates her extensive career in law enforcement technologies. Valerie makes her home near Boulder, Colorado. DRIVEN is her debut thriller.

More Mysteries

Rita Mars will return! To find out when book two is released, go to www.valeriewebster.com.

At www.valeriewebster.com, you will also find a mystery quiz! Discover if you have what it takes to be a private investigator.